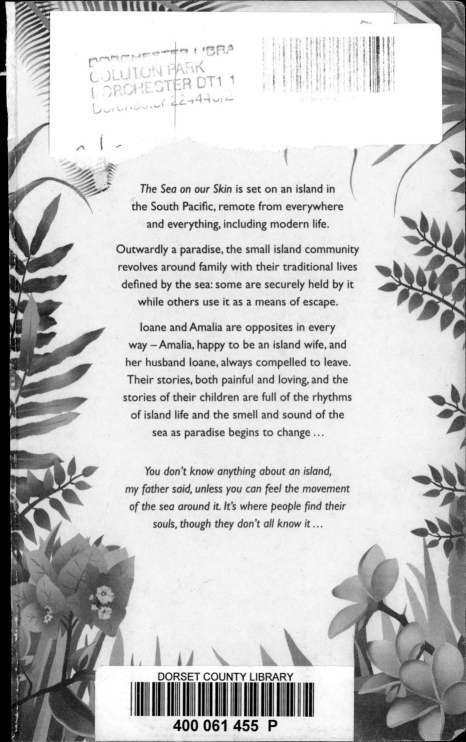

DORCHESTER LIBRA
COLLITON PARK
DORCHESTER DT1 1
Dorchester 224440/2

The Sea on our Skin is set on an island in
the South Pacific, remote from everywhere
and everything, including modern life.

Outwardly a paradise, the small island community
revolves around family with their traditional lives
defined by the sea: some are securely held by it
while others use it as a means of escape.

Ioane and Amalia are opposites in every
way – Amalia, happy to be an island wife, and
her husband Ioane, always compelled to leave.
Their stories, both painful and loving, and the
stories of their children are full of the rhythms
of island life and the smell and sound of the
sea as paradise begins to change ...

*You don't know anything about an island,
my father said, unless you can feel the movement
of the sea around it. It's where people find their
souls, though they don't all know it ...*

DORSET COUNTY LIBRARY

400 061 455 P

THE SEA
ON OUR SKIN

THE SEA
ON OUR SKIN

MADELEINE TOBERT

TWO
ROADS

www.tworoadsbooks.com

First published in Great Britain in 2012 by Two Roads
An imprint of Hodder & Stoughton
An Hachette UK company

First published in paperback in 2013
1

Copyright © 2012 Madeleine Tobert

The right of Madeleine Tobert to be identified as the
Author of the Work has been asserted by her in accordance
with the Copyright, Designs and Patents Act 1988.

All rights reserved. No part of this publication may be reproduced, stored
in a retrieval system, or transmitted, in any form or by any means without
the prior written permission of the publisher, nor be otherwise circulated
in any form of binding or cover other than that in which it is published and
without a similar condition being imposed on the subsequent purchaser.

All characters in this publication are fictitious and any resemblance to
real persons, living or dead is purely coincidental.

A CIP catalogue record for this title is available from the British Library

ISBN 978 1 444 73412 6

Typeset in Sabon by Palimpsest Book Production Limited,
Falkirk, Stirlingshire

Printed and bound by Clays Ltd, St Ives plc

Hodder & Stoughton policy is to use papers that are natural,
renewable and recyclable products and made from wood grown in
sustainable forests. The logging and manufacturing processes are expected
to conform to the environmental regulations of the country of origin.

Two Roads
Hodder & Stoughton Ltd
338 Euston Road
London NW1 3BH

To Tema and Tu for giving me a home in the
Pacific all those years ago.

And to all the Saumakis for welcoming me back.

Dorset County Library	
Askews & Holts	2013
	£8.99

PART ONE

THE WEDDING OF IOANE MATETE AND AMALIA HOKO

On the morning of the wedding of Ioane Matete and Amalia Hoko, it rained. The clouds that had been waiting, dark and swollen for days, gave in to their impatience and a torrent of water pounded the island. The damp between Ioane's toes made his feet itch and the itch in his feet made him desperate to move on. He was an explorer, not used to staying still. As soon as the wedding – by which he meant the wedding night – was over, he would leave his new bride and set out once more on his travels.

He changed in a stranger's house. He tied a garland of leaves over his *sulu*, a piece of cloth wrapped like a skirt around his waist; he had not worn one for years. He put on a clean white shirt, which the mud would soak and splatter the moment he stepped outside. He shaved off his beard and examined the skin underneath. It was as brown as his shoulders that saw the sun every day. He frowned. He was not looking forward to the ceremony. Tradition: he'd spent all his adult life trying to avoid tradition. 'It'll soon be over,' he said to himself.

He'd been an ocean away when the thought came to him that it was time a man like himself had a wife. He'd decided to return to the island, his island, his first visit in fifteen years. And he had been right to come to this isolated village, the village of Moana, which he had never visited as a boy. It was on the other side of the island from his home and known for its beautiful women. Ioane had scanned the thatched houses that stretched up from the beach, the rundown little school, the rowing boats bobbing on the water and the girls, who glanced at him with wide eyes. Yes, he'd known then that here he would find a wife. And it had been easy. Temalisi Hoko had met him on the shore and promised him her daughter. The men of the village wouldn't marry her because there was no one to give her away: no father, no brother, no uncle. The village expected her to remain unmarried. Tradition, superstition. Ioane Matete assured her he did not care.

In her own home on the beach, Amalia Hoko was having her face painted by her mother.

'Stay still, child,' Temalisi said, holding her daughter's cheek steady in her hand. 'This is an important day for you – you've got to look your best.'

'But it's raining. There is no point spending hours on my hair and face; it's all going to be ruined anyway.'

4

'Yes, it will be ruined, my girl. But as long as there is something to destroy, your husband will know we have made an effort. Better to have streaks down your face than to look like you do every other day. It's the island way.'

'But he's only seen me once. He doesn't know how I always look.'

'That's not the point, Amalia.'

As the bride got ready, the weather got worse. The rain clouds became storm clouds. A growl of thunder was heard and then a bolt of lightning was seen in the distance and another and another.

'This is a bad omen,' Amalia whispered. 'Maybe I shouldn't do this. The sky is angry.'

'Better you should,' her mother replied.

'I should stay single. My father died over a year ago. It's too late. There is no one to give me away. Why do you want me to shame myself by walking up the aisle alone?'

'You're meant to have your wedding today. I feel it. This is just a storm, my Amalia. The island isn't trying to scare you. It will stop soon.'

'Are you sure? It *is* scaring me. Look at the lightning. Why am I getting married? It's wrong.'

'No, it's not wrong. The lightning starts in the ground and rises up to strike the clouds. Put your fingers to the floor, you can feel the thunder. The island is fighting off the rain. It's blessing your marriage.'

'Perhaps.'

* * *

5

On hearing the thunder, Ioane Matete went to the door and let his hand feel the strength of the downpour. He was a man who knew weather. He had spent his life at sea. He had been in storms with sixty-foot waves, he had known winds that had driven him hundreds of miles off course and lightning that felled whole forests of trees. He had stood in the opening rain of the monsoon more times than he could remember and had felt the first fat drops hit his skin; plentiful, abundant, rejoicing rain. That was rain he recognised and it was not what was falling now. In all his life, Ioane Matete had never seen a storm like this.

There was no love in the rain he watched pound the village of Moana. This rain attacked the land, it tried to flatten the plants and drill through the roofs of houses. And this thunder did not rumble, it roared the bellowing clatter of a thousand crashing skulls. It made the ground shudder as though it was about to split open and swallow the village. And the lightning was now close and getting closer, creeping up on the village like the waves up the sand. It was menacing and deliberate. Ioane Matete knew that it wanted a sacrifice. He laughed, took a step outside and stared up at the heavens. He let out a howl and with his arms spread out and his head facing the sky, moved around in a slow circle, daring the weather to take him. Within seconds he was soaked to the skin and bolts of lightning had struck on either side of him. He smiled.

'So it's not me you're after.'

*   *   *

A small boy ran into Temalisi's house and announced that Ioane Matete wanted to have the ceremony on the beach.

'Why?' asked the bride.

The boy shrugged. 'He says he'll see you in half an hour. He says not to worry about the weather. He says you'll get wet.'

'Tell him we'll be there,' said Temalisi. 'Can you pass the message on to Tom Havealeta, please?'

'Okay,' replied the boy reluctantly, preparing to head back into the rain.

'What's it like out there?' Amalia asked quietly.

'The rain drops are bruising my skin,' came the answer as the boy launched himself into the storm.

Amalia stood up and ripped off the pretty white dress she was wearing.

'I'll be as good as naked in this,' she said to her mother's questioning glance. 'I'm going to wear my brown *lavalava*. It will be better. The village has turned to mud. Brown is the right colour. And my husband will see me with a *lavalava* wrapped around my waist every day. Let it start now. What top can I wear?'

Excitement grew slowly inside Amalia Hoko, starting as a small knot in her stomach and spreading throughout her whole body. It was as if the pores on her skin were opening and new life was being drawn right into her heart. She ran to the wide windows at the front of the house and stuck her head outside. The rain pummelled down, massaging her scalp. She reached out and grabbed the sea-spray at the window. She rubbed the salty water into her arms and inhaled deeply.

'That smell!' she called out to her mother, luxuriating in the aroma of ocean mixed with the crisp scent of fresh mud.

'Put some clothes on, little Amalia,' Temalisi softly scolded. 'You're getting married any minute now. Your father would be so proud.'

Amalia looked at her mother sadly and shook her head, 'No, Tema, he wouldn't be.'

Ioane Matete was the first to arrive on the beach. With a stick he drew an aisle in the sand – this would be his church if only for the few seconds before it was washed away. He stood at the top of it, waiting for his bride. He remained there, standing straight, impervious to the weather, without thoughts.

Tom Havealeta ventured down to the water's edge, holding a palm leaf over his head. 'What's the meaning of this?' he demanded, straining against the wind, wiping sand from his face. 'You can't expect to get married out here?'

'I do,' replied Ioane Matete. 'I've always dreamt of having my wedding on the shore.'

'Well, I'm afraid,' Tom gestured around him as a heavy gust of wind blew the palm leaf from his hand, 'that it is not going to be . . .' but then he trailed off. Ioane Matete was staring straight into his eyes and he saw that there was no point in arguing. 'Okay,' he said.

A few more people now left their houses and ventured to the beach, more out of curiosity than in belief that the wedding would take place. The largest family in the village, the Tatafus, had at first refused to leave their shelter, but theirs was the oldest house and their palm roof had not been able to withstand the rain and the wind. They weren't going to get any wetter, so they walked down, through the mud, to the sand.

'Come on, Amalia, it's time to go.'

'How do I look?'

Amalia Hoko, as she was for the last time, looked like a child. Her shoulder-length brown hair had gone even curlier in the rain and the frizz made her face seem younger than its sixteen years. Her *lavalava* was straight and shapeless, hiding her modest curves – she seemed as flat-chested and narrow as a boy.

'Like someone's wife,' lied her mother, holding tightly to her daughter's hand. 'Now, promise me you'll be good to your husband.'

'I'll try to be. If you want me to be. If you're sure this is right.'

'I do, I am.'

'And one day you'll explain to me why, why we are going against tradition?'

'Yes, my Amalia,' said her mother, stroking her arm. 'But I think you'll understand for yourself the day your first child is born.'

'But if I don't, you'll tell me then?'

'Yes.'

'Okay then.'

'Good girl.' The mother reached out and kissed the forehead of her daughter. 'Right, it's time for me to go.

The next time I hug you, you'll be a married woman. Goodbye, little one.'

She left Amalia in the doorway and hurried down to the beach.

Ioane Matete observed as his soon-to-be mother-in-law joined the rest of the villagers. He laughed at the wedding party shivering on the beach. They could have been the half-drowned survivors of a shipwreck. He knew they wanted to give respect to Amalia, the little girl who had grown up amongst them, who was as much a part of the village as they were, but look at them now, he thought to himself; shadows with downcast faces and clothes dragged apart by the wind.

As Ioane Matete watched, a group of pigs took advantage of a break in the lightning to run back to the shelter of their pen. They knocked into an old man on his way down to the beach. The man fell into thick mud. Ioane Matete laughed. 'This is how weddings should be,' he thought to himself, feeling the chaos all round him as something internal, primeval – something wonderful.

Amalia stepped out of the house as a bride and walked alone along the beach towards the man who would be her husband. Her *lavalava* was battered by the wind, her hair flew in all directions around her face and she quickly became as wet as those who waited for her. She saw her mother standing at the back of the group and a man of about Temalisi's age at the front, next to Tom Havealeta. He must be Ioane Matete.

'I don't remember what he looks like,' she thought, but then comforted herself by noticing that with their faces screwed up against the wind, with their brightly coloured clothes trying to fly away, with mud splashed all over their calves, everybody was almost unrecognisable. It seemed to her that the man she was going to marry was the only person who was smiling. 'It's a strange day,' she thought. 'We're going to be unhappy.'

Amalia stopped thinking about the wedding; instead she concentrated on the walk along the shore. She paid attention. She tried to feel each grain of sand that touched the sole of her foot, she tried to see each wave that broke, and tried to absorb every drop of rain that fell on her body. 'I am a part of the island,' she told herself, comforted by the idea that Amalia Hoko had never existed, that she was as unimportant as each tree, each bush, each piece of the island's whole. She was not a girl who would have to live with what she was doing. She was not giving her body and soul away to a stranger. She was simply a part of the island, nothing more, nothing less.

Ioane Matete saw that his wife-to-be was unaffected by the weather. Good. He wanted a woman like that. The lightning was moving away and she was walking confidently towards him, not rushing to get out of the rain, not in a hurry.

'We're ready,' he said.

'Very well,' replied Tom Havealeta and the service began.

Ioane Matete thought he had forgotten the details of the wedding ceremony. In his head it had mingled with the religions and traditions he had encountered around the world. But as he listened to the familiar Christian service, he realised that he had attributed a lot of the island's ways to other places. He remembered a great deal more than he expected – it was as though he had never gone away. The only part that was new to him was a tradition from the village. Tom announced he would tie their little fingers together. This meant it was almost over.

Amalia watched as her delicate finger was crushed against her husband's large, rough one. There was hair on his, and blood under the nail. She did not like the comparison between them. How could she have anything in common with a finger so unlike her own? How could she live with it? She imagined what it would be like to share a house with that finger, and could not. How then could she sleep with it? She glanced back at her mother for comfort and wished her father was standing behind her.

At that moment the thunder and the lightning returned, adding their voices to that of the wind and the rain. The thunder bellowed so loudly that Tom was forced to pause and wait for it to calm a little so that he might be heard. The lightning struck a tree in the forest nearby, splitting it in two; one half falling into the thick mud beneath, the other smouldering. The guests huddled together.

'Amalia,' Temalisi called out to her daughter. 'Are you okay?'

'Yes,' she yelled back, but while the wind had carried Temalisi's words to the bride, it took Amalia's away from her mother.

'Let's hurry up,' Amalia said to Tom Havealeta. 'I think we all want to be out of here.'

The lightning strode lazily, like a man on stilts, striking now and again on its way from the forest towards the huddled islanders. When it reached a point directly above Tom's head, it paused. The villagers looked up in terror. They wanted to run but Ioane Matete turned around and faced them. They stopped moving, stayed where they were; their legs wouldn't carry them away.

Tom no longer cared whether people could hear him or not, he just wanted this inappropriate, God-defying ceremony to end. He waved his hand in front of the bride and groom to attract their attention and declared them man and wife.

There was a clap of thunder, louder even than all the others, the sound of the sky being torn in two, and then lightning, drawing its legs up beneath it, pounced. The wedding guests were scattered, thrown away, blasted back across the beach. The village lay stunned on the sand.

When she came to, Amalia questioned whether she had invented the whole morning. The sky was blue, the sun was out, no trees seemed to have blown over and the sea was serene. She didn't know how long she had been unconscious or what had happened. Had she really just married in a storm? But, in the silence, there was a reminder of the wedding: the smell of burnt flesh.

Amalia stood up slowly and brushed the sand from her damp dress. She saw Ioane Matete, her friend Laita watching her and, further up the beach, the rest of the villagers. They were on their knees, huddled in a circle as if in discovery of treasure, or the dead. She turned her face to the sky expecting to feel rain but it was her own tears that were wetting her cheeks. Amalia vomited. She knew what she would find when she broke through the backs of her neighbours: her mother's body.

THE CRAB

Amalia Matete woke up alone on the first day of her life as a married woman. She peered down at her battered body and rubbed the bruises on her thighs. She felt sore between her legs. There was blood on the leaf matting beneath her. She put her nose to the stain and sniffed. The smell contained everything that had happened to her in the last twenty-four hours. She smelt her own pain and the end of her childhood. She smelt the sweat of her husband, the drops that must have fallen off his body from the effort of pinning her down and depositing his fluids into a hole she had hardly been aware of having. But below those smells she also sniffed her mother, who, up until last night, had slept on these reeds, had lived in this room. Amalia couldn't think of her as dead, so she tried not to think of her at all.

'I suppose it's my room now,' Amalia Matete said out loud.

Her gaze fell on the chest that her father had brought back from the sea. He had found it washed up on the sand bar just off their beach. Inside there had been six cans of blue paint, which had turned every room in the house the colour of one of those island mornings when the sun rose through thin clouds and its light bounced off the pale water below. Her parents had put all their things into that chest, making the room seem quite empty.

Amalia saw the window that her mother looked out of every morning before coming to wake her. Temalisi knew that her daughter's first question would be, 'how's the sea today?' and Amalia remembered her mother sitting next to her on the floor, leaning over to kiss her and saying, 'the sea, Amalia, is jumping with catfish', 'the sea is still asleep like you', 'the sea is cold today and grey', 'today the sea is attacking the house', 'in this sea your father will fill his nets', 'the boatman is out on the sea this morning'.

Amalia got up from her mat and, ignoring the pain, walked to her old room to find something to put on. She wondered if it was supposed to hurt this much. Laita Havealeta had told her about her wedding night and had talked about soreness, but she had said it was temporary, a momentary discomfort, nothing more.

That wasn't what this was.

All her clothes were hung on nails in the wall. Her father had hammered them in, hitting his thumb twice for every time he hit metal. He'd given up after five, claiming his hands were too important to lose, since his hands fed them all. The nails had lasted and he had died.

She had to stop thinking about her parents. She pinched the skin on her hand. She was married now and the last thing her mother had ever asked her to do was to look after her husband. She should have demanded to know why. She should have refused. But she hadn't and now she was stuck with her promise.

She was someone's wife. She would act accordingly, even though she didn't know what that meant. She thought she could ask Laita; she had only married a year ago – she would still remember when it was new. But something, pride perhaps, stopped Amalia Matete from leaving the house.

She dressed sensibly, putting on a blue *lavalava* and a white shirt. She thought about wearing shoes, but couldn't bring herself to put them on. It would feel wrong in this house. The wood panels under her bare feet were comforting. She'd trod on them every day of her life. Tying her dark curls up in a handkerchief, she headed to the back of the house, into the kitchen.

'I'll make my husband some breakfast,' she mouthed silently.

She made special food using pork that had been prepared for the wedding, and boiled yam. She remembered the villagers' eyes as her husband dragged her away from her mother and forced her back to the house. Why had he done that? What special cruelty was it? Did he not care that her mother had gone, did he not understand that she had to mourn? Was this dragging and beating what husbands did on the first night of their marriages?

One of the women had tried to talk to him. Laita? Amalia put her hand to her head feeling again how he had pulled her by her hair, how he had warned them all; 'Keep away. She is my wife.' *His wife, his thing*. And she had gone along with it. When the villagers had followed, had tried to protect her, had tried to take her home with them, she'd told them to do as he'd ordered. Why? So that he could throw her down on her mother's mat and touch her and make her touch him, when all she'd wanted to do was cry.

'My friends must think I'm an idiot, worse than an idiot, for getting married, for not running away. They're right. I am an idiot, an idiot covered with marks like an octopus' ink. Why did I do it? Why did Tema want me to? The island warned me. Tradition warned me.'

She set the food aside and waited for her husband to come back.

'He's probably gone to explore the village,' she told herself.

A shout, followed by the sound of feet entering her house, caused Amalia Matete to breathe in deeply. She put a smile on her face that made a cut on her lip ache and went out to greet her visitor. It wasn't her husband.

'Amalia Hoko—' began Tom, but he stopped when he saw the young girl's face. 'Oh, what has he done?'

'I am Amalia Matete,' she corrected, stepping away from the opening arms that were approaching her, knowing she'd be hurt if they touched her body, even gently.

'Oh, Amalia. Come home with me.'

'I'm married now. A wife can't leave her husband.'

'Well, fortunately, your husband has left you. He's taken my boat.'

'He must be fishing.'

'No, Amalia . . .'

'I'll get you some breakfast. I've just made some. It's delicious.' Amalia Matete put her thumb to her four fingers and raised her hand to her mouth, signalling that he should eat.

She ran back into the kitchen, stood by the door for a few seconds to let the wind hide the tears in her eyes, then brought out the plate she had prepared for her husband. She sat opposite Tom, careful to tuck her legs underneath her, the soles of her feet facing away from her guest.

'Amalia,' he said, his voice that of her friend, not simply a man of the church, 'I'm sorry about your mother.'

'Mmm hmm,' Amalia Matete replied.

Tom ripped the pork apart in his hands and took a bite. 'We cremated her last night. We thought it would be best, considering the state of the body.' He paused, waiting for Amalia to react.

'You burned her?'

'Yes.'

'Then how can I bury her? How can I put her next to my father and my grandparents? How can I lie next to her when I die?' she asked, her voice growing faster and faster with panic.

'We had to, Amalia. She had been hit by lightning, she was . . . But you can still bury her. The ashes are in the house next door.'

Amalia wasn't listening. She pictured her mother's body as ash. She saw it as a piece of barbequed *taro* that had been left in the fire too long. No one wanted burnt *taro*. The image would not leave her mind; her mother as some discarded vegetable. She could not understand why Tom had done something so savage.

'She won't be whole in heaven,' she said.

'Amalia, when we say that we are not talking about the body. The body remains here on earth. Your mother lived a whole life; she loved her father, then her husband and you. She was kind to the rest of the village and generous with her pigs. Your mother is whole, she always has been.'

Amalia slowly shook her head. She wanted to believe him but in her heart she knew he was wrong.

'Is there anything you need?' he asked.

'No. Not from you. I have a husband now.'

'Amalia, I think he might be gone a long time. He was seen heading around the headland through the coral. He's probably going to Laumua. His boat is there. We tried to follow him. Hosea Unga was out on the sea when Ioane left, but only some of the Tatafus can sail through the pass.' Tom paused. 'And Ioane Matete, it seems.'

Amalia stood up. 'Sorry, but I have to go . . . and make breakfast for my husband.'

'Amalia,' started Tom, 'I'm not a stranger, I . . .' but

she had already left the room. He finished his food slowly, in silence, hoping that she would return and speak to him. When she did not, he got up, stepped over the pig board on the side entrance and left the house.

This time Amalia Mátete cooked fish, frying it over her little stove.

'We're nearly out of oil,' she said, aloud once more. 'My husband can go and pick some up when he gets back. Perhaps that's where he's gone now. I must tell him about my father's boat. Imagine thinking he has to use someone else's. He'll be angry that I didn't mention it sooner.'

She started boiling water for more yams but decided to make him breadfruit instead.

'It'll give him energy; he's been up a long time.'

She left the food cooking and went back to her new room. She hesitated by the door, afraid to enter; that room contained the last traces of her mother and the only memory she had of her husband.

'I have to clean it out before he gets back,' she told herself firmly. But instead she went into her old room. She lay down and fell into an exhausted sleep.

Amalia Matete woke up to the smell of burning breadfruit. She rushed through into the kitchen, grabbed the pan and took it to the back door. No one was on the beach. She ran with the evidence of her failure into the sea and kept running until the weight of the water against her legs forced her to slow. Waist deep, she stared at the pan, half angry at herself, half afraid of what her husband would say. She dived under the water and scooped up some sand for scouring.

She swam down to the sea bottom, pulling herself along by digging the pan into the sand. She held her legs tightly pressed together and kicked them in unison, pretending to be a mermaid, imagining that she never need return to the world above. She opened her eyes and saw fish, coral, seaweed and seashells. She swam around a jellyfish. A curiously-shaped pink shell, the size of a frangipani petal, caught her eye. It was flat along the bottom with straight sides and a smooth circular top. She clamped her hand around it, like a shark pouncing on its prey, and held it in a closed fist. She wanted to stay down there, a mermaid, a shark, and pretend that her mother was alive, that she had never been made to marry. She wanted to stay down there so badly that she begged her lungs, 'just a little while longer, just one more moment', but her lungs wanted air.

Back on the beach she prayed that her soaking clothes would be dry before her husband returned. On the waistband of her *lavalava* she made a pocket for the shell she had picked up and then began to scrub away all the traces of burning from her pan.

By the time Amalia Matete returned to the house it was nearly midday and her husband had still not come back.

'What would he like for lunch?' she asked herself as she walked into the kitchen. She stood, dripping on the floor, shivering a little now she was out of the sun. There wasn't much to eat. Her neighbours had picked up most of the wedding food while she was swimming. It would feed the whole village for a few days. They had left her a flower on the kitchen floor. Amalia held it up to her nose then put it behind her left ear. No, she was married. She moved it to her right.

'Fish,' she said and began to cook the last of it, enjoying the heat from the stove and the smell from the frying pan. She was hungry. She stuck out her tongue and let the smell linger on her taste buds. She would make something for herself as soon as it was finished. But first, she put everything on her husband's plate and set it to one side for him.

The three women she liked best in the village put their heads around the door.

'Amalia,' said Laita, with sadness and love in her eyes, 'how are you?'

'I'm fine,' she replied, 'but very busy.'

'You're not fine. What are you doing? Let us help.'

'No. I need to sort the house out. My husband is exploring. I want it to be clean when he returns. Maybe you could come back once he's here. I'm sure he'd like that.'

'Amalia . . .' Zeno Tatafu, the schoolteacher who had taught three generations of Hoko women, tried.

Amalia turned her head away. Them or him? Their love or his beatings? The choice had been made for her on her wedding day. 'Please don't come back until then,' she said. 'He'll think I haven't been working.'

'Okay, Amalia. But you know where we are if you need us,' said Whinney, the doctor's wife.

'No, Whinney, it is not okay,' Laita said. 'Amalia, we're your friends. You can be sad in front of us, or confused or angry or hurt or even frightened. Why are you talking like this? This isn't you.'

'It is me. I am married now.'

'And—'

'Listen, Laita. I am not you. I did not marry a seahorse who I can drift with, who will court me and carry the eggs I give him. I married an eel and I am a crab. I tried to be myself last night. I tried to reason and to fight and be the "me" you know. You can see the results; the signs of the eel's teeth are all over my body. So what does a crab do? It changes its shell so that it changes its scent, so that the eel no longer wants to attack it. I am Amalia Matete now. I am in the only shell that will keep me safe and I need to clean the house. Please Laita. Please Whinney. Zeno, please.'

'Amalia, my lovely Amalia. Maybe you are right and maybe you are not, but don't forget it is not only the crab that changes. The eel has to change too as he moves from the river to the sea.'

'I know, Laita. But that part isn't up to the crab.'

'No, I suppose it isn't.'

So they left, and Amalia was about to start on her own food when she saw that the stove had gone out. There was no gas. There would be no more hot food until it was filled.

'My husband will do that when he returns. It's a

man's job,' she decided, remembering that it had been her father that had bought the new canisters from their neighbours before he had died. The gas was heavy. She had often helped her mother with it and both of them had joked about Amalia marrying whoever next walked along the road so her new husband could carry it the rest of the way home. Now she would never have to fill it again. That was a good thought.

Perhaps she'd cook on a fire outside until he got back. It would remind her of fishing trips with her father when they'd stopped off on uninhabited islands and camped, eating warm fish off large leaves. She thought that collecting the wood would take her mind off everything else, and she was good at starting fires, at building a pyramid of sticks that would light quickly. She'd find some leaves for kindling, then perhaps she would heat some pork. No: all the wood on the island was soaked from the wedding storm.

Her stomach rumbled. She hadn't eaten since before the wedding, she realised. She'd find something that didn't need heating. The sea would feed her. She ran outside, back into the sun, and up to her father's old boat, lying upside down on the beach. One of the fishermen, a Tatafu, waved at her and she waved back. She pushed the boat out before he could walk over to her. It was heavy but she was tough when she wanted to be.

Amalia Matete felt peaceful out in the little rowing boat. She felt natural in it. She had been born in this boat, she had lost her first tooth in it, she had spent hours in it being told stories by her father, and even her mother . . . Enough thinking.

Her arms were strong and she was a good rower, good enough to have been a fisherman her father had said. She pointed the boat to where she saw birds hovering over the surface, knowing that they were looking for the same thing she was and had probably found it. To stave off her hunger she took the little pink shell out of the top of her *lavalava*, put it in her mouth and sucked the salt off it. She enjoyed the sharp sour taste as she pulled on the oars. The birds flew off at her approach.

She put down a line and waited patiently. Amalia Matete was patience. She knew that to catch a fish she had to become a part of the ocean. She concentrated. She allowed herself to be absorbed by the water. Time passed without her noticing. She was no longer hungry. She was the waves. She was the sea. She felt a tug on the line.

It was a young tuna. She grappled with the hook in its mouth. It caught awkwardly and its blood spilled into the boat. It soaked into her clothes. She wondered where so much blood came from. Was it lucky to have a fish bleed on her? Or deeply unlucky? She had bled too.

She removed the hook and brought the fish's head down firmly on the deck. Then she leant out over the side of the boat and rinsed her catch in the sea. She watched the blood mix with the clear water. On an impulse she put her finger into the ocean and drew on the surface the outline of the shape the blood made.

Amalia Matete hacked off the head of the fish. It was no longer an animal, it was a beheaded mermaid, she thought, but then corrected herself: it was her dinner. She cut off the tail, sliced along its side and scraped out the guts. She took the shell out of her mouth and wrapped it once again in her blood-drenched skirt. She bit into the cold flesh of the fish and drank a little of the remaining blood. The meat tasted good. It lifted her spirits. She ate more. Now she was thirsty. She popped the eyes into her mouth and sucked out their moisture.

She stared back at the island and examined her house sitting proudly on the water's edge. It seemed so solid from here, so firm, as if it could protect her from anything. How close to the sea it was, yet it had never been swept away. Even on the night her father died, when the full moon had caused the tides to come right up into the village, it had remained undamaged. How strange that was, now she came to think about it. But the beach was a steep slope and her house jutted above the water, only the stilts that held up the front were touched by the sea. The large windows looked like benevolent eyes, smiling in her direction. She was ready to go home. She threw the bones, skin and head overboard and started rowing to the shore.

'My husband will be back by now,' she said out loud and felt the fish in her stomach twist and twirl.

The house was empty. Amalia Matete drank straight from the rain tank and went inside. She called out,

'Ioane Matete,' pretending that her marriage was like her parents', pretending she wanted him to be there. She listened to her voice reverberate, filling the silence. 'Husband,' she yelled. Amalia thought she heard people approaching the house, but no one entered. She picked up a pillow and put it over her face. She breathed in deeply through her nose and screamed into it from the bottom of her lungs for all the hurt inside her; for her abandonment, for the pain between her legs, for the loss of her mother, the enslavement of her body and for all the unknown things that were yet to come, and she kept on screaming until she could scream no more.

Amalia Matete spent the rest of the afternoon gathering and plaiting leaves, hiding as she did so from the people who loved her and came to wish her well. She would make a mat to sleep on. At first she thought of it as a mat for her mother's room, but that didn't feel right. Then she thought of it as her new mat, but that wasn't it either. Neither did the idea that it was a marriage mat seem plausible to her. Had she invented her husband? Had he ever existed? Was she married at all? She tried to picture him, but every time she did, all she saw was the storm and the faces of her parents. Her husband was a ghost to her. She pulled up her *lavalava* and touched her bruises.

'So you are real,' she said. 'But where are you?'

She felt panic rising up inside her once again. She was scared but didn't know of what. Did she want him to come back or didn't she? She wished her mother were still here. They used to make matting together.

'I am alone,' she said and carried on weaving. 'It is our mat but I'll sleep here without you.'

Once the mat was finished Amalia Matete took out the shell she had found that morning. She fingered it nervously, trying to make sense of her world through this piece of the sea.

'Tell me what to do,' she begged it, rubbing her thumb over its soft sides, 'tell me how to act.' But the shell did not speak to her. She pressed its cold surface to the side of her face and let it bump over her swollen skin. 'Fix me, please,' she asked it, 'don't leave me alone.' But the shell was just a shell. 'I need Tema,' she told no one, 'and my father, Tamatoa.' She breathed into the bottom of the shell and licked it, but there was no salt left.

Amalia put the shell down on the floor and lay beside it. She put her hands on her stomach and allowed herself to feel her emptiness. Then a warmth, which must have been there all along, revealed itself.

Amalia Matete realised that, in spite of everything, she was not alone.

BABY MATETE

Amalia Matete knew, instinctively, all of a sudden, that she would die during childbirth. Her grandmother had died giving birth to her mother; it was a common thing in the village, every family had lost someone that way. Death came to the young, it was how it was: babies died before they became children, children were killed in accidents on the plantations or in the water; and she, at sixteen, was still young. Besides, her wedding had caused one death, her mother's, why wouldn't it be the cause of her own? Why had her mother wanted her to marry Ioane Matete? Why hadn't she warned her about what having a husband would mean? When Amalia died in nine months she would see her mother again and be able to ask her. She wasn't afraid to die, and so now, knowing that she would, she was suddenly no longer afraid to live.

*   *   *

During the first month of her pregnancy, Amalia Matete grew to understand that Ioane was gone and might never come back.

She flung open the door and let the fresh sea air breeze through. Before her marriage, Amalia had never lived in darkness. She stood at the side door and breathed in her village. There, to her right, as it always had been, was the sea. Amalia liked to leave the big window open so that the spray made puddles on her floor, but today the water was far down the beach. To her left were the four other houses, connected by sand paths, separated by grass. Moana. Home.

It was just before midday and the women were all inside, cooking. Amalia could smell their food: *palusami*, (her favourite, how she loved the tinned corned beef cooked in an underground oven, with chillies and garlic, wrapped up in *taro* leaves), yams, fish in coconut sauce, breadfruit. She took a deep breath. The men who had been up in their plantations were walking back home. As Amalia watched them chat and joke with one another, a smile appeared on her face. She saw them call out to those who had fished at dawn, now sitting in a shady spot of grass at the top of the village, next to the graveyard and before the wilderness of trees. School had just finished and children were playing in the forest on the far side of her house. She could not see them but could hear their voices. She walked to her neighbours' houses and spoke to them for the first time in weeks.

Amalia buried her mother's ashes next to where her

father lay. To ward off bad spirits she decorated the grave with smashed pieces of glass in a kaleidoscope of colours. She invited the villagers to the graveside and was glad to be held in the arms of the women she had always known and be comforted by the steady, sombre faces of the men who had fished with her father. Together the whole village said goodbye to Temalisi Hoko, with stories of her life and with songs to see her on her way. They waited for her soul to leave the island and when the sun reflected off the glass they saw her moving heavenwards in a jagged beam of light that looked like lightning. A warm wind brushed Amalia lightly on her cheek and she felt Laita squeeze her hand. She knew then that as long as her husband remained at sea, she would be amongst friends. By the end of her first month she was almost happy.

During the second month of her pregnancy, Amalia Matete spent her days learning how to manage the house. The food that was left by her door once a week, food she had never questioned before, was from the first of her neighbours, the Unga family. The plantation that she thought was theirs, that their three grown sons farmed, was in fact her mother's and now hers.

Her second neighbours, the Tatafus, could get the things she needed from the island's town, Laumua. Only a few of the villagers were able to sail through the coral, so the Tatafus made the trip once every few weeks, weighed down with orders from their friends to buy this or sell that. It took them a day to get there and another to get back. Amalia always lost track of who exactly lived in the old rambling house and who had moved away. It was constantly awash with family; grand-children, great-grandchildren, cousins, brothers, sisters, uncles and aunts, all watched calmly by an old couple who'd had twenty-one children when they were young and had seen most of what was to be seen. Amalia repaid them for the cloth, the shoes, the cooking gas, which they carried right into her kitchen, and for all the little things they brought her, by giving them one of her pigs. The Tatafus always needed more food and Amalia's animals were the best in the village. Her family had owned pigs for as long as anyone could remember and although they just let them alone, they thrived. The villagers said that meant that the Hokos were lucky people.

Her third neighbours, the Havealetas, wanted to teach her to dance.

'Come on Amalia,' said her friend Laita.

'My mother has just died. My husband has gone. I can't dance.'

'If you don't dance now, when will you? To dance is to live, Amalia. You're alive.'

'My mother never taught me. She can't have wanted me to learn.'

'You didn't need to learn when she was here. You used to smile, you swam. Now, you need to dance. It will remind you how to live. It will connect you to God.'

So Laita taught Amalia and some of the younger Tatafu girls how to plant their feet firmly on the island soil and move their arms as if they were the waves and the wind. Amalia was good at it. She loved the slow pace of her arms drawing pictures in the air. She had strong legs and enjoyed the challenge of keeping her feet controlled and dancing with her knees. They would perform to the village during the festival next year. Except, of course, Amalia would have died by then. She was practising for no reason except the fun of dancing. She decided not to tell anyone about the baby just yet. She was enjoying her freedom.

Her fourth neighbours, the Vaites, liked her reed matting. Temalisi used to make it for them, but now Amalia was the only one in the village who knew the secret of weaving so tightly that a mat would not fall apart even in the strongest wind. They were old and needed her help. All their daughters had moved away and they had no sons. The old man was the village doctor. He had known Amalia's every ailment since she was born. She was glad she could finally pay him back for all his many kindnesses.

By depending on her neighbours, Amalia quickly grew independent. She got used to being alone in her house. She grew up. By the end of her second month she felt her life was in order.

During the third month of her pregnancy, Amalia Matete started talking to her baby.

'It's evening,' she said to her stomach at the end of every day. 'Let's go swimming.' And every evening she took her baby into the sea to get it used to the water at night.

'Anyone can swim during the day,' she told the little person growing inside her. 'But to really understand the ocean you have to know it at night. You have to be able to walk into the sea when the stonefish are out and not get stung. You have to know how to step over the rocks without stubbing your toe. You have to remember that the water lulls people into its rips and you must stand up to it. And you must know how not to feel cold. You have to *learn* not to be cold. You have to let the warm air into your skin but keep the cold water out. You have to boil the water around you, use the heat of your body to make the water hot enough to warm you and then your body hot enough to heat the water. If you don't understand the sea you'll think that's impossible, but I'm here and I'm warm. You'll know it's possible because you'll know the sea at night. You're going to love the ocean; I think I can feel you loving it already.'

She grew used to chatting away to her stomach and by the end of her third month it was a habit she couldn't break.

During the fourth month of her pregnancy, Amalia Matete decided to do something she had always longed to do. She had never climbed a coconut tree. Now she realised she was running out of time. She would be dead in five months and any moment now her belly might start to bulge and she wouldn't be able to climb any more. She couldn't bear the idea of dying without looking out at Moana from a height, without ever seeing the roof of her house, or the top of her neighbours' heads. She walked down to the beach and stared at a tree. She grew nervous just being under it.

'Shall I pick you one?' said a voice and Amalia turned around and saw Lave Unga standing next to her. He was always bringing her coconuts from the plantation. He was twenty-five, younger than Ioane Matete, she thought, broad shouldered and handsome. Even though they were both married, she imagined she would have liked him as a husband. She wondered what her life would have been like if she hadn't married Ioane. Were all husbands the same? Had her father been like Ioane before she was born? That was something she couldn't believe.

Nearly all the village men had tattoos on their legs, a tradition from another island far away that had trickled over the ocean to Moana, losing its meaning on the journey and turning to scribbles carved into the skin with a turtle-shell chisel. Amalia always thought Lave's were the most interesting. One was a pair of jagged inter-crossing lines, a sign of peace, another a small wobbly circle and the third could be a wave or a bird.

He saw her looking at them. 'You see this,' he said, smiling, pointing to the circle. 'This is a coconut.'

'You used to tell me it was the world,' Amalia replied.

'A coconut is the world,' he said without thinking, practised at making up stories about his tattoo. He never told the truth because his brother Mori had done the tattooing after they'd both drunk too much home-brew. 'A coconut tree contains everything we could possibly want. It has milk for drinking, meat for eating, *copra* for oil and feeding the pigs, leaves for thatching, plus we use the bark for cleaning ourselves once the food has passed through. What else is there in the world?' he asked and Amalia couldn't answer.

'I need to pick one myself,' she told him. 'I've never done it before.'

'Never? Really? Why not?'

'I don't know. I just haven't.'

'Well, the best way is to throw things up into the tree. But make sure you run out of the way as quickly as possible. You don't want a coconut falling on your head. That's how my grandfather died. They found him up on the plantation a few days later. Dead. As dead as could be.'

'I have to climb it. Can you show me how?'

Lave Unga took off his shirt and rolled it into a long thin rope. Amalia let her eyes rest on his chest. He hitched up his *sulu* and she lingered on his legs. Ioane Matete was the only man she had seen naked. Lave wrapped the shirt around the trunk of the tree and held it firmly in each hand. Then he started climbing, gripping with his knees, moving the shirt rope higher, moving his legs up to meet his hands, until he was at the top.

'It's easy,' he shouted and then loosened his grip and slid down the tree, as though it was a greasy pole. 'Use my shirt to begin with. Once you can climb with that, you won't need it any more. It's easier without it, but first you have to learn how.'

'I only want to get to the top once – then I'll be happy.'

'Then you'll be happy very soon! Here.' He handed her his shirt.

Amalia Matete found climbing exhausting. It took all her strength to hold her weight with just her legs after her arms let go to fling the shirt further up the tree. She kept slipping down the trunk and soon she was covered with scratches and bruises. She wondered if Lave was looking at her legs. She wished they were unmarked. Slowly she made it further up, then further up still. She got to just below half way.

'Lave, what do you think you are doing!'

'I'm teaching Amalia to climb,' he told his mother, who was bearing down on their tree.

'She's not a child any more. She shouldn't be climbing trees! She's a married woman.'

Amalia glanced down at Lave and he up at her. They realised at the same time that it was true.

'Sorry,' Lave Unga said.

'I'm sorry too,' said Amalia and she dropped to the ground. 'Here's your shirt. Thank you, eh?'

He walked away.

'I know you may not feel like it, Amalia, but you have to start acting like a woman now, not a girl.'

Amalia held her stomach and silently agreed. Her baby hadn't liked it while she was up the tree.

By the end of her fourth month Amalia had given up her dream of climbing a coconut tree.

* * *

During the fifth month of her pregnancy, mosquitoes started biting Amalia Matete. She had only been bitten before once in her life, on her first day in this world, when a perfect little red spot had appeared in the centre of her forehead. Her mother had thought it was good luck. But the insects noticed her now and tucked in. She reacted badly to the bites; blisters came up on her arms and legs. They itched and she scratched. She went to see Doctor Vaite.

'You're changing, Amalia. The mosquitoes think you're someone new. They don't recognise your smell anymore.'

'I'm going to have a baby. Is it her they can smell?'

'Are you sure, Amalia?'

'Yes. I know it.'

'You must be happy.'

'I must be.'

'And you think it's a girl?'

'Yes.'

'It could be the baby,' the doctor told her, 'or it could just be you. A lot has happened to you recently, Amalia. It's no wonder you're not who you were. How are you feeling? I should examine you.'

'I'm fine. Will the bites hurt the baby?'

'No, it'll be okay. You're young and healthy. You shouldn't have any problems. But don't scratch.'

By the end of her fifth month, the mosquitoes left Amalia alone.

During the sixth month of her pregnancy, the whole village knew that Amalia Matete was to have a baby.

The doctor had told his wife about the child and she had told one other woman in confidence and soon everyone knew. 'The coconut wireless,' Amalia thought when people started congratulating her. But she did not mind, she was showing now, it was no longer possible to hide the growth in her stomach. It was as though she had swallowed a melon whole and there it was protruding out of her small frame.

She stopped wearing her own straight tight dresses and put on her mother's, which were looser. Still her stomach bulged. At first she hated it. She hated the old women touching her and insisting she ate horrible things that would be 'good for the baby'. She hated feeling so large, being hot and uncomfortable, and she hated not being able to mess around with the younger children. She missed being agile. She missed her tiny flat stomach. She was going to be a mother, people kept telling her, but in her head she would rephrase it; she was going to have a baby. It wasn't quite the same thing.

But soon she started to enjoy her melon bump. It was fun to look so strange. She liked the tracks that snaked across her hips. They made her feel important. She was carrying a baby and because of that, the villagers crowded around her. She was scooped up by the women and made one of them. They all went into their storage chests and came out with their old baby things. The Havealetas gave her the clothes they had made for the children they never had. The Ungas sent everything that Lave's young children and their cousins had now grown out of, and even the Tatafus found some bits and pieces that had not yet fallen apart after being worn by count-less generations. The elderly Vaites had long ago sent their baby things to their daughters so the doctor's wife started sewing for Amalia, just as she had done for all the other girls in the village.

By the end of her sixth month, Amalia's child had everything it would need.

During the seventh month of her pregnancy, Amalia Matete started to think about who she would like to bring up her baby. Her first thought was the doctor and his wife. They would know how to take care of a child. They would be able to give it everything it needed. But they were old and resting at last after a lifetime's work. It wasn't fair to ask them to take on a little girl. Then she thought about the Havealetas who so desperately wanted a child. But if Amalia gave them her baby and something happened to them, her daughter would be all alone with no brothers and sisters. She couldn't risk that. More than anything she didn't want her baby to be lonely. Was that why her mother had wanted her to marry? So that she would have family? She thought about the Ungas. They seemed a good choice. Each of the three sons had a wife and three sons of their own. They all lived together. If her baby went there it would have lots of brothers to play with, but Amalia knew that the Ungas would not want her girl. They had been glad to have only boys; it meant they did not need to build any *fale*s. If a baby girl arrived in the house, all nine of the boys would have to move out into a hut as soon as they became men.

That left the Tatafus. She walked over to their house. It was midday and everyone was asleep. Bodies lay every- where. Babies slept in the arms of their mothers or brothers or sisters or cousins or aunts or grandmothers. The room was full of women and children, some snoring, some just enjoying lying in the shade. A few opened their eyes when Amalia stepped over them, but they thought nothing of her presence and dropped back to sleep. The family had once tried to keep track of which child belonged to which couple, but it was a useless task. The family resemblances were so strong that Amalia Matete wondered if she was even moving through the room or just passing over the same few children again and again. She made it across without stepping on anyone and sat down by the big open window that all the village homes had at the front of their houses, the one that faced the sea. She thought about this family, where all the boys were Vete and the girls Zeno. If she named her daughter Zeno they would presume it was theirs. She fell asleep in the sticky heat of the hot sun made warmer by many bodies, cooled occasionally from the breeze coming off the beach. Her own house was cooler, it was nearer the water, but she liked it here.

By the end of her seventh month she slept every afternoon with the Tatafus. Amalia knew that they would take care of her baby.

During the eighth month of her pregnancy, Amalia Matete did hardly anything at all. By now she was huge and had little energy for more than sleeping and eating. She started craving mangoes. Two of the Vetes swam over to the nearby island where they grew in abundance and picked them for her. She loved their sweet sugary taste, she loved letting their juice drip all over her hands and down her face and neck. The fruit cooled her and was the only thing that would stop the baby kicking.

'She's longing to swim,' she said and the women told her that meant the baby was strong.

'Your mother kicked your grandmother all through her last month. And you kicked your mother in the same way,' the doctor told her. 'It's taking after you both.'

Amalia did not like the idea that the baby would be like her mother because it made her want to live to see it.

'We've been friends,' she told her baby. 'But you'll have to live without me soon. I hope you'll be okay, baby Zeno. You're going to live with the Tatafus. They'll look after you. I have to go.'

The thought made her sad. She reminded herself that it was not just her mother she would see soon but her father also. Her father had rowed away when he knew he was dying and had never come back. She really was going home. By the end of her eighth month she was as tired as death and ready to give birth.

Amalia Matete gave birth exactly on time, on the day Dr Vaite had predicted. She screamed her way through the labour. The pain was unlike anything she had experienced.

'So this is death,' she thought as she pushed the baby out of her body.

But she didn't die. She lived. And a tiny perfect little boy was placed into her arms. As she kissed his bloody head, Amalia Matete realised she knew nothing about her own body. How could she ever have thought that he was a girl and she would leave him behind? As she held her son, she knew why her mother had wanted her to marry Ioane Matete. Tradition did not matter, she realised, and neither did years of bad luck. All that mattered was that she had a child. This was what her mother had wanted for her.

She never thought about death again and forgot that she had ever dreamt of a daughter who would kill her.

naming the baby

On the day after his birth, Amalia Matete named her baby Ioane after its father, but Ioane was far too adult a name for the little wrinkly-faced creature that she held in her arms. Ioane was a man's name, a rough name, a violent name, and her perfect little baby was none of those things. She tried to find traces of her husband in her son, but his little hands would never beat her and his tiny legs would never pin her down. She wondered if the lightness of the brown in his eyes, that was so different from the darkness of hers, was his father's colour. She could not remember Ioane's eyes and so chose to believe they were from her mother. It wasn't entirely true.

'You look just like your grandmother,' she told her child, and he gurgled back at her. 'If you were a girl I would name you after her. I'd name you Temalisi Matete. But you're not a girl and you're not an Ioane, not yet. Not ever. Don't be like him. Be you. But what are you?'

Amalia's child had been born with a full head of

curly hair, curls that the baby, as a boy and then a man, would hate and shave off, but which his mother could happily play with for hours.

'Shall I call him Curly?' she asked the doctor's wife, Whinney Vaite, who had moved into the house to help Amalia during the first couple of weeks.

'No,' came the definitive reply. 'These curls will fall out soon. A baby that is born with hair loses it quickly. Your baby may not end up with curls at all. Besides, what kind of name is Curly? Honestly, Amalia, think of the child.' And the old woman tutted and fussed and shook her head. She picked up the broom and began sweeping. 'Amalia, this house is a disgrace. You need to put something down on this floor, and the walls need repainting. In a few months the baby will eat everything that peels off them, and as soon as he crawls he'll get splinters.'

Amalia Matete did not reply.

'Are you listening to me?'

But the mother was too absorbed in her child to notice anything else. 'Have you smelled him, Whinney?' she asked. 'He smells wonderful. Like coconuts and mangoes and earth all mixed in together.'

'He'll smell like his own shit soon if you don't change him,' replied the doctor's wife. So Amalia cleaned him, found a new cloth and threw the old one out of the window into a tub full of water.

The baby hardly seemed human to Amalia. He was like a curious little fish, floundering out of the sea. He rasped for breath and she worried he was drowning.

'He's asking for milk. Feed the poor thing,' said the

doctor's wife, so Amalia lowered her simple brown dress to her waist and offered her breast to the baby. With nothing to hold it up, the dress fell to the floor. Amalia watched as her son's mouth searched for her nipple, found it, and began to drink.

'You shouldn't wear dresses while he's young. You'll spend half your life naked or taking clothes on and off. I'll bring you over some plain tops. Do you have material for a new *lavalava*?'

'Yes, I've made some out of my mother's old things. Watch him drinking. It tickles a little.'

'Soon you won't even notice.'

'I like noticing. Should I call him Fish? It's like he's been in the water for too long.'

Whinney Vaite sighed.

Amalia Matete had a permanent stream of visitors coming over to see the baby. All of them had different ideas about what she should call him.

'Name him Vete after my relatives,' suggested an elderly Zeno Tatafu.

'No, call him Tamatoa, after your father,' said the doctor.

'Hosea is what we'd call a boy,' confided the Havealetas.

'How about Vete?' another Zeno said.

'I like Simione,' Grandmother Unga added.

'No!' exclaimed her pregnant daughter-in-law, 'that's what I want to call my son.'

'Vete?'

'No, Simione.'

'They can have the same name. Anyway you might have a girl.'

'All us Unga wives have sons!'

'That's true enough,' said Grandmother Unga.

'Anyway, you've already named him Ioane, haven't you?' someone else asked.

'Yes,' replied Amalia. 'But I can't call him that. It's his father's name, not his.'

'Why not just call him Baby while he's little until another name sounds right?'

'Because Baby sounds so wrong! And what if he never becomes Ioane? I couldn't call him Baby for more than a few months.'

'Maybe he's not supposed to be named,' said Laita Havealeta quietly, thinking of her own dead children.

'Don't say that, please,' said Amalia growing fearful. 'I'll think of a name.'

When the midday sun drew her visitors back to their houses for an afternoon sleep, Amalia Matete stepped outside. It was low tide. She sat in the shade under her house. The sea danced hot and glittering. On the damp sand she felt cool enough to stay awake. She didn't want to sleep. Closing her eyes, even when she could still feel his reassuring weight in her arms, meant missing precious seconds of her son's life; she wasn't ready to do that just yet. She could scarcely believe that this was what had grown inside her. Waves collapsed gently onto the sand.

'Look at the sea, baby Matete,' she said. 'We belong

next to the sea. We are sea people. You'll be a fisherman one day. Like my father was. He used to spend most of every day in his boat. "You don't know anything about an island," my father said, "unless you can feel the movement of the sea around it. It's where people find their souls, though they don't all know it."

'Every year after they were married, my parents would row all the way around the island. I was born in my father's boat. The sea so relaxed my mother that her labour began right there. She said I swam out of her. She said I was so desperate to see the sea that I swam right out into the boat. My mother fainted overboard and I followed her into the waves. We swam. You'll never drown unless the sea wants you to. "Now that you're born, little one," my father said, "there's no need to go home." I was three weeks old before I spent a day on dry land. Whinney thinks I'm going to drown every day and she'll probably tell you the same thing. But you mustn't listen to her. You'll swim . . . Come on. I'll show you.'

Amalia Matete stood up and waded with the baby into the sea. When she was up to her chest, she took a deep breath and knelt down, submerging her head below the waves, holding her baby firmly in her hands. She let out a steady stream of little bubbles to keep below the surface. She opened her eyes and forced them to focus, through the blur, on her boy. He was staring back at her, his thick black curls floating above his head, his mouth wide open. She smiled at him, but couldn't quite tell if he was smiling back. She began to worry and rose up quickly. As she broke the surface, she heard a sweet sound that could have been his first laugh or a gull calling out to its mate.

'You were like a sea urchin,' she said. 'Shall I call you that?' But she knew that she wouldn't. That name belonged to a boy she had once known; a boy who had long ago left Moana.

The following day was a Sunday, so Amalia Matete took her baby to the service that was held on the far side of the beach from her house. She joined the rest of the villagers lolling on the sand and watched the children stand up and sing for the adults. They were all dressed in their finest Sunday clothes, white shirts and white *sulus*, with woven-palm waistbands decorated with different coloured cloth. Most were barefoot. Amalia wondered which of these children her son would most resemble. She could hardly wait to see him standing there, singing and grinning with the rest of the little boys. One of the Tatafu children sang particularly loudly and badly. The adults smiled and Amalia smiled with them.

Amalia was surrounded by the rest of the young mothers. She cooed over their babies and they over hers. They talked about the children and only half listened to what was being said. Tom Havealeta was talking about angels. She heard sentences about being half way between a man and God. About the devil being a fallen angel. About them being everywhere. She heard something about them helping mortals. But when she started to listen properly he had moved on to telling the children a story she loved.

'God created the countries,' Tom said, 'and then the seas. And he made this ocean huge so that there'd be enough room for the whales, enough room for the fish to swim in peace and enough room for coral to stretch out over its floor. But when God had finished with the oceans, he needed to get back to the countries because he still had to add trees and grass to feed his animals. He stepped across the water, and wherever he put down his foot, land rose up to meet him. And he was so thankful to the ocean for keeping him dry that he gave his footprints the best plants and the best weather. His footprints are these islands, and that is why we live in paradise.'

Amalia Matete, scanning the village where she had lived all her life, agreed. She loved the turquoise blue of the sea on a calm day and the dark shadows made by breadfruit trees standing out against the clear sky. She loved that she always heard only one bird singing at a time, but could never see where it was. She loved the faces of the other villagers as they shut their eyes and let the sun caress their eyelids as they sang. She wondered about the other countries that she knew so little about, countries that had not been given the best of everything and she felt sorry for the people who lived there.

'We're lucky to be islanders,' she whispered to her son, and later on in his life he claimed to remember her saying it.

*   *   *

The next evening Amalia Matete and her baby were sitting on the beach, when the doctor came stumbling out of the Ungas' house, saw the young pair and came to join them.

'I am too old for so much *kava*,' he announced and Amalia heard the narcotic slur in his voice as he sat down, moving as though in slow motion. 'But little Zeno Tatafu is pouring today, and she always gives everyone a full cup.'

Amalia laughed at the bloodshot eyes of her old friend. 'When I used to pour, you demanded I fill them up,' she told him.

'I was younger then, and considerably more foolish. A full half-coconut shell, each round – high tide – it's too much for me now. I begged for the sea to be out, but she doesn't listen.'

'It wasn't long ago,' Amalia said.

'Long enough for you to grow up though,' he replied, 'and long enough for me to grow old. Excuse me a moment.' And he walked into the trees, either to pee or to be sick; Amalia did not want to know which. He returned a few minutes later and sat back down again.

'Look at that tree, Amalia,' he said to her, pointing at a coconut palm a few metres from them. 'That tree is an angel.'

Amalia, puzzled, waited for the explanation. He shut his eyes, then forced them open again.

'That tree is what links the islanders to God. It is not God, but it contains the spirit of the island.'

The palm stood as it always stood, unaware it was being discussed.

'That tree saves us,' the doctor continued. 'Where would we be without coconuts? A coconut is the finest thing. It is more than food. It is spirit.'

'I think I know what you mean,' Amalia said remembering Lave Unga and the tattoo of a coconut world on his leg.

'A coconut is fun!' the old man shouted, raising his right arm triumphantly. 'And life, Amalia, a good life, should be fun. I love coconuts, they are a treat. Whinney puts one in the fire for me every Sunday. I make her burn them. I love them burnt. So coconuts, burnt coconuts, are my religion! They make me smile and that is an angelic thing to do.' The doctor laughed.

'I think *kava* might be angelic as well then,' Amalia said.

'It might well be! I must drink some more. Goodbye.' And he stood up and swayed back to the Ungas' house.

'The doctor is mad this evening,' Amalia told her son. 'And one day *kava* will make you mad too. It will make these crazy curls of yours stand up straight,' she said as she played with them. The baby squirmed in her arms. 'You don't like it when I play with your hair. Already you're the man of the house!' she said and laughed at his cross little face. 'I think you might be my angel,' she told him and then she said it again, 'My angel.' And it felt right and the baby became known as Angel Matete.

THE RETURN OF IOANE MATETE

'It always rains on this island,' thought Ioane Matete as he sailed around the coast, back to Moana. He had arrived in the town of Laumua a week earlier and had planned to stay with his mother until the rain cleared. She had a house near the old fort that had been built before time began and then rebuilt and rebuilt again by whichever settlers needed it for the protection of their trade. But the rain didn't clear and he discovered his mother was dead, so, since he had nothing better to do – he'd washed his clothes, eaten his favourite food, been bought as much rum as the town would shout him – Ioane climbed into his boat and went to see his wife. He had been married for four years and had only spent one night with her. He wondered if the rumour was correct. It told him he had a son.

The rain was unrelenting, a persistent drizzle that soaked into his clothes and clung to his beard. The sea was neither rough nor calm, but every now and again a wave came over the side and hit him in the face with a salty smack. The sky was grey; the darkness made the cliffs around the island appear steep and dangerous. It was early evening but felt later.

'The island hates me now,' Ioane thought. He remembered how it used to be before he left Laumua for the first time. He remembered growing up with clear skies and a loving sea. With family and friends. With fresh fruit and plenty of pork. 'It will never be like that again,' he said and for the first time allowed himself to be frustrated with his current life. It wasn't that he had done things that an islander should have been ashamed of. It was that he no longer cared. Somewhere deep within he thought he should care, at least for something. But when he searched for that centre inside him he couldn't find it. That, he supposed, was what he should regret.

When he was a boy, Ioane was the only one of his friends who had ever jumped from the cliffs into the water below. And he'd survived. No one else made the leap – everyone knew that rocks just below the surface waited to break the legs of those foolish enough to throw themselves down the sixty feet. But Ioane jumped. And he wasn't scared. He was exhilarated, buoyed up by excitement and the terror of his friends. The water swallowed him like a shark and chomped the base of his spine as he went down. He kept the pain to himself; pain was for the weak. When he returned, his friends rushed around him, congratulating him. He shrugged them off, walked straight back to the cliff edge and jumped again.

A fish flew into the boat and its flailing brought Ioane Matete back from his memories.

'I should know what type you are,' he told it as it suffocated. 'But I can't remember. Today everything is grey and you are nothing more than a fish, not one that deserves a name. Are you grey? Or when you swim are you slick and silver? Is there blue on your stomach?' The fish stared at Ioane, only its mouth moving, slowly opening and closing, trying to concentrate on something other than the pain of its own death.

'Die fish,' Ioane shouted suddenly from the bottom of his lungs as he stood up in the boat. 'Die in the rain,' and he laughed as he wondered how much rain it would take to keep a fish breathing and why there was no salt in the clouds.

The intensity of the water pouring from the sky increased and the bottom of the boat began to fill up. A large wave splashed over the side and created a pool. The fish was now half submerged and kept its head below the surface, able to breathe again.

'No,' said Ioane Matete and he scooped the water back in the ocean. When the fish's gills were still, Ioane picked it up. Its eyes were pearly grey and dead. He threw it into the sea.

He sat back down in the boat and started rowing once more. A boy, standing on the cliff, waved down at him and Ioane Matete waved back.

Once, how many years ago Ioane could no longer

remember, he'd been standing on a cliff when he'd seen a rowing boat moving very slowly around the headland towards the town of Laumua. An old man sat in the boat, wrapped up in a thick black cloak, and he seemed to be struggling with the oars. Ioane was driven by a sudden desire to help. Despite it being a warm day, the ocean was still freezing; it was early, the sun had not yet heated up the world. Ioane gasped as he felt the coolness against his body but soon the power in his arms distracted him as he swam out to the old man.

'You've come to help me,' called the rower as Ioane drew close. 'Are you sure you want to do that? This is one job you won't be able to walk away from until it's finished.'

Ioane did not reply but swam right up to the boat and hauled himself over the side in one graceful move-ment.

'Hello, Ioane,' said the old man, and Ioane saw the wrinkled face of a stranger smiling down at him. 'Drink this.'

Ioane drank the water offered to him and did not ask why the man was covered with shells, why he was wearing a wet cloak.

'Now, come on, let's row,' said the stranger.

Ioane took one oar and the old man the other. Ioane put all his strength into it and his companion effort-lessly matched his force. The rowing boat hardly moved.

'Why is it so heavy?' Ioane asked, exasperated.

'We're towing something,' the man replied.

'What?'

'Look behind us and you'll see.' But all Ioane could see was a dark shadow on the sea floor as big as a whale. It was tied to the boat by nothing more than a regular fishing line.

'The line will snap,' Ioane said. 'What is it anyway?'

'I'll show you when we get to land,' said his companion, which they did five hours later.

Ioane collapsed on his back on the sand, breathing heavily.

'What is it?' he asked again, propping himself up on his elbows.

'You'll see once we get it out of the sea. Come on.' And the old man walked back into the water, up to his waist. Suddenly half the town was gathered around. Together they pushed it, whatever it was, out of the water, to the far side of the houses where it could dry. They left it between the giant skeleton of a cruising ship that had washed up a few years earlier and a derelict hut where it was said the ghost of a madman lived.

Ioane and the rest of the town investigated what the sea had brought them. They examined its frame, which was rusted, with only the flaky remains of white paint clinging to patches here and there. They walked down the side of it, found a door that opened and climbed in. Ioane sat on a seat in front of a wheel the size of a large saucepan lid. His feet rested on a floor of sand. The inside walls were matted with seaweed. He pulled at a few of the weeds and threw them outside.

'What's it for?' Ioane said. But the old man was nothing more than a silhouette on the horizon.

Ioane Matete was now so wet that his clothes were clinging to his body, and his hair and beard had stiffened with salt. Soon the village would come into sight. He waited for the moment when he would be able to see the beach where his wife lived, the house where she had produced a son in his absence. He began to think about his child, his boy, and wondered what he'd be like.

'Will you be as I was, or as I am? Which one do I want you to be?' he asked. 'I have been two people,' he thought. 'In my past I was an islander, but in the present a traveller. Which will you be? Will I take you travelling with me?' Ioane Matete turned to the sea for an answer, but only saw a school of fish dart out of view. 'I'll need two sons,' he decided. 'One can stay here, work the plantation, marry a girl and have sons and daughters who will stay on the island forever. The other can come with me. He'll be an explorer like his father and learn languages and see skyscrapers and snow, forget where he comes from and be rained on when he returns.

'When did the rain start?' Ioane wondered, but he knew the answer. 'There was no rain before the truck was dragged out of the sea and after the truck it never stopped.'

The boat hit the sand with a crunch. There was a boy sitting on the beach.

Ioane Matete meets his son

'You must be my son. Well, aren't you going to say hello to your father? My brother Pena had the same faraway look and that light hair. My mother thought that was what killed him, that he'd been born meant for heaven. Actually he drank himself to death.'

Angel Matete sat under his house and watched the stranger on the shore talking to the Tatafu baby. He seemed friendly although Angel could not be sure. There was a beard covering his face and his skin was coarse and brown. Angel wondered what was underneath.

'Amalia, my wife, your mother, must have called you Ioane after me. It's a good name. It's served me well. My whole life, everyone has called me by the same name. Not like other people who are called one thing by some people, another by others. But Little Ioane, my son, perhaps it is more important to be one person than to be called one name. I am two people . . .' he trailed off and then continued in a quieter voice, 'though perhaps half of me is dead.

'But that was before I had you! When a man has a son he starts again, his sins are forgiven. You and I, Little Ioane, we . . . You must become a man. You must learn to fish and provide for your family. Or I'll take you with me. Would you like to be a traveller?'

The man's feet sank into the sand so that only when he wriggled his toes did they break the surface. Above his left ankle, Angel saw that a word was tattooed. He wanted to know what it said.

Ioane Matete moved closer to the boy. The child raised his arms, wanting to be carried. Ioane lifted him up and held him against his chest. He smelt his skin and kissed his head.

'My son,' he said. 'I have a son.'

The boy pulled on the hair at the back of his neck.

'I know Little Ioane, I need a haircut. I don't normally look like this. Soon I'll cut it off and shave my beard and your father will be a new man.'

A woman was walking down to the beach. She shouted, 'You, who are you?'

Ioane frowned. 'I am Ioane Matete.'

'Then say hello to your own son, he's sitting under there.' She pointed towards the house. 'Pass Vete to me.'

Trying for a Son

Amalia Matete was sitting on the floor of the kitchen, sucking the last milk from a coconut, when Ioane Matete entered the house.

She stood up and forced a smile onto her face. 'Ioane,' she said and then faltered. Her legs felt weak as he leant forward and kissed her lightly upon the cheek. 'You've met our son?'

'Yes,' he replied, but did not turn to the boy standing behind him. 'He tells me he is called Angel.'

'Yes.'

'And not Ioane. How can my firstborn son not be Ioane?'

'He is. That is what I named him.'

'But you call him Angel?'

'Yes, I'm sorry. It suits him. He isn't an Ioane. I tried to call him that.'

Amalia and Ioane stood in silence facing one another. He was different from the husband she remembered. He was wilder in some ways, his hair, his eyes, even though this was the first time she had seen him being still. She waited for him to talk, but he did not. There was a meaning behind his quiet that Amalia did not understand.

'Would you like some food?' she asked her husband. He nodded.

Amalia filled a plate with food she had prepared for Laita and herself.

'Here,' she said and put her thumb against the rest of her fingers and raised her hand, 'eat.'

'Thank you, Amalia. I'll eat, shave, then sleep. Later—'

He was interrupted by Angel holding out his little hand to his mother. When she took it he pulled her gently outside. Ioane Matete did not say a word. Angel took Amalia away from his father, down to the sea.

The day after Ioane Matete's reappearance, Angel crossed the beach and went up to the house of Doctor Vaite.

'Good morning!' called the old man.

Angel did not speak but took off his shirt and showed the doctor his shoulder. The night before, his father had dragged him out from his hiding place. Angel had heard a pop like a coconut splashing into water and felt his bone coming out of its socket. The doctor lifted him up and placed the boy on his knee. Angel leant into his chest and smelt the familiar woody odour of the old man. His shoulder was snapped back into place and then Doctor Vaite's arms were around him and he was being held.

'I heard your father was back. So it's true then?'

Angel nodded but kept his head lowered. He felt his eyes stinging and hid them behind his wrists.

'Cry now,' Doctor Vaite said. 'Cry all you need to but then stop. Do not cry in front of Ioane Matete. Be the opposite of that man, but be strong like him. I hear you've been looking after your mother. Good, Angel, keep her safe.'

Angel brushed the tears from his eyes and sat up. For once he did not see a smile on the doctor's face.

Amalia and Angel Matete spent whole days together in the water or walking along the cliff. The boy would appear just as Ioane Matete entered a room, and lead her out. Amalia watched her husband as this happened. Each time he met Angel's gaze and looked away. They have the same eyes, she noticed. But nothing her son did could stop the night stealing over Moana and when night came, it was Ioane's turn to take Amalia's hand.

'I want another child,' he told her the first night as he took off her clothes. 'Did you know that the baby in your womb is easily influenced? If you are around too many women we will have a girl. The baby changes sex over and over again,' he told her.

'I didn't know that.'

'It makes me wonder how little Ioane is male.'

'It must have been the doctor. He took care of me.'

'It better be. I don't want to find out that there has been anyone else around here. Especially those Tatafus. There are too many unmarried men in that house.'

'We'll need them when we have daughters,' Amalia replied.

'We're having a son,' Ioane Matete answered angrily and hit his wife around the face. Amalia did not allow herself to cry. She put her hand to her cheek and remembered what it was like to have a husband. Ioane believed that violence was male. His fist would prevent them from having a daughter.

But Amalia knew she wasn't pregnant and didn't feel like she would be soon. She went to talk to Whinney Vaite. Laita was with her.

'What has he done to your face, Amalia? He's hit you.'

'Yes. He's my husband.'

'What does that mean? That your face is his to turn purple whenever he wants? Where did you get that idea?' Laita took her friend's cheek in her hands and moved her thumb over the swelling by her eye. 'Don't let him do this.'

'Doesn't Tom ever hit you?'

'No, of course not. Men must "love their wives as their own bodies. He that loveth his wife loveth himself."'

'But Tom's different, Ioane doesn't follow those rules. And Tom's not from here.'

'It doesn't matter where he's from,' replied Laita.

'Your father was from here and he never hit your mother. And the doctor is from here,' Whinney said. 'In the first week of our marriage we had a fight and he raised his hand to me. I walked out the door and stayed away for a month. When he came to find me I told him if he ever did that again it would be the last time, and if we had children by then I'd take them with me. He knew I meant it. Men have their responsibilities and we have ours, Amalia, but not one of us is better than the other. Do not let a man hurt you.'

'I could never talk to Ioane like that.'

'You should.'

'My mother told me to obey him.'

'Your mother is dead. But you're alive and have a son. If you let this happen again he'll grow up like his father.'

'Ioane wants another boy, but I'm not pregnant. What should I do?'

'The first thing you have to do is to stop him drinking *kava*. He was at the Ungas' last night. I saw him stumbling home with Vete Tatafu at dawn. If he drinks like that every night, you'll never have another child.'

Amalia knew that what Whinney was telling her was true, but the nights when her husband crashed onto their mat without touching her were precious to Amalia. When his body lay vulnerable and exposed beside her she wondered how he had ever hurt her; how that man whose skin next to her own seemed old, could yield such power. She felt something for him then, when he lay quietly, passed out, defenceless. Like that, he was her husband. She gently kissed his neck, came to know his blemishes. She compared the dark of his chest to the lighter brown of his hips and wondered if she was the only one who had seen this side of him. He had a mole above his left nipple and if she positioned her head level with it, it became huge and filled her entire view. She searched for the Angel in him and thought she saw it in his eyelids. They moved slightly in his sleep, just as Angel's did. And in the flaring of his nostrils she also saw her son.

When he was *kava*-sleeping, Amalia would bring their child and sit him next to his father. She would make up stories about someone who took care of them, who Angel should respect.

Life was different for Amalia Matete with her husband in the house. In his absence she had relied on the villagers, had spent her days at the Tatafus' or talking with the Vaites or Laita Havealeta. But now that Ioane was back, people stopped visiting her, except Laita who made a point of it. When the Ungas dropped off food they used to eat with Amalia, but now they would leave what they had by the side door and slip away. Amalia began to wonder if the village was as open as she had once believed it to be. Ioane was an outsider. They didn't want him there.

But Ioane Matete was not a man who cared.

When it suited him, Ioane played the part of a villager. He went with the men around the houses and took all he could from them. But Amalia saw that her husband wasn't returning the village's generosity. Ioane had all kinds of potential gifts. He had sent himself a parcel of strange and wonderful items from his trips, none of them available even in Laumua. But when someone asked him for something he found a reason not to give it. It made her uncomfortable. She thought about when she'd watched him talk to Lave Unga on the beach. Ioane had been walking down to the waves with a board tucked under his arm. Amalia had seen him on it before, riding the surf like a dolphin charging towards the shore. Everyone had thought he had some kind of special power.

'No, anyone can do it. Surfing is easy. You just have to learn how.'

'Oh, I would love to do that. Can you teach me?' Lave had asked.

'I won't have time to give you a lesson,' Ioane answered. 'But give me that melon. Surfing is thirsty work.' So Lave Unga gave Ioane his melon.

Amalia tried to pay back the villagers with little kindnesses of her own, but all she had to offer were her *pandanus* leaf mats.

'Why do you keep making them?' Ioane asked her one day as she sat by the window at the front of the house, weaving in time with the sea, her boy asleep next to her. 'We don't need any more.'

'I like making them and I can give them away,' replied Amalia. 'I want to do something for our neighbours.'

'You don't owe them anything. And you've better things to do than that. Look after your son,' Ioane said. But as he spoke he ignored the child.

Amalia glanced at her Angel and wished he took up more of her time. She knew children, there were hundreds over at the Tatafus, but none of them seemed like him. All Angel ever wanted to do was gaze out to sea. It didn't matter what the weather was, he watched and clapped happily at every sparkle of light on the water and pointed to every bubble that could be a fish. Amalia sometimes carried him away just to make him cry. Then she could comfort him.

Now that her husband was back Amalia tried to find excuses to be busy so that he would leave her alone. But as he hardly let her out of the house there was little she could do. Twice a day she was dragged into their sleeping room where she shut her eyes and lay still and waited until Ioane was finished with her. After a few weeks of this he got angry.

'Don't just lie there still and straight as a palm. Enjoy yourself. Move!'

But Amalia didn't know how she should move. She tried wriggling.

'What are you doing? Don't you dare try to run away from me!'

She tried bouncing.

'Ow! Why are you trying to head butt me?'

She tried all sorts of movement, but none of it was right. For weeks Ioane got angrier and angrier and hit her more and more frequently, until one day he stopped. She was naked and afraid. He sighed.

'Amalia, you are my wife. We are trying to have a son. This is a great moment.' Amalia flinched as he raised his hand to her cheek, but he only ran his fingers gently across her skin. 'Relax.' And he kissed her neck. 'Imagine you are in the sea. My hand is the water caressing your body.' He stroked her side, around her breasts, ribs and hips. 'My weight is the weight of the sea all around you.' He climbed slowly on top of her. 'It is a calm day, but the tide is coming in. The waves want to reach the beach. They are rocking towards the sand, and you go with them, you give yourself to the waves. Move with me, Amalia.' And finally Amalia Matete knew how to move and conceived a second son.

Angel was told by his mother that soon he would have a brother. The little boy took this information with him to the water and decided he was glad. A brother would love the sea as he did: the waves, the fish, the coral beneath the water. Together they would follow the outline of a shark and feel the salt rubbing between their toes. When he had a brother, Angel would have someone to sit on the beach with, to swim with and to grow with. Angel and his brother would be sea people together, like the stories he was told by Amalia.

When Amalia was three months pregnant, Ioane Matete announced he was leaving.

'I'll be back to pick up the boy. This second one is going to be an explorer like me. This one will be mine.'

And with that, Ioane Matete left.

arun

Amalia's son was a perfect boy, born on an imperfect day on the island.

A week before she was due, Amalia took Angel out in her father's old rowing boat for one last fishing trip before the baby came. She knew that as long as they were on the water, Angel would amuse himself staring at the waves. She was tired now and didn't have the energy to play with him. She threw out a line while Angel watched. When there was a tug she reeled it in and handed the fish to her son. He piled it neatly in the corner with the others.

'You're going to be a fisherman,' she told him, remembering her father talking about the importance of order on a boat, 'like your grandfather.' And she laughed as he played with the rudder. He was steering.

It was raining Amalia's favourite kind of rain, the sort that simply hung in the air, that did not seem to fall. But it was not like some rains that only added to the heat; this one was cold and it lay on her forehead like a cooling cloth. She needed it.

'I hope it stays like this forever,' she told Angel as she lay back in the boat. 'It's been too hot.'

'That's because there will be a storm,' a voice replied and Amalia saw another boat coming towards theirs. There were two men in it, and both were Vete Tatafus. They had the same broad shoulders as each other, the same proud, flared nostrils and those eyes that the Tatafus were known for, deep and dark like a moonless night. She knew one of them well. Little Vete, tall as a coconut tree and round like a *kava* bowl, had been her neighbour for many years. But Amalia didn't believe she had seen the other.

'Hello,' she said.

'This is my elder brother,' her friend shouted across at her. 'He's been working in Laumua. Don't you remember him?'

'I remember you,' the brother said before she could answer. 'You're Amalia Hoko. You once made me put a sea urchin in my mouth. We'd found it up in the trees, all dried out. You said it needed to be put in water straight away.'

The man was talking so easily to Amalia that she felt uncomfortable. She did remember him now and wanted to laugh with him, to tell him that he had been the one who had thought of his mouth as a water hole. His eyes smiled at her. He had a dimple on each cheek. She liked this man.

'My brother's been telling this story for years. Now

we call him Urchin,' Little Vete added and they waited for her to say something.

But they were all grown up now and she had no place talking to them like this. Yes, she remembered him, remembered growing up with him, spending all her time with him when they were young. But he was over eighteen by now, moved out of his home to keep him away from the women. He might have done to some other girl what Ioane did to her. But even if he hadn't, it did not make a difference – she was married. She could no longer have male friends. She could no longer reminisce about her childhood. It was gone. And that meant that this man with floppy black hair and a biteable chin was out of her life. She could not stroke his shoulder as she had when they were younger, or lay her head on his chest.

'I'm Amalia Matete now,' she told them. 'I'm married. This is my son Angel.'

And saying that, her waters broke. It was time for the baby inside her to stop swimming and be born.

'It's okay,' Urchin said, looking directly into her eyes. 'Row up to her boat,' he told his brother.

Little Vete paused. 'A man shouldn't see this,' he said.

'She needs us, Vete,' Urchin said and, steadying Amalia's boat with one foot, he gently picked her up and moved her into his.

She panicked and squirmed and wriggled in his arms as though trying to fall into the water. But Urchin held her tight, and sitting down, made her breathe calmly.

'My baby,' Amalia cried out, not talking about the boy who was slowly creeping out of her body, but her other son, who was still sitting in the bottom of her boat, playing with dead fish.

'My baby,' she shrieked again. 'Bring Angel into the boat. Where is he? Get him!'

'We'll tow in your boat and your son, Amalia,' said Little Vete. 'A boy shouldn't see his mother like this. Not if he wants to grow up to be a man.

'Angel,' he called out to the boy, 'throw me the rope.' And Angel stood steadily in the boat and his four-year-old hand hurled the rope to the Tatafus.

'Good arm!'

While Urchin reassured Amalia, Little Vete looked around him at the sea. The storm was coming closer, the waves were now merely choppy but he could see that they would get larger and larger. He looked at Angel; the child was not afraid. Good. He needed to make the tow long so it wouldn't snap. He didn't want the waves to strain the fibres, he didn't want the boats to collide. He secured the rope and sat down to row, focusing only on his arms, the sea and getting them all to the mango island nearby.

Angel had enjoyed throwing the rope. He had done well. It had gone far. He wanted to throw more. He threw one fish into the sea. Then another. He didn't enjoy throwing them as much as he enjoyed throwing rope. Fish were lighter and slippery and they didn't go far. He waited for the rope to slacken and untied it a little. Then it was tight again and he stopped. He'd hurt his fingers on this rope before. He remembered what Amalia had told him. 'You can only untie a rope when it wants you to. Sometimes it does, and sometimes it doesn't. You have to learn to tell the difference.' Slack again, and it was loose. Angel picked it up. He threw the rope as far as he could and saw it splash into the sea. His arm felt good. He looked around for more things to throw.

And so it was that Amalia and Angel were separated by water for the first time in their lives.

Through the spray and the waves and the wind, which was now howling into their faces, they did not see that Angel's boat was missing until they arrived at the mango island. Little Vete ran into the sea. 'Angel!' he shouted at the sky and the heavens and at God himself. 'Angel, where are you?' But his voice was lost, unanswered, as he knew it would be. He could not turn again to the land. He could not look at the tears on Amalia's face. He could not bear the weight of what he might find in his brother's eyes. He pushed the boat back through the waves. To himself he vowed, 'I will find him.'

Amalia heard the thunder. Where there was thunder there must be lightning. Memories flooded back and she cried out in fright, terrified lest something happen to Angel. But this storm was not hostile as her wedding storm had been; it was simply weather, simply the sky letting go of its load and pouring water down onto the earth. Yes, there was thunder but it was far away and as it continued Amalia believed that the growling was just the noise of her stomach tightening, the birth pains of her body amplified across the sky, and that Angel would be okay.

* * *

75

While his brother was coming into the world, Angel was sitting in the bottom of his grandfather's boat, alone on the ocean. He watched the storm with wide eyes, trying to imitate the roar the sky made. He laughed happily as his boat toppled this way and that over the waves. When he was thirsty he opened his mouth and drank the rain and when he was hungry he chewed on the tails of the fish. If there was too much water around him he scooped it overboard as he had seen his mother do. The tide took him out to sea, further and further from Amalia and the new baby, further and further from the island.

Urchin Tatafu had worked in the hospital of Laumua. He had been a porter and had seen how babies were brought into the world. He did not believe that it was unlucky for a man to be present at the birth of a child. He knew that what was happening was natural. He did not think, like his brother, that men should have no part in it. Amalia was hurting and she needed him. He got behind her, massaged her head and kept her under the shelter of trees when she started to crawl around, howling like a beast and ripping her *lavalava* away from her body. He gave her a stick to chew on when she wanted one and let her squeeze his fingers until he could no longer feel them.

'Don't lie to me, Urchin,' she begged, 'tell me about the storm, tell me about my boy. Will you find him?'

'The storm is not so bad,' he lied, 'and there is no finer sailor than Vete. He will find your son and bring him safely home. Don't worry about him. You have a new life to worry about.'

Saying this, Urchin realised that he did not want the baby ever to be born, he wanted to watch her like this forever, panting and crying out, so tired yet so full of energy. He stared at the sweat on her forehead and the moisture that covered her top lip. Her eyes wouldn't focus for a long time but then would suddenly stare at him and see him, see everything in him, right to his very soul. When she charged into the sea, Urchin brought her back, sure that it would be better for the child to be born on land – born in the sea and you longed for it your whole life. He calmed her, he settled her. And the baby slithered like an eel out onto the sand, caught by Urchin Tatafu, separated from his mother with a fishing knife and cleaned with sea water. Then Amalia cried, but her tears were not for the baby on her breast, but for her other son, out at sea. The newborn heard her sadness, he tasted it in her milk and he started to sob.

Little Vete Tatafu could not see Amalia's boat. The wind had risen and stronger waves now broke up the horizon. He headed in the direction of the tide and raised his sail. There was no sign of the boy. He knew the task was hopeless, that he should turn back and he would have, but for Amalia. How could he return without Angel? He moved deeper into the storm, hardly daring even to pray – and there it was, just for a moment – Amalia's boat, lifted on a wave, as visible as a house on a headland, before it plunged back into the sea's furrows. Vete moved closer, so close he could see the boy sitting with his fish. He knew that if he stretched out for Angel he would capsize them both. He changed course and approached again. Again and again the sea, throwing up giant waves between them, allowed him so far but no further. Finally he was driven away, out of reach, beyond all hope of ever reaching. He knew then, with all the certainty of his being, that a child alone in a small boat could not survive, and he also knew he could not come back without him. Holding the mast, he stood up in the centre of the ocean and said goodbye to his brothers, to his sisters, to his father and his mother, his wife and their children, to the sea and to the fish, to the wind and to the rain. And, begging her forgiveness, he said goodbye to Amalia Matete.

'Arun is not an island name. How did you think of it?' Urchin asked Amalia as he watched her talking sadly to her baby.

'I found a bottle on the beach and it was full of writing. One of your cousins took it to Laumua with him and found someone who could translate it for me.'

'What did it say?' Urchin asked as they watched the storm move off.

'The message was from a man named Arun. It talked about where he had been born, somewhere far away from here. He talked about the beach in that far-off land and the sea and the colour of the water and the sky. He talked about palm trees and his family and the other people in his village. He was leaving Laumua and going back there. He sounded like a good man. Like the kind of man I would like my son to be. The letter was a goodbye to this sea. It was brave. The name sounds strong to me.'

'This little man will be strong. He was born in a thunder storm; he'll fight his whole life.'

'I don't want him to have to fight, just to be able to. Ioane is going to take him away with him next time he comes back. Maybe he'll see this village Arun describes. I can't give him an island name when he'll see the world.'

'Then Arun it is.'

'Yes. Arun. The letter is full of love, for a friend who betrayed him and for the island. I want my son to know love, to talk about his heart as this man does.'

'Have you known love, Amalia?' her friend asked gently, needing to know the answer, knowing that once his brother returned he could never ask the question.

She tried to read his eyes. 'Of course I have. I'm married now. I have children. Have you?'

'No. I thought I would return and find it. I thought it would be waiting for me, but I was wrong. It seems I stayed away for too long. The girls I knew are women now. They have husbands and babies of their own.'

'Is it hard moving back?'

'The hardest thing I've ever done.'

'My Arun will have to do that one day.'

'Will your husband agree to the name?'

'I don't know. Maybe he'll make him be another Ioane like his brother, but—' a giant wave formed out at sea and the wind roared again. 'Angel!' she cried, 'Angel! Where are you?'

Amalia stood up, her baby in her arms and screamed.

Angel was not found that day or the next, despite all the fishermen in the village searching for him. They returned instead with the body of Little Vete Tatafu and bits of a broken boat. No one knew if it was Amalia's, the Tatafus' or parts from both. No one knew if Little Vete had seen Angel and if the boy had shared the fate of the man.

Amalia Matete waited for her son on the beach, under her house, holding Arun to her chest and crying into the head of thick, straight, black hair he was born with. The tears washed over the baby and into his skin. The sadness that surrounded his entrance to the world flowed into his heart and stayed with him. He cried silently along with his mother, both of their bodies weak with grief, one for the loss of her son and the death of a friend, the other because he did not know how to be happy. He had only learnt how to cry.

Amalia understood, deep inside her, that her son was not dead. She knew that he was alive, but she did not know if he would ever find his way back to her. She was sure that if someone found him they'd want to keep him. She imagined him sitting under another woman's house as he had sat here, staring out at another woman's sea. She waited.

After a week had passed the villagers tried to get Amalia to go inside.

'He's not coming back,' they forced themselves to tell her. 'You've got to think of the new baby now.'

Amalia did not listen.

The sea always brought gifts to Moana. Most days something new washed up; pieces of boat, the letter from Arun, her mother's chest with the blue paint inside. Laita had found a dress lying on the shore one day and Lave Unga a set of oars. The Tatafus had a rocking chair in their house that the sea had given them and the Vaites a bag full of needles. Tom Havealeta had once discovered a telephone on the shore. He was keeping it for the day when Moana would be connected to the rest of the island. If the sea could bring all that, Amalia knew that it could bring her Angel back to her. You only drown if the sea wants you to. The sea would not take her son.

Laita Havealeta took to sitting with Amalia and encouraging her to eat. She tried to take the baby so that it could spend one night indoors but Amalia would not let her. She had lost one child and swore never to lose another. Laita wondered if the boy had eaten anything and forced her friend to show the baby her breast. It clung to it greedily and drank and drank. It was so hungry that Laita almost believed this was its first meal.

'Amalia, you can't go on like this. Come inside please. I'll wait for Angel, you need to worry about Arun.'

But Amalia was silent in grief and deaf to the pleas of those around her. Day and night she waited for her son.

* * *

A month later a small rowing boat approached the beach, with a withered old man in a damp, dark coat covered in limpets, drawing on the oars. It was the middle of a moonless night and Amalia only saw him when he landed on the sand.

'I think he belongs to you, Amalia Hoko,' a quiet voice said and Amalia jumped up, leaving her baby, to run and grab her boy. She covered him in kisses and held him tightly to her.

'Angel!' she cried and then turned to the man who had brought him. 'Thank you, thank you, eh?' She held the boy to her. 'I'm so sorry, my Angel.' She hugged him and covered him in kisses once more and then turned to the old man again to ask how he had found him but all she saw was the silhouette of a boat rowing out to sea.

Amalia walked back up the beach and picked up Arun.

'Angel, this is your little brother, Arun. You're to look after him. Arun, this is Angel, my eldest son. You're to respect him.'

Amalia held her two boys in her arms. She carried them to the house and kissed both of their heads. She lay on her large mat with her sons; one, no longer a baby, with light hair and bright eyes, smiling and awake, the other, tiny and vulnerable, with hair as dark as his tear-filled eyes, nodding off into his first sleep indoors.

'We've missed you, Angel.'

a Funeral

Amalia Matete took her two sons, a mat and a dead pig to the funeral of Little Vete Tatafu. She stood with the women and children. Urchin was with the men. She looked at him across the crowd. He did not look at her. Amalia tried to free herself from her body and float across the villagers into his head. She got as far as his ear and he raised a hand and flicked her away like a mosquito. What did he think of her now? She could not guess. She had not seen him since they had returned from the mango island. She had her two sons and he had lost a brother. Anger seized her – perhaps he wished Angel had not returned, perhaps he wished Arun had not been born – but it was quickly replaced by something sadder. Little Vete; his laugh, his fish, his badly fitting clothes, the noise he made when he spat, his way of fixing nets, the canoes he dug out of trees – all were lost to Moana, to her, to his wife and to his brother; to Urchin who stood there bearing it all without a word and for whom she suddenly felt such tenderness that she wanted to hold his head in her arms and to comfort him as he had comforted her while his brother was alone on the waves.

She looked at Little Vete's sons, one day they'd be as tall as houses just like him, and at his daughter. Fatherless. Amalia looked at his wife, the opposite of her husband, small – tiny today, hunched up and crying. She saw that Urchin was also looking at her. Jealousy flew into Amalia Matete. Would Urchin feel he had to marry her? Would Urchin, her Urchin, leave her to become a husband? No.

After the ceremony Amalia sat under a tree feeding Arun and let Angel run off around the village. He returned later. Urchin Tatafu was holding him by the hand. When he saw Amalia he turned to leave, but she stopped him.

'Please, sit.'

In silence they looked at one another. Tears formed in Amalia's eyes and in her friend's.

'I'm sorry,' she said.

'I'm glad Angel came back.'

'Thank you for waiting to have the funeral.'

'Little Vete would have wanted it like this. Angel was . . . his last thing.'

'Will you be Arun's godfather?' Amalia asked suddenly. 'Angel doesn't have one.'

'I know – but I want you to . . .'

'I'm not his father or your husband. You are Amalia Matete and I am a Tatafu. Ioane will come back.'

'And take my son away. You could stop him.'

'I have to worry about my nieces and nephews now. I have to look after my own family. Everything has changed, Amalia.'

'You cared for me just a few weeks ago. I felt it on the mango island.'

'Yes.'

'And now?'

'I should not be here, Amalia Matete, you are feeding your son. You have a husband. Let me go. Today I just want to bury my brother.'

As Urchin stood up to leave, Amalia felt the space between them grow and the ropes that held them together stretch. She shut her eyes tightly, don't let them come loose, don't let them snap, she begged. She swore that one day, even if it was years from now, she would close the distance. For now, she, like Urchin Tatafu, had to look after her own. He was right, she was married. She was Amalia Matete.

Brothers

There had been water between Angel Matete and his mother and the boy could not pretend otherwise. He knew what it was like to be at sea alone and could not now sit on her knee and let her play with his curls. He looked at her hair and his own and saw how similar they were. He went into the house and searched among his father's boxes. Under Ioane's surfboard, on top of a whisky flask, wrapped in a jumper too thick to ever wear on the island, Angel found a razor. He cut his hair as close to the scalp as he could. He would never have curls again.

Amalia's two sons grew together like the roots of neighbouring trees, breathing in the same air, tangling around one another. Angel tried to make the little boy smile; for Arun was still as miserable as the day he was born. The older child saw it as his job to stop the tears that ran down his brother's face. He spent hours poking his damp cheeks to interrupt the flow of water or pulling silly faces at the baby.

'He throws Arun around like a doll,' Amalia told Grandmother Tatafu.

'Don't worry, it's natural. Babies are stronger than they look. Trust your sons – they know what they're doing.'

Amalia did not want to trust them. She wanted to join them. But when she was there, Arun's cries grew louder.

'Is it me who's making him sad?'

Angel nodded.

Amalia Matete felt pushed away. More and more she left Arun in the hands of his brother. They played on their own or with the Tatafu and Unga children.

And the years passed.

Amalia was staring out of the front window of her house when Urchin Tatafu walked along the beach.

'You look bored,' he said to her. They had hardly spoken since Little Vete's funeral.

'I am,' she answered.

'Come for a walk.'

'I shouldn't. I'm still married.'

'Do it anyway. I'm bored too. We can walk into the forest. Let's pretend we're young again just for a moment. I want to have as much fun as them.' He pointed to the group of children, just out of school, laughing and playing with a wheelbarrow. 'Let's make some better memories.'

'Okay.'

Amalia went walking with Urchin Tatafu. And once turned into twice, and twice to three times and soon they set out together every couple of days, quietly moving into the trees by Amalia's house, walking through the forest, out to the cliff on the other side.

'This cliff is why I went to Laumua,' he told her. 'It made me feel trapped. I would run through the trees trying to escape the village only to end up here, hemmed in, with nowhere to go. Laumua is a town. It has phones and shops and lots of people. It has a busy port. It has roads out to some of the other villages. Nowhere else on the island is as hard to get to as our village. The cliff, the swamp, the coral – we're stuck here.'

'I've never thought of it like that.' Amalia paused. 'So why did you come back? Why not stay in Laumua?'

'I didn't feel trapped there. I missed the feeling!' Urchin laughed at his own foolishness. 'What about you? Have you ever wanted to leave? Don't you mind that your husband comes and goes and you just stay here?'

'I could no sooner leave than change the direction of the tides.'

'You've never thought about it?'

'No. My parents are buried here. My children were born here. I'm not even from the island; I'm from this village, from Moana. This cliff is the edge of my world and always will be.'

'I always wanted to jump off it.'

'And die?'

'Exactly. But I wanted to be sure.'

'Sure of what?'

'Sure that it really was impassable. Sure that I wasn't just trapping myself. That this cliff really was the end of my world.'

'Well, I'm glad you didn't jump, Vete Tatafu,' and saying that, she blushed. Amalia reached over to Urchin and took his hand. As his rough fingers clasped her own, she felt safe. His nails were clean. He had Moana tattooed along the back of his hand. She raised her face upwards and felt the sun on her nose. He leant forward and, as he did so, over his shoulder, Amalia saw a boat at sea. Her heart pounded. It was Ioane Matete's boat. He was coming back to the island. He was coming to take his son.

arun matete leaves with his father

Ioane Matete was excited to meet the son that he would take travelling with him. He was also nervous. His son. What would this boy be like? He must be five, walking and talking, old enough to leave his mother. Ioane wouldn't want the child's company when he travelled far, but he could leave him with his mother's sister in Laumua or, better still, with a woman he knew a few weeks' sail away, who had a daughter of the same age. His son would get used to moving around, he wouldn't grow roots. He would not become a villager but a traveller, like himself, while his brother stayed on the island and worked the plantation for his mother.

'Amalia,' he shouted as he beached his boat by the house. 'Sons,' he cried and enjoyed the word. 'I have sons,' he repeated more quietly to himself.

Amalia Matete heard Ioane calling as she ran through the woods, Urchin Tatafu following behind her.

She turned around. 'Stay here. That is my husband. Let me go and greet him alone.'

'Can't I come with you, Amalia?'

'No. I don't want you to.'

'You're scared of him.'

'Yes, I'm scared of him, you know I am. But what does that matter?'

'You matter, Amalia.'

'Stay here, Urchin, I beg you. Don't come between me and my husband. Nothing good can come of it. Not for my sons and not for you. You don't know Ioane as I know him.'

'Amalia, wait.' But she had already run out of the trees.

'Amalia,' her husband said, smiling as she ran towards him. He opened his arms as she ran into them. Amalia thanked the sea for bringing Ioane home just in time.

'How is my son?' Ioane asked.

'They are both wonderful! You'll love them.' She turned away from him and called out, 'Angel, Arun.'

Ioane Matete froze. 'Angel, I know about. But Arun! You call him that?'

'Yes,' she said in alarm. 'I do.'

'I knew an Arun when I was younger,' he said. 'He grew up with me in Laumua.'

'Where is he now?' Amalia asked.

'Gone. Where are my sons?'

At that moment a group of children ran around the corner of the house and collapsed in front of Amalia, breathless and laughing.

'Get out of here,' Ioane said to them. The little brown

bodies disentangled themselves and walked back up into the village. The two Matete boys stayed behind.

'Angel, you remember your father?'

'Hello,' said Angel.

'You're too old to be playing with the children. Why aren't you out working with the men?'

'He's only just nine,' Amalia said, for she knew that Angel appeared much older. He was almost as tall as she was, broad and strong. 'And he goes to school.'

'He should be working,' Ioane Matete repeated. 'Arun, come forward and meet your father.'

'He's a little shy,' Amalia said, as Arun hid behind his brother. 'There aren't many new faces here.'

'Well, he can't be scared of me. I'm his father. Come here, boy.'

Arun took a step closer and Ioane Matete was pleased with what he saw. The boy was dark so the sun wouldn't bother him, his eyes were serious, stained by tears; there was no hint of humour in them. They were as solemn as fate. Ioane liked that. Nothing frivolous, nothing weak. That was good. He was his son.

'Arun, you are to come travelling with me.'

'No, Ioane, he's too young,' Amalia said.

'He is not. I'm sure he wants to come, don't you boy?'

Arun said nothing.

'Good. Then we'll leave in a week. Now your mother and I have things to do. Go and work, Ioane. I don't want to catch you playing with those children again.'

Angel took his brother's hand and led him up to the plantation.

'Let's collect some coconuts,' he said to Arun and they walked among the palms, picking up the coconuts that had fallen and lobbing them up into the trees to knock down more.

'Do you want to go with him?' Angel asked.

'No,' Arun replied and the tears that his brother had managed to stop started again.

'Don't ever cry in front of him. Promise me. Come here to cry when you want to, okay? Cry to me instead.'

'Okay.'

'But you don't need to cry anyway. It won't be so bad. You'll get to travel the world. I think our father goes to all kinds of places we've never even heard of. It'll be fun. It'll be just like being here, only better.'

'I want to stay.'

'You can't, Arun. He wants you to go with him.'

'Why not you?'

'He doesn't like to be around me. Watch him and you'll see it's true. So I have to work on the plantation. Just do what he says, but run if he looks angry. Don't fight him. Then when you come back we'll sneak up here and you can tell me all about it. I wonder if they have coconuts on the other side of the sea.'

'Maybe they do.'

'I'm sure they do.'

'And mangoes?'

'Yes, and mangoes. And white sand like ours.'

'And pigs?'

'And banana trees.'

'And yam.'

'And breadfruit.'

'And . . .'

'And the sea? I wonder if it is the same there. Maybe it's purple instead.'

'Or red.'

'Or as orange as the sun.'

'Or grey.'

'Or, maybe over there it is pink.'

'Or blue.'

'It's blue here, Arun!'

'I know.'

'You're right. I bet it is blue there too. Only a more interesting blue because it will be one you've never seen before. That will be my first question when you get back. "How was the blue?" So you'd better pay attention. Okay?'

'Okay.'

'Come on, we have enough coconuts now. Let's carry them back.'

'How?'

'Oh. We forgot the net. Race you to the beach to get it, go!'

And the two boys ran back down to the sand.

When Amalia Matete thought about what she had almost done, she shivered, but she didn't know if she was shivering out of fear or regret. She would have liked to feel Urchin's skin on her own, feel his strength and his gentleness. And yet, this time, when her husband lay beside her, he was different. He was kind. He moved softly. She wondered what he wanted.

'I missed you.' He kissed her. 'How has it been here? Tell me about the village and our family. Sometimes when I'm away I think I invented my Moanan wife.'

'The village hasn't changed. It never will. Same people, same trees, same sea. Our pigs are doing well. The Tatafus think we should sell them in Laumua.'

'We don't need to do that. I can give you money if you need it.'

'Good. I'd miss them. And I don't need money. I have everything I need right here.'

'You'd miss the pigs?'

'Yes. I like to hear them rooting under the house in the morning.'

'Amalia, Amalia.' Ioane pushed her hair from her face and kissed her again.

'Ioane, can I ask you something?'

'Anything, my wife.'

'Leave Arun.'

'No.'

'Please. He and Angel are close. They're each other's family.'

'No, Amalia. Don't ask me that again. He's coming with me.'

'Please, Ioane.'

'Never question my decisions, Amalia,' Ioane said, in a voice his wife remembered from all those years ago. 'Now get up and cook some food. And no fish. I've had nothing but fish for months.'

*   *   *

Angel and Arun huddled together at the back of the little wooden classroom, behind the tallest of the Unga boys. They whispered to each other quietly, their voices hidden under the drumming of the rain on the tin roof. They knew they only had a small amount of time before teacher Zeno would notice and send them back to their right places. Arun was supposed to be reading a story and Angel should have been working on some maths, but instead the boys were imagining what their father's ship might be like. The day before, teacher Zeno had read to them about pirates and Arun and the Vete next to him were drawing Ioane with a wooden leg and a parrot. Angel added a picture of his brother up a sail, wearing an eye patch.

Within two days of her husband's reappearance, Ioane's anger was back and Amalia felt she was pregnant again. She worried about herself in a way she wouldn't normally, as though her body knew she had something to protect. She tried to cover up but this only provoked him more. He hit her, in the face, in the stomach. 'Not there,' she screamed. 'Not there, I'm carrying your son.' She tried to keep him calm. She cooked, she let him do what he wanted to her and never talked back to him. When she saw Urchin Tatafu walking along the beach every day, she looked away. She asked Laita to stop coming to see her. She was Amalia Matete, Ioane's wife, and she would be nothing else. That way she could protect her baby.

Angel and Arun watched their mother fade before

their eyes. Angel blamed Ioane Matete. He talked to
Arun but Arun found he didn't dislike his father. Instead
he watched how he acted. The anger of Ioane matched
something that had always been inside him since the
day of his birth. The thunder he had been born into
was back and Arun was comfortable lying in the storm.
He did not recognise the woman that Angel described
as their mother. He did not feel the warmth that his
brother felt and did not remember the moments of love
that Angel talked about. When Arun thought about his
life, he thought of his brother: but now he had a father.
He took to following him around, going with him to
kava parties and out on the boat. Ioane let his baby
son join in and did not try to protect him from anything.

'You and I are going to be a good team,' he told Arun
when the *kava* got to his tongue and he couldn't stop
talking. 'Ioane and Arun, leaders of the sea! We're going
to see the world,' slurred Ioane before passing out. The
little boy took the coconut shell cup from his father's
hands and drank the remains. He too promptly lay
down and slept.

Angel Matete hated to see his brother moving away
from him. He had hoped they would be able to spend
this last week together. Instead he watched as Arun
stuck to their father like a limpet. Angel wanted to drag
him away, to protect him, for he knew that Ioane would
hurt his brother in ways that could never be undone.
He knew this as surely as he knew that a fish in the
bottom of a boat would die. Whenever Arun went
somewhere with Ioane, Angel would go up to the

coconut plantation and wait for him, in case he ran there to cry. But no matter how long he waited, Arun never came. Soon the day arrived when he had to leave. Angel would never again be able to protect Arun. There would be an ocean between them.

They gathered on the beach to say goodbye, Amalia with her Angel and Ioane with his son Arun.

'Please, Ioane,' Amalia begged her husband, 'please, leave him here.' She held a hand out to Arun and pulled him towards her. 'He's my son,' she said, 'I can't lose my son.'

Angel watched as his mother pressed Arun into her legs. With her eyes she tried to persuade Ioane. Angel knew she would never succeed.

'Come on, Arun,' said the boy's father.

As Amalia cried, something stirred inside her youngest son. He remembered her tears from the first days of his life and was glad to be leaving. He wriggled free from her grip and ran to his father.

'No! Arun!' Amalia cried. She ran into the house.

'Goodbye,' Ioane Matete said.

'Goodbye. Goodbye, Arun.'

'Bye, Angel.'

And the father and son got into their boat and rowed away.

THE TWINS

—

Inside Amalia a baby had been forming. It had started growing when Ioane was around. It had felt its father. It had felt his presence in Amalia's fear, his fists on her stomach, his voice in her head. The baby's chest was small where Ioane's hand had crushed it. The baby's legs were weak because its mother had not been allowed to rest. The baby had realised that it would have to protect itself. It had chosen to be male.

But now everything was changing. Ioane Matete was an ocean away and for the first time the baby felt its mother. It felt love and peace and it grew to know the sea, the rise and fall of the tide, the soft comfort of water. A new baby began to grow from the first. This baby was large and healthy, with no fists to shy away from. This baby had no memory of its father's anger, all it knew was its mother's womb and its brother. This baby felt safe. It chose to be female.

LIFE WITHOUT arun

The morning after Ioane took Arun away, the sun rose in a cloudless sky and light bounced off the sea. The fishermen hurried to their nets. Teacher Zeno moved the school outside. And up on the plantations the men did not sweat as they normally did, for the earth yielded to their spades, the trees to their axes. Fruit fell into their hands.

But the morning passed Angel by. He lay on his back in the room he had shared with his brother. If he closed his eyes and drew in a giant breath he could still smell Arun. There was his matting. There was the cloth that Angel used to wipe away his brother's tears. There was Arun's bag still full of his schoolbooks. There was the pile of clothes that Angel once had worn but were now his brother's. Angel tried to imagine his brother seeing the world, but all he could conjure in his head was the picture they had drawn: Arun as a pirate on a boat made from three lines.

Later, when the sun was high in the sky and the island was once again as hot as it usually was, Angel picked himself off his floor and left the quiet, too empty house. He went up to the plantation as his father had told him. Perhaps if he never went to school again, Arun would come home.

When Amalia Matete woke up, she was happy for a moment. Her face would have a chance to heal. The scratches on her legs would not get infected now as long as she stayed out of the sea. Her babies would be safe. Ioane Matete was an ocean away.

But so was Arun.

She closed her eyes, trying not to think of him. She fought against the panic deep within her. It was okay. It'd be okay. She would bring him back. She would go and get him. But she had never left Moana. She had never passed the cliff that Urchin Tatafu had once wanted to throw himself off, or tried to cross the swamp, or even been rowed through the coral. She could not leave. She would never see the ship that had her son on it or understand where he could have gone.

'Ioane Matete will come back,' she told herself. 'He'll walk up the beach with my son.' She held her stomach as she thought of her husband. Her babies would be born by then. 'He won't hurt them once they're out of me,' she thought. 'And Arun will be okay spending six months with his father. Then he'll come back. He'll come back. I know he will.' She dreamt of dark eyes and tears.

* * *

Amalia Matete did her best to be a mother to the twins that had grown inside her. Doctor Vaite was worried about them; they weren't lying correctly. He feared for her life during the birth.

'There is something not right with these babies, Amalia. I don't think you're going to be able to have them naturally.'

'I will, don't worry. They'll be fine.'

'I don't think they will be. I think you should go to Laumua. One of the Vetes can take you.'

'No. Let's just see what happens. I feel good about them.'

'This is a mistake, Amalia.'

'Maybe.'

'Both their heads are here.' He touched her at the top of her stomach.

'Then you better move them.'

So the doctor started massaging Amalia to give her babies a chance to live. He gave her herbs. The herbs worked. The twins came into the world, the larger of the two dragging her brother feet-first behind her. They were attached. The toes on the girl's right foot fitted into a space on the boy's left, a space where his toes should have been. The girl had four perfect toes, was large and healthy. The boy had only one.

'No more children, Amalia,' said the doctor, weeks later, when she'd recovered. 'Another one will be the end of you. No more, do you promise?'

But they both knew that that was not her decision to make.

The babies were named after Amalia's parents, Tamatoa and Lisi. Amalia held one in each arm as they gurgled and giggled and kicked.

'They remind me of you and Arun,' she told Angel as he came back into the house after dark.

He smiled at his mother and walked straight past, taking the food from the plantation to the kitchen.

'They're inseparable,' she said to the empty room. She put the twins on the floor and watched as they lay on their backs. 'You two are talking to each other, aren't you?' she asked her babies, 'through that foot of yours.' She got down on the floor next to them and tickled where they were one. Both babies squirmed contentedly. She then played with Tamatoa's right foot and both babies reacted. The same happened with Lisi's left. 'You two are not two at all, are you? You're one little baby.' She laughed at the twins, but then stopped herself. She shouldn't be happy when Arun was away.

'Angel,' she said to her son another night. 'These babies speak for each other.'

Angel nodded as he put down a net full of coconuts.

'Lisi was crying. But she was clean, she didn't want any milk and nothing was wrong. So I checked Tamatoa. He was thirsty. He drank and drank and then Lisi was silent again.'

Angel kissed his mother on the cheek and went into his room.

Amalia watched her babies grow. Days passed and months and soon Lisi and Tamatoa were rolling onto their fronts, then crawling, one forward, one back. More months passed until they were over a year old and they had worked out a way to stand and to walk, facing one another, one going forward, one back. They held each other by the elbows for balance and bashed into walls and people because their whole world was the other's face. Amalia laughed.

'It can't go on, Amalia,' the doctor told her. 'We have to separate them. It's better to do it now, before they've grown too much.'

'But they are so happy. I can't imagine hurting these babies.'

'It'll hurt them more in the long run if we don't. Look at how they're walking; it's not human, it's not natural. And, Amalia, it is unlucky to keep them joined. The villagers are getting nervous.'

'They're babies.'

'It is a bad sign. If they stay together the crops will fail, the fish will die. We can't risk it, Amalia.'

'I won't let you hurt my children.'

'They'll survive it, Amalia. It will be quick and I'll make it as painless as possible.'

Amalia agreed to let the doctor separate her twins.

Doctor Vaite numbed their feet and sent for Mori Unga to help him keep them still. He made Amalia take a walk with Whinney, his wife.

'Don't come back, no matter what you hear,' he told them. 'I'm sorry,' he said to the babies. They gurgled and smiled and clapped their hands together. They had just been fed and were about to fall asleep. The doctor nodded at Mori and pushed down on the knife. With one cut he freed Lisi's big toe and the one next to it from Tamatoa's foot. With a second Tamatoa's middle toe no longer touched Lisi's foot. With the third stroke Lisi's two smallest toes were released.

Such howling had never before been heard on the island. It was the sound of two hearts betrayed. The twins were separated.

Amalia heard the noise from the other side of the village. Distraught, she raced back. Her babies were in the front room in a pool of blood.

'It was a success, Amalia,' shouted the doctor over the din. 'It is perfectly natural for them to cry.' 'But he knew that the babies were doing more than crying. They were breaking, and this was not something he could heal. He bandaged up their feet and left them to their mother.

The babies did not stop crying for five months. Tamatoa lost his balance. His left foot now had only one tiny toe in the centre. Amalia gave him a stick to lean on but even so he cried and fell. Lisi could still stand; between her four toes there was only a small gap. But she wobbled. She was used to Tamatoa's elbows to hold. Without the support of her brother she couldn't walk.

For five months the twins lay just as they had done before they were separated; Tamatoa's toe between Lisi's. Their crying broke the spirit of the villagers. *Kava* parties stopped; no one could sing or tell stories while they listened to the twins. The fishermen no longer caught anything in their nets. The fruit of the trees fell withered and dry to the ground. The villagers feared that if the noise did not stop soon, Moana would be washed away by tears. The sound drained the energy from even the strongest. Grandfather Unga, who'd always been the first to rise and the last to sleep, grew tired and died. The village slowed. People did less and less. No one went up to the plantations unless it was to try and walk away from the noise, or down to the water, except to plunge their heads into the silence below. The Havealetas, whose house had always been full of music and dancing at night, no longer opened their doors. Urchin Tatafu and four of his brothers moved away to Laumua and the Unga wives regretted their latest pregnancies. No one wanted any more babies.

But of everyone, Amalia Matete was affected the most. She lay down next to her children and cried with them.

'I'm so sorry, my babies, I'm so sorry, eh? I thought it would be for the best. I'm so sorry. Please stop crying Lisi. Please stop crying Tamatoa. The doctor told me it would be okay. I'll never listen to him again, I promise. I'll never let him near you again.'

And she kept her word, turning the old man away when he came to check on their bandages.

'It was for the best, Amalia. Now they'll be able to have a normal life, to walk. They'll stop crying soon.'

'When Doctor? When? It's been months. You did this. Leave us alone.'

'Amalia.'

'Leave us!'

One person enjoyed the crying and that was Angel. Though their tears were different, though the twins were loud and his had been silent, Angel couldn't help but be reminded of Arun. When he saw tears, he saw a little boy with jet-black hair and dark sorrowful eyes. The sound that was the whole island's constant companion became Angel's brother returned. He played with the noise; went running in the trees with it, took it up to the plantation with him, or down to the sea to swim. He talked to the crying as though it was his friend and for the first time since his father had returned to take his brother away, he did not feel lonely.

'I'm glad you're back, Arun,' he told the sound. 'Don't go away, please don't go away.'

STOPPING TEARS

When Ioane Matete landed at Moana he was surprised
to see that the paths had not been raked, that the leaves
had not been swept from under his house and that,
across the beach, boats were scattered, their bottoms
covered in bird droppings. The village was deserted and
there was no sound but one: a constant howling. It came
from his house. He walked up and entered the side door.
In the main room was his wife, her face red and puffy,
lying next to two soiled screaming babies.

'What's going on here?' he demanded, and Amalia
raised her head. When she saw it was her husband she
ran to him and clung to his chest.

'Ioane,' she cried. 'Help, please. I can't make them stop.'

Ioane Matete held his wife her by her shoulders and
examined the desperation on her face. She was crying
almost as much as her children.

'I've been away too long this time,' he said to himself
and then asked her, 'How long has this been going on?'

'Since the operation. Five months.'

'They've been crying for five months?'

'Yes.'

'And how long have you let them lie here like this?'

'I don't know.'

'They're dirty, of course they're crying. Pull yourself together, Amalia.' And he slapped her across the face. She fell to her knees in stunned shock because, for the tiniest moment, her children were quiet.

'Now I want you to go out and have a swim. Wash. And don't come back until you can behave like my wife.'

Amalia ran out of the house and into the sea and held herself underwater where she could not hear the crying. Her husband turned to the babies.

'What do we have here?' he asked them. 'You're a little girl,' he said as he picked up Lisi. 'My first daughter. Hello my sweet darling. Why are you crying? May I wash you? Okay.' And gently as he could, he picked her up and dressed her.

'Now you stay here. I'll change your brother. Then the three of us will sit down and get to know each other. Okay?' And as he kissed his daughter, she stopped crying and as her father's new moustache tickled her face, she laughed.

'Now, you my boy,' he said. 'You need to be a man and not wail like this. Come on.' And he picked up his tiny son and washed him as well. Tamatoa, hearing his sister laughing, laughed.

The whole village held its breath, not daring to believe that the noise might be over. But when half an hour had gone by they started to hope. After an hour, one or two allowed themselves a hesitant smile. Half way through the night it was still quiet and one of the Unga children sneaked to the Matete house. He tripped over the pig board. Everyone braced themselves for crying. Silence. In the morning they decided to believe their ears. They shook off the lethargy that had been plaguing them and set to work repairing the neglect of half a year.

Ioane Matete found that he loved his daughter more than he thought he would ever care for a girl. Her large eyes and mouth had smiles just for him. He spent hours holding her in his arms, staring down into her little face. His new son didn't interest him at all and he wondered why, for he knew that the two children were very similar. But the boy was too small, much smaller than his girl. And his son never settled in his arms. What use was a son with a limp? How could he ever compare to his first daughter?

Amalia gradually overcame her fear of the twins and while her husband doted on their girl, she spent time with Tamatoa, who she found she liked for exactly the reason Ioane didn't. She kissed his poor deformed foot and promised she would love him more than anyone else in the world ever could.

Angel continued to feel nothing for his brother and sister. He wanted to know where Arun was. Why hadn't he come back? He had heard Amalia asking his father this question time and again, but Ioane never answered.

Angel was now ten and felt that it was time he stood up to his father. It took him a week to work up the courage, a week of pretend dialogues up on the coconut plantation, but eventually he asked Ioane.

'Why didn't Arun come back with you?'

'No room in the boat, was there Lisi?' Ioane had taken to addressing everything through his daughter.

'Where is he?'

'Oh, not too far from here.'

'When's he coming back?'

Angel had asked one question too many. Ioane raised his head away from his daughter towards his eldest son. Their eyes met, both filled with anger.

'Where's Arun?' Angel asked.

'Forget about him,' the father told his son. 'Arun doesn't live here anymore. He's not coming back.'

For a second Angel thought about fighting his father, about grabbing his hair and punching his fists into that face. He thought about standing on the neck of his father and demanding an answer to his question. He imagined Lisi howling as Ioane spat out the name of some island or some town that would mean nothing to him. But more than anything, Angel wanted Arun back, and he knew that that was not the way.

When he left the village, Ioane was determined to return soon to see Lisi.

'Look after her, Amalia.'

'I will.'

'Properly this time. You are their mother. Keep them

with you, hold them if they cry. I never again want to get home to my children sobbing.'

'I'll make them happy this time.'

'Make sure you do.'

As Ioane sailed away he thought about his children. He'd miss Lisi, but at least he would soon see his son Arun, a much better boy than his other two. Although he wouldn't admit it, Ioane was always afraid that one day he would not be able to find Arun, that when he returned, his son would not be there. Arun. Where had his wife got that name from? Did she know what had happened all those years ago? Arun, his childhood friend. Arun, swimming with him. Arun, walking with him. He and Arun eating at his mother's house. Ioane Matete and Arun Nepali, rulers of Laumua. Arun, covered in blood, accusing him. Arun's eyes as he walked away. Arun Nepali had been willing to do anything for him. But now he was gone.

'If only the truck had never been dragged from the sea,' Ioane thought to himself. 'If only I'd never seen Vahine.'

When Ioane Matete was fifteen he had noticed a girl in one of the inland villages a few miles from Laumua. He walked over there every weekend hoping to catch a glimpse of her. The driver of the village's only truck felt sorry for the boy; so obviously love sick, too scared to approach the girl or her family. So he let him drive. He taught him about gears and steering and how to fix the truck when it broke down, which it would do at least twice on the muddy road before they got back to the coast.

Ioane told Arun Nepali about the truck and the boy wanted to try it as well. The next time Ioane went to the village, Arun went with him. They spent the day there.

'Look at her,' Ioane said to his friend, 'Vahine is the most beautiful woman I have ever seen.'

Vahine was inside her house, trying her hardest not to notice the two boys sitting on the wall outside, watching her. She carried on washing her family's clothes as she always did. She swept the front room, just as she did every day. She mended a blanket that desperately needed repairing. And of course she washed the clothes at the front of the house, because it was where the sun was and she didn't want to be in her usual shady spot around the back. And the floor nearest the window was particularly dirty so that was why she spent so long there. As for the blanket, well, why shouldn't she sew in the front room? Should she be forced to hide herself away in the kitchen just because two boys were watching her? One of them came every weekend and if she hid from him now she knew she would have to hide forever. He would keep coming back, she was sure.

'Vahine, who are those boys outside?' her father asked when he got back from the plantation.

'I don't know. I think the tall one wants to meet me.'

Her father smiled at her, his eyes twinkling, 'And do you want to meet him?'

'Well. Yes. I suppose I do.'

So Vahine's father went outside and invited Ioane Matete to the village's next *kava* party where his daughter would wash water through the powdered root, stir the mixture and serve the men their drink.

'Woooooohoooooooooo,' Ioane shrieked as soon as the old man had gone back inside. 'I'm going to talk to her, Arun! I'm going to sit between her and her father. I can't wait to watch her serve.'

'If she gives you a full cup it means she likes you,' Arun Nepali advised, 'and you should carry on as you are. But if she serves you half, then she does not think you are a man and you still have to prove yourself.'

Ioane laughed at his friend. 'What do you know about *kava*, Arun? You've never even been to a party before. You're too young.'

'Well, neither have you,' said Arun Nepali, 'so I know as much as you do.'

'She'll give me a full cup. I know it. By the end of the night at least. And then I'll marry her and bring her back to Laumua with me. I can't wait to marry her and build our own little house on the beach, right next to my parents and sisters. We'll get a plantation and maybe I'll learn to fish and we'll have hundreds of children and—'

'Okay, okay, enough,' laughed Arun Nepali. 'First you have to talk to her. But before that, we've got to get back home.'

'Let's find the truck.'

separating the twins

Lisi began to talk to other people, to Angel, to visitors, but Tamatoa clung to his mother's *lavalava* and begged to be picked up. He still could not walk. It was difficult even with a stick.

Every evening the twins lay down to sleep with their toes pushing against each other but, as skin touched skin, they remembered what was lost. Tears pooled in their eyes. Amalia pressed their feet together to try to mend their broken hearts. But they could no longer talk through their toes. It was only in grief they were joined and only Ioane Matete could stop them from crying.

The twins waited for their father, crying a little or quiet and sad. But when a few weeks had passed and there was no Ioane to hold them, they started again, that howl that everyone in Moana knew too well. It hit the village like an unbearable memory and left them stunned and unable to react. Amalia saw the eyes of her neighbours deaden as they had deadened before and knew that they could not survive more tears. And neither could she. As long as Lisi and Tamatoa were together they would be in mourning. She had to reverse what the doctor had done and the only way to do that was to repeat it. Amalia knew that to make them stop, she would have to keep them apart.

She called out to a girl, playing with the other children in the mud.

'Zeno,' she said, 'take Lisi with you.'

When the children left with Lisi tucked, still screaming, under their arm like a doll, Amalia took Tamatoa and hurried to the Havealetas' house. As he got further from Lisi, Tamatoa grew quieter, until on arrival he was as silent as a shell.

'Amalia,' Laita said. She was smelling a flower but stopped and tucked it behind Amalia's right ear. She then took Tamatoa in her arms, wiped his face, then blew on his stomach. He clutched a handful of her hair in his fists and tugged lightly. She laughed. 'He's so like Angel, isn't he?'

Amalia had never thought so. 'Maybe,' she said.

'Shall we go for a walk?' Laita asked. 'I want to watch the sunset this evening. I think there'll be a green flash. Tom and I usually go together but Vete brought some rum back from Laumua yesterday so I don't expect to see him tonight.'

'Okay. Where do you want to go?'

'What about to the cliff? It will give us the best view. We think it's going to be a great one tonight. The sky is so clear, the sun should set right on top of the water.'

'It'll be hard to get back through the trees once it's dark.'

'It'll be fine. Tamatoa will lead the way, won't you?' Laita held the baby out in front of her and walked out of the house.

About half an hour later the two women sat down with their legs hanging over the edge of the cliff, Laita with the baby on her lap. She held tightly to his little stomach, suddenly afraid lest she drop him over the edge.

'You're good with children,' Amalia said to her, thinking of Arun, imagining him on a foreign cliff, slipping from the arms of an unseen woman, breaking his bones on rocks he didn't know were there.

Laita said with a confused expression, 'Everyone is. They're children.'

'Do you like having them around?'

'Of course I do. Jesus said, "Let the little children come to me, and do not hinder them, for the kingdom of God belongs to such as these." I make bread so that they'll visit me. They fill my house with light.'

'I think you're the only person who does. I only eat it when the Tatafus bring some back from Laumua.'

'They're getting more and more things from there now. Vete must go every week. Yesterday he brought me Spam.'

'I was given a jelly mix for the children. You add it to water and drink it.'

'That's what they were putting on my bread this morning. It made it go pink like the sky is now.'

The sun was sinking lower towards the sea.

'What is this green we're looking for?' Amalia asked.

'As the last of the light disappears it is there for an instant, a tiny moment. Once in a lifetime, if God blesses you, you can see it.'

'You and Tom look for it every night? Together?'

'Yes. Tom loves the idea. And I like being with him. Not every man is Ioane Matete.'

'What idea?'

'That at the moment of death, there is something else.'

Amalia's expression was blank.

Laita started to explain. 'Look at the sky now. What colours do you see?'

'Pink, red, orange, blue, grey.'

'Yellow, white. Are there any others?'

'Purple over there.' Amalia pointed to one side of the sun where the sea looked bruised and beautiful.

'But no green?'

'No.'

'Green has no place in a sunset. The sun is all bright fiery colours, the sea at this time of day is always a sort of bluish grey. But for that one moment, just before it sinks and is gone, there is green. Tom says that you don't know what's inside a person until they've died. I don't think that's true. I like the sunsets but I disagree with him. A hint of green doesn't stop the sun being red. It's going now.'

The sun was sucking its colours off the end of the world, preparing to leave the sea in the dark. Amalia tried to glimpse the green flash, but the sun disappeared without either of the women seeing a thing.

'Laita, will you have Lisi?' Amalia asked.

Laita paused. 'Yes,' she replied.

'But I need her back when Ioane is here. He'd kill me if he found out about this. She's his daughter.'

'Then why do it? He'll find out.'

'I need to. Angel and Tamatoa are mine. I can look after them. But I can't stop Lisi from crying. When the twins are together that's all they do. Will you take her?'

'Okay.'

'Are you sure?'

'I've always wanted my own child. Of course Lisi can come.'

'Tom won't mind?'

'No. But won't you, Amalia?'

'No. I've thought about this. I can't look after her. But you can.'

'Yes, I can.'

'Thank you, eh? We'd better get back. It's dark. I'll take Tamatoa.' The little boy had fallen asleep in Laita's arms. 'Can you lead the way?'

'I'll try,' replied Laita, less sure of herself now. They headed into the trees, aiming for the village. Laita stumbled and would have fallen, except that a man caught her arm. It was Angel, who in the darkness looked nothing like a child. He went with them.

Back in the village, outside Amalia's house, Laita took Lisi.

'She's very beautiful. And calm. She's not crying now. Are you sure about this, Amalia?'

'I'm sure. I know it makes no sense and you must think I'm an awful mother . . .'

'Of course not. Plenty of women here get help, you know that. Didn't I have Baby Zeno until she was two? And Whinney always has an Unga boy or two at her house.'

'Yes, you did. She does. It's better if I just have my boys here. I know it is. But Lisi . . .'

'We're just up the village.'

The women had forgotten that Angel was there. 'I'll bring you back,' he whispered to his sister.

Once inside the house, Amalia got down on the floor next to Tamatoa and lay staring at his little face. He had Angel's curls and Arun's eyes. Except that Angel had shaved his head. And now that Lisi was gone, Tamatoa seemed happier. His eyes shone; dark, mournful pools no longer.

THE END OF IOANE MATETE

Ioane Matete was gone for five years. He arrived back on the island early one morning and was immediately suspicious. It wasn't raining. The sky was clear from one end of the horizon to the next. There was not even the possibility of bad weather. The beach was clean and calm. The trees were bulging with fruit. He listened; the only sounds were the laugher of children on their way to school and the singing of a bird. He turned and faced the perfect sea. Ioane was used to travelling in storms but the ocean had helped his journey today. Each wave had propelled him towards the village and away from the rocks and coral. He saw his house. He thought he smelt fish cooking. He thought about seeing his daughter and was excited.

'Morning,' said Angel, who was walking down the beach towards Ioane carrying a little girl. 'Someone wanted to come and say hello to you.'

Ioane held out his arms to his daughter. Lisi accepted

cautiously at first, but then seemed to recognise something in the smell of the man and cuddled into his chest.

'She remembers me,' Ioane said.

'You could always make her smile,' Angel replied, trying to understand why his sister loved their father, 'of course she does.' He wondered what would have happened if Ioane had arrived and found Lisi with Laita Havealeta. His relief that he hadn't made him speak more gently to his father than he would otherwise have done.

Ioane sniffed his daughter's hair and kissed it. She giggled and started talking to him about a shell Angel had found for her. Ioane nodded and listened as he moved up the beach and into the house. He stood in the doorway for a few moments, letting his eyes adjust to the darkness. There was a shadow on the floor. It was a boy asleep.

'Who's this?' Ioane asked, nudging him with his toe.

'Tam,' Lisi told him. 'We are the same, but have a different house.'

'That's Tamatoa, Lisi's twin. They're five now,' Angel said as he gently woke his little brother. The boy sat up, not saying a word.

'I know how old my own children are. Where does he live?' Ioane asked.

'Here,' Angel replied.

'Where does my daughter live?'

'She lives where she is happy.'

Ioane turned to face Angel but there was something in his son's eyes, a deep determination, or was it hatred, that made him think better of it. He went to find Amalia.

Amalia saw him and was afraid. She held out a plate of fish to him. He put it on the ground.

'Where does my daughter live?' he asked again, so quietly that Amalia had to strain to catch the words.

'You're back. Laita has been helping me with her. It's okay. It happens all the time here. The village is so small it doesn't really matter where someone sleeps, does it? And Tom's been away. She was all on her own. She's okay. I just thought it would be better to have the boys . . .' she trailed off.

'I'm going to kill Laita but first I'm going to kill you,' he said in an almost tender voice, and held out his hand to her. 'Come with me. We'll go to our room.'

Amalia had never known her husband like this. Normally his anger was as tangible as the rain. She could see it coming like a cloud and could work out how wet she might get. She used to count the blows she received so that she'd know when it was over. Normally he was loud and aggressive, but as he led her silently to their room, she felt a fear she'd never experienced before. 'I'm going to die today,' she said to herself as she walked out of the kitchen. She saw Angel watching her, and for the first time there was something else other than fear. Amalia Matete felt anger growing within her, anger that her husband should treat her as nothing, anger that he should humiliate her in front of her son.

'Wait,' Angel said, moving between his father and the door.

'Take the twins down to the beach,' Ioane commanded.

'Don't talk to anyone, especially not to Laita. Do you understand me?'

Angel didn't move. They stared at one another. Amalia watched her husband and her son. They have the same eyes, the same powerful gaze, she thought to herself. But he shouldn't have to protect me. Not yet.

'Angel,' Amalia said gently. 'Please take the twins outside. It's okay. I'm okay.'

Angel did not move.

'Please,' she said again.

He looked at his mother. She smiled at him. Turning, not deigning to look at Ioane, Angel went into the main room and held out his hands to the twins. Tamatoa rubbed his eyes and picked up his stick. Lisi skipped out of the door. On the beach, Angel thought, 'If he hurts Amalia, I'll kill him. I shouldn't have left her alone with him. Where is Arun? When will he come home? Has he killed him too?'

'Lisi, we're going swimming,' he said. 'Put your arms around my neck. Tam, stay here, we'll be back soon.'

Angel picked Lisi up. She laughed and he lifted her onto his back. 'Take a deep breath,' he said and dived down to the bottom of the sea, where there were no thoughts except the thoughts of sea urchins and crabs, and no noises at all.

'Take off your dress,' Ioane said in a quiet voice.

Amalia fumbled with the buttons. It was a dress her husband had brought back for her, which she rarely wore. It got stuck in her hair and she couldn't pull it over her head. When she was naked she stood before him waiting for what would come next.

'I asked you to look after my daughter,' he said. 'You didn't, Amalia. It will be the last time you disobey me.'

His voice was calm, but his fingers were shaking.

'I did,' Amalia replied firmly and the sound infuriated Ioane, it broke his quiet fury. He grabbed her hair with both his hands and forced her head back. He held her there until her pupils fell into her skull and all that could be seen of her eyes was white. He hit her across the face. His actions were no longer guarded and composed. His face was red, his breathing heavy.

Amalia's pain as he entered her reminded her of the first night they were married. She felt as young and vulnerable as she had then. Would it ever stop hurting like this? He punched her again and she felt her cheek grow tight and swell up. His nails punctured the skin on her back and she became aware of drops of blood pooling in the cuts. Then, whether from weariness or from pain or from the understanding that these were her last moments on earth, the anger that she had contained inside herself since their first night together, burst out and blossomed like a fire that has suddenly caught hold. She struggled, she fought, she clawed at her husband, Ioane Matete. She saw him lunge towards her and with all her remaining strength she drove her thumb into his eye and kept driving it deeper and deeper until he turned away screaming. Then he hit her but, even as she fell, she knew with a final satisfaction that each time he looked at himself he would remember who had damaged him. She felt his hands grabbing for her throat and tightening. She tried to breathe. She passed out.

When she woke she found her husband slumped naked on top of her. It was midday, the room hot and the sun bright. She pushed him off her and rolled out from underneath his body. She stood up. She kicked him as hard as she could. He didn't move. She kicked him again. He just lay there, rasping for air. Something was wrong with him, something more than scratches and teeth marks and his eye that was covered in blood. He tried to say something, but Amalia could not make out the words. She bent down and looked into his face. It had changed; it was as if the muscles on one side had collapsed and turned the other into a grotesque mask. His arms were not moving. There was a plea for help in his one good eye. She noticed a touch of green in its dark brown.

Amalia stood for a few moments, counting her breaths, feeling the damage he had done to her body. She did not think of the pain. She listened to the movements of the sea and the sounds of the village carrying on without her. She had now been married to Ioane Matete for fourteen years. She touched her face. She would heal. She almost smiled as she thought how angry he would be if he knew that he had taken her past the point of submission, past the point of even caring. She felt invincible. She had feared that Ioane was going to be different, was going to torture her in a new way this time. But now she saw that he was not original, not capable of anything new. His anger today was the same old anger. She realised that he would not have hurt Laita as he had claimed. She saw that the village was not scared of him as she had been for all these years. She imagined Tom trying to force his wife to do anything. Laita would slap him round the face, pray to the Lord for patience and refuse to make him food. Why hadn't Amalia been stronger with Ioane at the beginning? She thought that in his own way he did love her; maybe he would have listened. Or at least she should have let her friends help her, let them stop him as they had tried to do, right at the start when he had dragged her away from her mother at their wedding.

'Ioane,' she said to him, 'tell me now, quickly, while you still can, where is Arun. Please, Ioane. Tell me so I can bring our son home. Where is Arun?' But Amalia saw that Ioane could not speak.

Amalia Matete found her children in the sea outside. Angel ran up the beach when he saw her and took her into his arms. She rested her head on her son's shoulder and wondered when it was he had become a man. The twins followed him.

'Your face is ugly,' Lisi said.

'What happened?' asked Tamatoa.

'Where is he?' demanded Angel.

'Your father is ill,' she told them.

'Dr Vaite?' asked Lisi.

'No. Ioane doesn't need him. He'll be fine. Let's go back into the sea.'

'I'm going up to the house,' Angel said.

'No, Angel. I need a swim. Now. I want you to swim with me.'

Angel walked into the ocean. Amalia took the twins' hands and went in after him. She threw her youngest son's stick onto the shore, then let the salt water slowly soothe her. They kept swimming deeper and deeper, Tamatoa holding tightly to his mother, afraid of the water, Lisi relaxed and happy on her eldest brother's back. 'Will Ioane die?' Amalia thought. 'Where's Arun?'

They swam to escape and they swam so far that they reached the mango island. They waded up its beach.

'Arun was born here,' Amalia said.

'Who's Arun?' asked the twins, and Amalia's only answer was tears. She had not told her children about their brother. If Ioane died, Arun would never find his way home. The twins would never meet him. She saw that she was scaring them but could not stop. With her eyes she asked Angel to look after his brother and sister. Angel picked four mangoes and sat down next to his family. They ate together in silence. And this eating and their togetherness calmed her. Amalia stopped crying. Tamatoa leant his head against his brother's arm. Lisi and Angel concentrated on their mangoes and juice ran down their chins. It was time to leave. They swam back to Moana.

Before she went inside to see if her husband had died, Amalia Matete stood in the sun and let her dress dry. She opened up her arms and twirled on the spot, trying to remember doing this as a child in this very place. It was too long ago. She remembered how she'd felt when her father died and she wondered if her children would cry if Ioane was dead. Where was Arun?

Inside, the house was still. Amalia noticed that the floor needed sweeping, there was dust in the corners of the room and the pig board was falling apart. It should be mended. The colours of the cotton cloth that hung in the doorways were faded. The paint was falling off the shutters on the front windows. Her dress was ripped and her feet dirty. She needed to start again, to sort out her family and her house. Was Ioane dead?

Amalia Matete went into her room and saw that her husband hadn't moved. She lay down next to him. He tried to turn himself around and she helped him until they were lying face to face. She ran her finger down the side of his cheek, tracing the lines that had formed during his years at sea.

'Where have you been, Ioane Matete?' she asked him. 'Have you come home now?'

They stared at each other and Amalia watched tears pool in the corner of the eye that was not weeping blood. She kissed him then, softly on the lips and tasted his sorrow with her tongue. She touched his hair, ran her hands through it and found streaks of grey. She wondered how old he was and was surprised she didn't know. She had always thought he must be much older than her; but then, when she was sixteen everyone had seemed old.

'I was so young,' she said. 'You should have been gentle with me.'

Ioane Matete tried again to speak but Amalia could not understand.

'It's your turn to be quiet,' she told him. 'Rest now. You'll get better.'

She looked at him.

'I'm not sure I've ever seen what you look like before,' she said. 'I've never stared at you. Do you know you are beautiful? You have the face of a powerful man, and thick lips. I want to kiss them.' And she did.

'Am I beautiful?' she asked. 'You've never told me. Or do you think I'm ugly? Maybe you've never looked at me either. Look now. Look at my hair, and my forehead and my swollen cheeks and my nose. Look at my chin and my eyes. What do I look like? Look at my face now. Am I beautiful?' She stood up and took off her dress. Then she lay next to him. 'Do you like my body? You have to ignore this bruise,' she said as she pointed at one on her hip, 'and this, and this. You did those, Ioane. But look at everything else. Do I have nice breasts? Is my skin a good colour? I'm very thin. I'd look better fatter, but perhaps you don't mind. Perhaps you dream about my body when you are away from me. Or maybe you don't, maybe you've had other women who are rounder with fewer scars. Do you love me, Ioane? You've never kissed the end of my nose or blown into my ear. Why is that?'

She stayed talking for the rest of the afternoon, long after Ioane Matete's gentle breathing told her he'd fallen asleep, until finally she whispered one last question. 'Where's Arun?'

Outside it started to rain.

ama matete

Amalia Matete was pregnant again.

'This is going to be our last child, Ioane,' she told him.

She found it easy to talk to her husband now. She chatted at him as she plaited *pandanus* leaves into mats. He had become an ornament of sorts, slumped there at the side of the room in a chair made for him by Mori Unga. When Angel moved him each evening to their room, Amalia tried the chair out for herself. She wasn't used to resting above the ground.

Lisi now lived once again with the family and she played with her father as if he was a giant doll, finding shells and leaves to present to him, hiding between his legs. Even Tamatoa had begun to approach Ioane and now and then joined in with his twin's games. Amalia fed Ioane the vegetables that the Ungas gave her.

She opened up the doors of the house and let the villagers return to her life. At first they felt awkward in

Ioane Matete's presence, as if stared at by the statue of a one-eyed god. But slowly the house became full again. Lisi and Tamatoa let the other children play with their father, until they got bored and ran outside. Lisi went with them, but Tamatoa, walking with his stick, could not keep up. The twins had grown close again since Lisi's return. She was the leader, the bossy strong one and weak-chested Tamatoa was her toy, who she dragged around as she wanted to. Tamatoa did not mind, he would always be a few moments behind his sister, there was no catching up now. Things that were easy for her, he found difficult, but as long as she was near he did not worry about anything. Lisi took care of him and both liked it.

Amalia tried to persuade Angel that he did not need to work on the plantation as much as he did, but the boy never stopped. Slowly he and the Unga boys were taking over the workload from Lave, Mori and their brother Hosea. The twelve Unga cousins had made Angel their thirteenth and they planned to learn everything they could in the next few years so that their fathers could stop working.

Hosea found the earnestness of the boys touching but ridiculous.

'We're not old, boys; we've got a good few years ahead of us yet. You lot, especially the youngest of you, only need come up once a week or so, not all day every day. I want you in school. There will be plenty of time to farm when you're older.'

'If they're keen let's make the most of it,' Mori said. 'Do you remember how our father had to force us to start working? We hated it. Well, brothers, if our children carry on like this we'll be able to stop soon and drink *kava* during the days as well as the nights. They know what they're doing, let them do it.'

'We started when we were fifteen, didn't we?' said Lave. 'Only our youngest sons are below that age and the rest of our boys are at least that. We'll only climb trees for fun now! Come, let's gather the men and pound some *kava* roots. It is time to drink.'

Angel hardly came back to the house. He divided his time between the plantation and the sea, scarcely seeing his family, except to come home each evening with coconuts or fish, to move his father and ask him, 'Where's Arun?', knowing that Ioane could not answer, praying that one day he would.

Laita spent a lot of time in the house, to see Lisi, as did many of the Zenos. Sometimes Whinney would come around, but Amalia felt awkward in front of her. She still had not spoken to the doctor.

'The twins are seven now and happy,' Whinney said. 'Lisi can walk perfectly. That is because of my husband. When will you talk to him, Amalia? The village is too small for this. And he is an old man who deserves your respect. What would your father think?'

Amalia didn't know any more why she wouldn't go to see the doctor. She wanted to and almost did several times but at the last minute she always invented a job that had to be done first. She was growing larger and larger and felt that the baby wanted her to stay away. She still heard the howl of the twins.

'I won't let it happen to you,' she told the new baby. 'I won't let anything bad happen to you.' And then she ran inside and asked her husband, 'Where's Arun? Please, Ioane, try to tell me.'

His lips formed shapes but no words came. It appeared to Amalia that he was saying, 'okay, okay' over and over again.

Amalia worried about having another child. She thought about Angel: young, strong and beautiful, now the man of the house, working to feed them all. But except for rare moments, Angel was a ghost to her. She had lost him the day he had floated out to sea. He was out of her reach, an untouchable stranger she was longing to know but who was impossible to meet.

Every evening Angel came in to move his father.

'Angel,' she whispered. But Angel said nothing. He just picked up the body of his father and carried it into the other room. He turned it to face the setting sun and bent down to whisper in its ear. Ioane's eyelids twitched. On his way out, Angel looked at Amalia but she felt that his eyes were empty, that they were seeing not her but some far-off place.

One day she asked him, 'What are your secrets?'

'I don't know.'

'But you have some?'

'Yes.'

'You're lost in your head somewhere.'

'Yes.'

'Can I come with you?'

'I need to go alone.'

'Will you come back to me?'

'If I can. I'm waiting.'

'Don't wait too long.'

Each day, as soon as he had moved his father, he left again.

She thought of Arun: would she recognise him? She remembered him as she had last seen him; hair growing long and straight; eyes, dark and fearful; skin, still young and innocent; back, unbending and proud. He would now be twelve, almost a man. She tried to imagine him grown, but all that came to mind was her little boy on a beach far away and alone. What has happened to him? Where is he? And then she thought, even if he comes back it will be too late to get to know him. I have lost him forever.

But she still had the twins. She knew Lisi would be fine. She was happy and beautiful enough to marry anyone she chose. It was for Tamatoa that she worried.

'He's going to be lonely,' she thought. 'He keeps being left behind.'

One day she asked Tamatoa, 'Why don't you go out with Lisi?'

'They run.'

'Go out, try.'

Tamatoa left with the children the next day. Amalia watched from the front room of the house as they played on the beach. She saw them throwing rocks across the water. Tamatoa's fell short. She saw them running across the sand. Tamatoa fell over. She saw them go for a swim and when Tamatoa's head sank below the water she brought him back inside.

'I've been a bad mother,' Amalia said to Ioane one day. 'Why are we having another child?' But as she spoke the baby kicked her and she cried out happily. 'I'm going to look after you,' she promised. 'I'll never leave you.'

She turned to her husband. 'Where's Arun? Please, Ioane, tell me!'

Amalia Matete had been pregnant for nine months and still the baby did not arrive. She was now so large that the skin over her stomach looked like it could stretch no more. She felt as though she would burst. It was October and very hot. Amalia could not move without being drenched in sweat.

'I need the baby to come,' Amalia moaned to Laita, who now spent a large part of every day looking after her friend. 'Why isn't it here yet?'

'Amalia, I need to get Dr Vaite. Okay?'

'No. Not yet. Let him come tomorrow,' Amalia said every day. When Laita finally ignored her request and sent for him, the doctor had just left the village on a fishing trip.

'He'll be back in a few days,' Whinney told Laita. 'If he'd known she wasn't well, he wouldn't have gone.'

Eventually the labour began. Amalia had forgotten the pain of her other births, but was sure that they had not been as bad as this. The women gathered outside, calling out advice or running errands. The children were made to leave. Whinney came to the house and took over from Laita. She calmed Amalia down but was unable to help her with the pain.

'Someone needs to find my husband,' she told the women. She didn't like the look in Amalia's eye. The girl was leaving herself, was becoming wild. She had seen it happen before and knew it helped to leave your body for small periods of time. It was an escape from the brutality of giving birth. But only some women could do it, and they had to return every few minutes or they would not be able to get back. It was something that happened automatically during the birth of a first child and could then be called upon later. But Whinney knew that Amalia had not done it with Angel, nor, from what Vete Tatafu had told her husband, with Arun. When the twins were being born, she was hardly conscious. It was a bad sign that she was doing it now.

'Stay with us, Amalia,' she said firmly to the girl, and was relieved to see her return. 'Now push.'

The labour went on and on and no baby emerged. Amalia screamed as day turned to night and when it turned back to day she was still screaming and still there was no baby.

The labour took forty-eight hours, but eventually a girl forced her way out and into the light. She was large and healthy.

'She's beautiful, Amalia. Look, she's perfect,' said Laita. Whinney agreed. They cleaned up the baby and cut the umbilical cord.

'Mmmm, smell her, Whinney. I love baby smell.' Laita wrapped the child up in a little white cloth. When they turned to her to hand over the baby, Amalia pushed it away. Her brown skin had turned as pale as the newborn's.

'Amalia, are you okay?' Whinney asked.

Laita ran through into the main room and placed the baby on Ioane Matete's lap.

'Ama,' he managed to say.

'Quickly, Laita,' called Whinney.

The doctor arrived, straight back from the sea, smelling of fish. He ran to Amalia. 'Amalia, Amalia.' He kept repeating her name as he held her head and kissed her brow. 'What have you done, my girl?'

She took hold of his fingers and squeezed.

Amalia was bleeding and the doctor could not stop it.

'She's going,' he told the women.

'Can you leave us please?' Angel was at the doorway. Laita, Whinney and Doctor Vaite wanted to refuse, to demand to stay with Amalia as she died, but Angel looked at them with his father's old stare and they nodded and left the room. Angel sat down next to his mother and stroked her hair. She opened her eyes one last time and saw her son. He smiled at her and she smiled back. She opened her mouth to try to speak but no words came. Instead she laughed and Angel laughed with her. Then, with her eyes fixed on his, she lowered herself gently into death.

Once she was gone, Angel put his hand over her face and calmly closed her eyelids. But for the blood around her, she might have been asleep. Then he stood up and walked outside. He found Laita in the main room, trying to pick up the new baby from the arms of Ioane. He moved her out of the way and took the child.

'She's called Ama,' Whinney told him.

He nodded at her and left the house. He walked along the beach and showed the baby the sea for the first time. The sun was setting. He took the child into the water and rubbed salt all over her little body. Then, just as the last of the light was leaving the sky, Angel went to find Lisi and Tamatoa.

PART TWO

THE ROAD

It should have taken three years to build the bridge that would connect Moana to the rest of the island. One year to determine the best route through the swamp, another to lay the foundations, and a third to complete the bridge and connect it to the island's other roads. But in the end, because this was the island, because the sun shone and *kava* flowed, five were needed.

Eventually the bridge was built.

Its first crossing took the villagers into the realms of fable, to places some had only heard about in stories – but that which to start with caused the hairs on their arms to stand up in wonderment, became commonplace soon enough.

No one rowed through the coral any more, except for an old man wearing a thick coat covered with limpets.

There was no going back.

Most were glad of the change. New clothes could be

bought in Laumua, and light sandals. Foods that had been rare delicacies before – Spam, noodles, crisps – were soon everyday snacks. Jewellery that once only townsfolk had worn now decorated the necks of the Moanans. Chickens were brought and the villagers were able to sell, in return, their fish, mats and pigs. A phone was installed near the Havealetas' house and families that had hardly seen each other in a generation could now speak each week. Moana was no longer the end of the world.

But some of the villagers, especially the older people, were saddened by the changes. Children moved away and something died in the spirit of the place, or so they thought. Or perhaps it was just the noise they did not like.

The noise came from strangers.

Sitting cross-legged on a woven mat in the middle of the village, under a hastily constructed palm shelter, Tom Havealeta watched as Mori poured water though the cloth that contained the pounded *kava*. He cleared his throat and addressed the men gathered around.

'Almost six years ago the government decided to visit our little village. They told us they would build a road and connect Moana with Laumua and the rest of the island. This, for better or for worse, they have done. As we all know. Now is the time – long past the time – when we should ask the island to bless it.'

He clapped and received a coconut shell full of *kava*. He raised an eyebrow at Marau Unga who giggled. 'It is high tide, Tom,' the younger man said, gesturing to the beach, 'so we must have full cups all night.'

Tom laughed and raised the *kava* to his lips. 'To change,' he said, 'and to tradition.' He finished the bowl, clapped a further three times, then sat back and watched as the cup circled the villagers.

There was a call from beyond the mat and Funaki appeared.

'Mori,' she said. 'The phone rang. It's the doctor for you. Come.'

Change, thought Tom. There it is: the phone, that necklace around Funaki's neck, the very fact that Dr Vaite and Whinney moved away. Where would it end? Tom knew he could not answer that. It was only just beginning.

There was another shout and a new face with a bundle wrapped in newspaper, sat down at the back of the mat. He knelt down on the floor and addressed the village.

'I'd like to present this *kava* to introduce myself to Moana. My name is Fono Vata and today I moved here with my wife and my son and daughter. I'm sure you heard of the storm on the other side of the island. Our house was destroyed, our house is always being destroyed. I would like to ask your permission to rebuild here, live with you and be a part of the village. My family and I are greatly looking forward to our new life.'

'You are welcome,' Tom said to him and another round of drinking began. Tom saw Angel walk down to the mat with Ke and Tevita Unga. They handed a guitar to a Vete and the four of them began to play. The rest of the men sang. Tom relaxed back into the music. Maybe not everything would change. The men had always sung their songs together and always would.

There was another round and another. Tom felt the *kava* meandering through his body, slowing him down, making him smile. He called Fono Vata to come and sit next to him. The two of them drank together in silence. Tom, his back perfectly straight, his legs still crossed, found his head nodding forward into sleep. He felt the newcomer lean onto his shoulder and pushed him back against one of the shelter's poles. Fono grunted and opened his eyes.

'Okay,' he said, coming out of his daze. 'I have to sleep.'

'Go, sleep. We'll see you tomorrow.'

'Goodnight Tom. Goodnight boys,' Fono called as he weaved his way to the Doctor's old house.

Tom looked around him. He was one of the oldest men there. How had that happened? Before the road had been built, Tom and Dr Vaite competed each night to see who could stay on the mat the longest. And who could keep their eyes open. The Doctor had left. Tom had outlasted him and would win their competition every night from here on in. It made him sad to think like this and although the moon was still bright in the sky and the sun far from dawning, Tom felt no desire to carry on drinking. Feeling a hundred years old, he stood up, said goodnight and went to sleep.

THE VATAS

Earlier that day, in the house by the sea, Angel, Lisi, Tamatoa and Ama Matete had been sitting half in, half out of their kitchen, when a truck they did not recognise drove up. Out of the vehicle jumped four people: a man and woman who stood close to each other, their shadows touching, at all times glancing at one another and smiling into the other's eyes; following them their two children. The boy was eleven and full of energy. He had sat still for too long and wanted to run around the village, yelling. He needed to whoop to get out the noise that had built up inside him. Just unloading the truck was too stationary for him, so he shouted, cackled with laughter and ran around his family – until his father merrily grabbed his shoulders and ordered him back to work. After him came his sister, five years older and twenty years calmer. She stood motionless, smiling broadly, only her eyes moving as she took in her new surroundings: the sun, the sea and trees, the pigs rooting, the chickens fluttering about and the villagers walking past, stopping to talk to her parents or waving at her. Lisi caught the girl's eye and gave her a half smile.

'Pay attention, Lisi,' said her twin. 'You're burning the coconut.'

'I am not.'

'Do you want me to cook, Lisi?' Tamatoa asked. 'I just want to eat one thing this month that isn't black.'

'Tam, I'm the cook. You like my food.'

The twins were twelve, but only Tamatoa looked like a child. Lisi had become beautiful, had one day woken up a woman. She was ageless, like a mermaid who was both forever young and eternally old, a woman whose fresh face didn't quite match the knowing light in her eyes. She had black hair and fair skin. She had small hands with long fingers. She slopped out the pig food, fed the hens with grace and the eyes of the men and women of the village followed her as she went about her chores. But Lisi was unaware of this. To herself she was just a girl who saw looking after her brothers and sister as fun, and cooking as the best part.

'We can give that one to Ioane,' Tamatoa said.

'No,' said Lisi. 'I've made him something different. He needs the best food. Ama, take him this.'

Ama was only seven and, unlike her sister, was not the slightest bit striking. She was a child of shadows, happiest when standing behind Angel or Lisi. She was so quiet that most of the villagers could not remember her ever speaking and, if asked, they would be unable to say exactly what she looked like. No one remembered her coconut-bark hair and her sea smell. Ama mixed with the colours of the island. She worked on being invisible and, from the background, watched.

She took the food to her father, lolling, as always, in his chair in the main room on the other side of the house. She smiled apologetically at Ioane as she raised Lisi's mushy orange soup to his lips. One of her father's eyes stared back at her as if he had never seen her before, the other did not see her now. After a while he opened his mouth and swallowed. Ama put the spoon into his hand and encouraged him to feed himself. She wiped his mouth and put a towel over his legs, then went back into the kitchen to force down her own lunch.

Angel found it strange that people were moving into the Vaites' house. For him it would always be the Doctor's. After his mother died he had gone there every afternoon. He'd fall asleep with Ama crawling over him and wake up being fanned by Whinney who had made him food to take home for the twins. But now Lisi cooked, Ama looked after herself, the Doctor and Whinney were gone. But he could tell that the new family was right for the village, especially the girl, who appeared as comfortable as if she had already lived here a hundred years. He wanted her to serve at a *kava* party. It was time he met a girl like her.

'Why don't we ask them for something?' enquired Tamatoa as more and more possessions were unloaded from the van.

'We don't need anything else,' said Lisi defensively. 'We have everything.'

'We don't know what they have.'

'It doesn't matter,' Lisi said. 'We won't take anything, Tam. I like having space in our house. But we'll go and help them after this. Okay?'

'Okay,' said Tamatoa.

'And you two?' Lisi addressed Ama and Angel.

'Okay,' said Ama.

'I have to go to the plantation,' said Angel. 'And you have to go to school.' He got up and started to leave. 'Tamatoa, I want to make a table for in here. Marau Unga is coming round when he gets back from the sea. Will you help us?'

'Okay.'

Angel grinned. 'Bye.' He left the kitchen and shouted back, 'Go to school!'

Lisi swatted the comment away with her hand. 'We'll go afterwards,' she said.

The twins stood up at the same time and each held a hand out to Ama.

On the way to the Vaite house they shooed the pigs off the path and picked a breadfruit.

'Hello,' said the boy as they came closer. He had bright brown eyes that suggested trouble, but a button nose that told them it was innocent. The rest of the family were indoors. 'I'm Mano,' he said, examining Lisi, Ama and then Tamatoa. The girl came out of the house, tying her wavy brown hair behind her as she did so. 'This is my sister, Meleane.'

'We've come to help,' Lisi said. 'I'm—'

'Don't help,' interrupted Mano. 'It's too hot to work.

You,' he pointed to Tamatoa. 'Who are you? Will you show me the village?'

Tamatoa and Mano started talking. Mano then scampered off with Tamatoa limping after him. Lisi wasn't used to being the one left behind. 'Remember school, Tam,' she said.

Meleane saw her frown. 'We'd love your help. Come inside, please.'

Lisi, Ama and Meleane Vata went into the house.

'This is my mother, Vahine,' Meleane told them, 'and my father, Fono.'

'Hello,' Lisi said. 'I am Lisi Matete and this is Ama, my sister.'

'Good,' Fono grunted, pulling a four-poster double bed into the next room. The girls moved out of his way.

'Matete?' Vahine asked. 'I knew an Ioane Matete once, long ago. But he left the island.'

'He's our father,' Ama said.

'He came back? He married?'

'Of course,' Lisi replied. 'Because he loved Amalia.'

'Not me,' Ama added. 'Our mother.'

'She's dead now.'

'Oh, girls, I'm sorry,' Vahine said. 'But Ioane Matete, he's here then? In Moana?'

'Yes. He's at home.'

'Then I'll have to visit him. I never thought I would see that boy again.'

a gift from the sea

Every year, five of Laumua's most distinguished residents travelled around the island and visited each village. They were searching for the most beautiful. Moana had never before been considered – the judges could not get to it.

In preparation for the competition the beach was being cleared, sand tracks were being laid between the houses and sprinkled with coral, and the muddy spots where the pigs wallowed covered over. Little flags marked the entrance to the village by the new road and each house was encouraged to put up decorations. The village wanted to win and to mark its arrival as part of the island, and to this end the plantations were neglected and the fish left uncaught. The men raked and built and the women tidied and planned what food they would serve the judges. It was decided that every house would make a dish. Except the Matetes'. Lisi did not know this yet.

The benches that Angel and Tom Havealeta had made for the beach looked perfect and they tied a red ribbon around each to accentuate the dark colour of the wood. Once the sand was clear of seaweed and kindling, they hoped it would shine. Dark benches, light sand – they felt this would impress the judges. Angel spent hours of each day on the beach, clearing it of leaves and coconut bark, making sure the fishermen left their boats in the right place. But, every now and then, he would be distracted by the dark brooding colour of the sea and stare into it, watching the rise and fall of the waves against the shore. Time passed without him noticing and when he snapped out of his trance he was annoyed with himself. The competition was important. He remembered how proud Amalia had been of their village. He would work hard for her. It was time to show off Moana, to let the rest of the island see that here they lived the island way: relaxed but hardworking, in the most beautiful village of all.

With only fifteen more days until the competition, Angel woke up early. He had built his sleeping *fale* two years ago, the day he had turned eighteen and had his first tattoo carved into his shin. Moana. He traced his fingers over the letters now. He yawned. He had not slept the night before. A storm had rattled the planks of his hut. He had gone to sit outside, cold and wet, listening to the thunder and watching the lightning strike the sea. I pity anyone out there tonight, he'd thought.

By dawn it was calm again. Angel went down to the water's edge until he was ankle deep in the gentle waves.

The mango island was the only shape on the horizon. He gazed at the point where the sky met the ocean. The blue of both was so pure it was hard to see where one ended and the other began. It looked like the end of the world.

In the village a couple of coconut palms had been knocked over by the force of the wind. Angel thought about the different things he could do with the wood; hollow out a canoe that the girls could use for fishing, fix the side wall of their toilet *fale*. But perhaps it would be better to give it to the Havealetas. They needed a new pig board and had a hole in the floor of their kitchen.

The storm had washed all kinds of debris up onto the sand. Angel buried his feet, wriggled his toes and knew that the beach had to be cleaned again.

Angel started to examine some of the things that had come ashore: a big fishing net that was only slightly ripped, four jellyfish that he would let the tide deal with and a cage with two small drowned yellow birds inside. He took them up to the top of the beach and buried them deep in the sand. Ama loved birds. He didn't want her to find them. He'd give the cage to the new family as a gift. He imagined the girl he had seen yesterday morning, placing it, empty, door open, by the Doctor's window.

He ran into the sea, enjoying the stretch in his legs and feeling cleansed by the chill. He put his head under water and then let his body follow, diving to the ocean floor, eyes open. He saw a school of little silver fish and swam into them, their scaly bodies tickling his skin. He swam out to the coral. The crabs were large. He would catch some for breakfast. He walked up into the house and came back with a small net and a bucket. With these he stood in the shallows and soon had a few fish. He took one out, speared it with a stick, then left it in the wet sand, just at the water mark. He sat down above it, very still, and waited for the crabs to come.

Angel, as he always did when he had time on his hands, watched the sea. He thought about the storm again, how angry the island had been at night, how calm it was now. The village was bruised, but also replenished and hopeful, and standing there on the beach Angel felt the same. After each storm you could start again.

One crab scuttled up to the fish and nibbled on its white flesh. Angel decided he would wait for five and then put them in the bucket. The crabs were large, the size of both his hands held together and bright red – the best kind to eat. He'd boil them before Lisi woke. Maybe he'd make a fire and stay down here instead of going back to the house. The beach was calling him today. He didn't want to leave it.

Something was lying on the far side of the sand that he hadn't noticed before. He left the crab and walked towards the shape. He tried to work out what it was, perhaps another log. He wanted to have the beach cleared by the time the other villagers awoke.

Angel found himself looking into the face of a girl, a face unlike any he had ever seen; as white as coconut meat, with hair that was golden like banana peel. Her skin was uncooked – not of this world. She was lying with her cheek down on the beach and was covered in seaweed. The lower part of her back was exposed and the beginning of a big purple bruise was showing. Angel turned her around. She was fatter than island girls. He was sure she must be from the sea. He carefully removed the seaweed from her body. She was human; the trousers she was wearing clearly marked her two separate legs. He looked once more at her face and brushed the hair away from her eyes. They were shut. Angel wondered if she would ever open them and look at him. He wanted to know about this girl the sea had brought him. He pulled off a limpet stuck to her arm.

'What do you want me to do with her?' he asked the sea, and as though in answer, the next wave came up higher than the rest and pushed the body further up the beach. The girl's chest moved, barely, up and down. Angel realised she was alive.

The girl understood that she was no longer in the water. She could taste sand on her lips and feel its gritty texture between her teeth. She must be on a beach. Strong arms raised her head. They patted her back firmly, but gently. She vomited seawater. She was in the arms of a man. He smiled at her. She passed out.

When she woke up again, he was there still, his face reassuring. Words came out of his mouth, words she couldn't understand. His hand reached down and caught a tear. He held her to his bare chest and whispered as she cried still more. She felt she would never stop, that there was nothing she could do with her confusion, her fear, her grief, but cry. She passed out again.

Later she felt calm. She was now lying next to him on the beach, his arm her pillow, his kind eyes looking down at her. She reached up and touched his face. He smiled as she ran her fingers over his cheeks, up to his short dark hair and down to his chin. She felt his neck and paused on the bump there. She put her hands on his lips. He kissed her fingers as she traced them. Her hand dropped down to her side again.

She stared at him without embarrassment and his deep, dark eyes stared back at her. She started to cry once more. To forget the pain in her body, she focused on his face and memorised it, so that even after her death she would still see exactly how he was that day. She would see his skin, the colour of lightly toasted bread, the colour of wet sand, dark next to her own. And his forehead, a sturdy, heartening space that made her trust him, that made her feel safe. She would recall his hair: dark and controlled in its shortness, but hair that wanted to curl, to frizz, to gain a life of its own. And his nose, made wide by the nostrils being always slightly flared, the nose of a man who breathes deeply, who smells the island wind and the island ocean every day. She memorised his ears, which fitted perfectly to the side of his face, ears that had heard her mute cries for help, so that he had come to rescue her. And his shoulders, perfect for joining strong arms to a firm body, next to the hole created at the base of his neck, the space between his collar and shoulder bone, the space that told her his body was perfect. She committed to memory his chest, solid and toned. And as she looked at all these parts of his whole, she thought that she had been saved from the sea by an angel and she fell in love.

He lifted her up and carried her from the beach.

Angel took the girl into the room his sisters shared, woke them up with a shout and put her where they had been sleeping.

'Who is she?' asked Lisi.

'I found her on the beach.'

'Is she a mermaid?' Ama asked. 'Or is she dead?'

'She's alive. Ama, go and get Mori. Lisi, find some water and bring clothes that we can change her into. She's cold.'

When his sisters left, Angel sat down next to the girl. She tried to open her eyes but was too exhausted. Her hands grasped for him and Angel took them. She calmed down, smiled and fell asleep. Her hands were so small in his. She had a scar across the back of one and a few cuts on the other. He tried to think if he had ever held a hand like it, played over in his mind the girls who had let him walk them home from *kava* parties, whose skin he had stroked before they ran into their houses, but they had not felt like this. No other hand had needed to be held as this one did, had clutched at him in this way, had squeezed his fingers with all their strength. No other hand had ever wanted him as this hand wanted him.

Lisi came into the room with water and Angel quickly

stepped away from the mat. A few moments later, Mori Unga and his wife, Funaki, arrived.

'Let's leave them,' Angel said to his family.

Since the doctor had moved away, Mori had taken over caring for the sick. Now that it was easier to go to Laumua, it bothered him that most of the villagers still turned to him. He wished they'd make the trip to the hospital to get proper care, but the village had its traditions and somehow he had become one of them. Mori knew only the little that Dr Vaite had taught him and continued to teach him over the phone, but he was lucky in his wife. At moments like this, she would take over.

In the main room, Lisi sat against her father's legs. He was, as always, in the corner of the room, on his chair. His good eye was fixed on his daughter's head in front of him, but occasionally it flitted upwards towards his eldest son.

'Angel, tell us about the sea people again,' Ama asked.

'You know the story.'

'But tell us again. While we wait for the sea girl to get better.'

And so Angel began to tell the story, as he always did.

'When I was a little boy, our mother and I would sit under the house and look out to sea. She told me the story that her father, a fisherman, had told her when she was a little girl, sitting under the house with him, looking out to sea. One day I'll tell it to my daughter and she'll tell it to her son, but first I must tell it to you girls, whose father cannot speak any more,' he paused as he considered Ioane, 'and to you, Tamatoa, whose mother has died.

'Once men lived underwater. They breathed like fish. They ate seaweed. They were happy and they were free. Underwater, people did not have to work or do anything they did not want to. They were content just to swim and eat and play for they knew that if they ever put their heads above the surface they would die: men could not breathe above water. But one boy believed that people did not drown unless the sea wanted them to and so he trusted the ocean with his life. He raised his head above the waves, he breathed fresh air for the first time and he saw the island and how beautiful it was. He realised that the beliefs of the sea folk were not true. He was not suffocating, there was no death above the sea. He was entranced by the sand, by the coconut palms, by the mangoes and the bananas and by everything on the land, all its creations that he had never seen before. He watched creatures flying above him, he saw shapes in the clouds and when it grew dark marvelled as the sun went down and the moon came out. He stayed on the surface for five days until, exhausted, he swam back to the ocean floor to tell of his adventures. Everyone listened to his story but didn't know if they should believe it. Many claimed it couldn't be true, but first one person, then another, swam to the surface to see for themselves. After a while, some of them dared to go up onto the shore. Later they spent the night on land, then two nights, then a week, until some people moved there permanently.

Others joined them and then more followed, until there was only one girl who refused to leave. She wanted to make sure that there was always a home for the people to come back to. Our mother told me that she's still there, guarding the underwater world, welcoming back those who return.'

'And is this girl the one you found?' Ama asked.

'She could be,' Angel replied.

'When people die, do they go back into the sea? And meet the sea people?'

'I think they do.'

'So Amalia is in the sea, with her father.'

'Yes, Ama,' said Lisi. 'And I think she sometimes puts her head above the water and looks at us.'

'Maybe she sent the girl with a message for us?'

'Maybe.'

'Yes,' Angel said. 'It's—'

They were interrupted by Mori coming into the room.

'She'll be fine,' he said. 'She just needs to rest. Funaki will sit with her for a while. Lisi, make sure she gets plenty of water. We daren't move her so she'll have to stay here with you. Come and find me when she wakes up.'

'What has happened to her?' Angel asked.

'She'll have to tell us that. But she's been in the sea a long time.'

When the girl woke up, she started talking, she started pouring out words. Funaki listened and nodded, hoping that the girl would not know she did not understand her. But soon tears poured from her eyes again. Funaki tried to comfort her but it was no use. The girl cried and spoke and spoke and cried and it seemed that she would never stop, until eventually Funaki thought she recognised one word said over and over again. She left the room to find Angel.

'How is she?' he asked.

'Upset,' Funaki replied. 'I think she wants to see you.'

'Okay.' Angel got up and started to walk into the room.

'Don't,' Funaki said. 'You can't go in there. She's a girl, without family.'

'She needs me.'

'I'll have to stay with you.'

'No. Leave us. It'll be fine. She's ill. I won't touch her.'

'This is wrong.'

'No it isn't. I'll draw back the curtain.'

'But there'll be no one else in the house.'

'Ioane's here. Go, Funaki. Thank you.'

Funaki was tired and knew she could not help the girl any more. 'Okay,' she said finally.

Angel immediately broke his promise. When he entered the room, the girl's face lit up in a sad smile and she held out her hand to him, speaking words he didn't understand. Angel let the curtain fall closed behind him and walked towards her. He took her hand then and sat next to her on the mat. She spoke and he replied and both emptied themselves of words, knowing it didn't matter what was said. She pulled herself up to sitting and put her arms around his neck and he held her tightly to him, careful to avoid the bruise on her back. Soon she moved out of his arms so there was space between their faces. Hesitantly he put his right hand to her cheek. She leaned towards him and they kissed.

THE MANGO ISLAND

With only ten days to go until the Most Beautiful Village Competition, the whole of Moana was busy building and cleaning, raking paths and burying the animals' mess. There were fences to be fixed and gardens to plant. There was so much going on that no one in the village was excused.

'It's fun for my parents, I think,' Mano said to Tamatoa, 'they're good at this kind of thing. And I think Meleane likes it too, but—'

'It's good for all of us,' Tamatoa replied. 'Our village has to win.'

'But why does it matter? It's just a village.'

'You're not from here. It matters.'

'But don't you ever get fed up? Don't you ever just want to walk down to the beach without being given something to do?'

'I don't mind.'

'It's boring. Even school is better than cleaning all the time. Let's do something we want to do.'

'We could go up to the plantation,' Tamatoa suggested. 'We need more food for the house. Angel hasn't time to go any more.'

'No. I don't want to do anything helpful. I want to do something fun.'

'The plantation is fun.'

'No. It's work. What about over there?' They were sitting on the beach and Mano pointed at the mango island. 'Let's swim out there. Then we can do what we want.'

'I'm not a very good swimmer, I—'

A voice was calling them from the village.

'I'm going. Come if you want.'

Mano ran into the sea and started swimming. Tamatoa hesitated. It really was too hot to work and the tide was going out. He threw down his stick and swam after his friend. The boys pretended not to hear Meleane calling.

'Keep swimming, Toes.'

Mano's old village had been inland and he was not used to the ocean. His swimming was mad and uncontrolled, but it worked. Tamatoa thought that his friend could do anything. It wasn't fair. He'd spent a lifetime living by the sea but couldn't keep up.

'I'm too weak,' said Tamatoa to himself, cursing his thin, feeble legs, one foot with only one little toe.

'Come on,' encouraged Mano, swimming on his back to talk to his friend. 'The sea is so calm today we'll be there in a second.'

Mano did not understand the island tides and

Tamatoa was too tired to tell him that he was wrong, that even when there was not a ripple on the surface, the tide was as strong as on the roughest day. It was with them now and that was why they seemed to be moving so quickly. They swam on and on until they collapsed onto the sand of the mango island.

'See, we did it,' said Mano and they both fell asleep.

Tamatoa woke up a few hours later when the sun was at the top of the sky and its heat had doused him in sweat. Mano was not there.

'Mano,' he called out.

There was no answer. Tamatoa limped to the nearest tree and tore off a branch to lean on.

'Mano!'

He picked a mango, peeled it slowly and bit into the fresh fruit. 'I like it here,' he thought.

'Hey, Toes!' came Mano's voice from above. Mano landed at Tamatoa's feet. 'I saw snakes. Let's go back to the sand.'

'I came here with my mother before she died. A mango made her stop crying. And I think Angel was born here; no, not Angel, someone else, I don't remember who. That's all I know. Not many people come here. There isn't much reason to, except for fruit.'

'Perfect, we can come here all the time then. It'll be our escape route. I wonder if this is where the girl at your house is from.'

'No, she's from the sea.'

'Don't be silly, Toes. I thought you Matetes just pretended to believe that. She swam from somewhere.'

'I don't think so,' Tamatoa said to himself. Then, out loud, 'We should go back. The tide will change again soon. We have to go with it.'

'We will in a minute, but first let's explore. Give me some of that.' Mano grabbed the mango from Tamatoa's hand and ate around the stone. 'I want to find the best beach.'

'I can't swim against the tide.'

'We'll be quick.'

The boys walked around the island, up and down the shore and into the trees. They found a secluded cove with a cliff where they could jump into the water below. Time passed, the sun began to set and when the boys were finally ready to leave, the water was against them.

'I don't think we should swim.'

'We have to get back,' Mano said. 'My parents won't know where I am. Let's try at least.'

Tamatoa and Mano walked back to the beach and waded up to their knees. They could feel the pull of the tide.

'If we swim now, we won't make it back, Mano. I promise you that.'

'We can't wait any longer.'

'We have to wait until tomorrow.'

'But we have no shelter here and it's going to rain. And what about the snakes? Please, Toes, let's try and get back.'

'Don't worry about snakes, worry about the stonefish in the water. The rain won't drown you, but the ocean will.'

But Mano did not listen. He kept walking.

'Mano! Wait.'

'I'm going, Toes. My parents worry if I don't come home. It's not like your house. Please come with me.'

'I can't.'

Tamatoa watched as Mano went up to his neck, glancing behind him only once. Tamatoa begged him with his eyes to return. He sank to his knees. As he watched Mano becoming smaller and smaller, dragged out into the vastness of the ocean, Tamatoa yelled for him, knowing that he could not be heard, hating himself for letting him leave, hating Mano for not listening, for dying.

Tamatoa sat on the beach for hours in the darkness, wet from the rain, the sea and his tears, trying to stay awake but slipping in and out of exhausted sleep, still kneeling, still facing the cruel sea.

As morning came and the sun rose, he saw an old man rowing towards the shore.

'I'll take you back,' the old man said.

In the bottom of his boat, was Mano, wrapped in a big black cloak.

'Don't wake him.'

Tamatoa tried to thank the old man with a mango. He asked who he was, but when he received no answer, Tamatoa lay down next to Mano and closed his eyes.

Ioane Matete and Vahine Vata

Vahine Vata cautiously put her head around the Matete door and called out, 'Hello!' When no one replied she knocked on the wall and stepped over the pig board into the main room of the house.

'Ioane Matete,' she said quietly, aware that the white girl was sleeping. 'Lisi, Ama?'

There was no response. She lingered in the doorway a moment, letting her gaze fall around the room. So this was where Ioane Matete had ended up. She took in the view of the sea and the chair in the corner of the house. Something, someone, was sitting on it.

'Ioane,' she said and went over to the man. 'Is that you?'

He was sitting as he always sat, without noise, without movement, only the rise and fall of his chest betraying that he was alive.

'What happened to you, Ioane Matete?' Vahine whispered.

He turned his hazel stare at the sound of her voice and Vahine gasped as she saw that one of his eyes was dead and unseeing. A flicker of recognition crossed Ioane's face and for the briefest of moments he was again the boy who had sat on her wall and his ghost of a smile the smile that had once caused her to blush. But a second later his expression was blank as though Ioane Matete existed no more. Her heart tightened a little and then released. At least now she knew.

'It is good to see you again,' she said, moving the hair across his forehead as if he was a child. 'It's been a long time.'

Kara

'My name is Kara.'

'Kara.'

'I'm not going to tell you my surname.'

'*Kara* means sand.'

'Because I think my family is dead, and a surname connects me to them, so I don't need it anymore.'

'And you're the colour of sand. Not on this beach but on one a few coves over. It's lighter there.'

'Have you seen them? Have you found their bodies?'

'I'll take you one day. There is a waterfall near it.'

'I sometimes feel that I have drowned too. That this is heaven, you are an angel and I'll see them again any second.'

'I used to go with Ama when she was a baby. If I stayed in the village my neighbours would all offer to look after her, would tell me to go to the plantation. They were being kind.'

'But I know I'm not.'

'But I wanted to be here with her and the twins. It's important being together. And I don't like leaving them with Ioane. Be careful around him, Kara. His eye has changed recently.'

'I'm glad I'm here. It's good to be somewhere so far away from the world I know. It helps me forget all of the things that have happened.'

'I'll keep you safe.'

'It helps to forget my home, my friends – they'll think I've moved to the other side of the world and forgotten them.'

'The green in it is fading. He's either dying or coming back to life.'

'Here I don't have to think about my brother, Charlie. How he'll never grow up, how he'll never have a first kiss or a job, or children of his own.'

'I've never met anyone like you, but I know the sea and I know that's where you're from. I feel I know you, even though I don't understand a word you're saying.'

'Or my poor dead parents.'

'I imagine you living down in the coral, wrapped in the seaweed dress I found you in.'

'I suppose I'll make my life here. Alone.'

'Talking to crabs, tickling fish.'

'No, not alone, with you.'

'And then rising to the surface to visit me on the beach.'

'You are my family now.'

'To become my family.'

'I feel safe with you. I feel at home.'

'You've come home.'

nimian

'This road leads us right into Moana,' the driver said, leaning back into his seat.

'So we're nearly there?'

'Any moment now you'll see the sea.'

Nimian looked around her at the road, carved thinly amongst the trees. 'You'd never guess that people lived here. It feels like we're going further and further into nowhere.'

'When really, we're going to the only place that matters.'

'You're from here? I thought you were from Laumua.'

'And I was driving to the other side of the island, why?'

'Well, I don't know. To be nice?'

The driver laughed deeply. 'No one's that nice to strangers.'

'Some people are.' Suddenly a thought struck her. 'What's your name?'

'Vete.'

'Vete who?'

'Tatafu. But people call me Sun.'

'Sun?'

'Sun.'

'I'm Nimian.' She looked away from him, out the window.

'Nimian who?'

'Rairi.'

'No! You're from Laumua! You can't be. But I was wondering why a girl like you spoke our language.'

Nimian turned back to him with a frown. 'No, yes. Not really. My mother was born on this island. It's her name. I grew up overseas.'

'Your father is white?'

'Yes,' Nimian laughed. 'Where I'm from, that would be a rude question.'

'But it's not here.'

'That's good, I like that. I should have come here long ago.'

'Why didn't you?'

'My mother sort of got stuck where she was. My father left her over there before I was born and she didn't know how to come home, years passed and then there was no reason to. She thought all her family must have died and it was too late for me to become an islander.'

'So, Nimian, why are you coming to Moana now?'

'Well . . .'

They fell into silence as the truck rounded a corner

into the village. The trees were no more and now Nimian could see houses, animals, people, and beyond it all the sea, stretching out to the horizon.

'Welcome to Moana,' said Sun.

'Finally here!' She started to open the door.

'Nimian . . . Your clothes?'

'What about my clothes?'

'Take this.' Sun reached into the back of the truck and pulled out a *lavalava*. 'Put it over your skirt.'

Nimian blushed, she should have realised.

Sun leaned heavily on the horn. A crowd of men, all with his features, appeared from every corner of the village and started unloading.

'Thank you, Sun,' Nimian called and, with her legs covered, slipped away from the crowd, back out of the village, into the trees. She climbed one – she had long ago been taught to climb – and sat in its branches. She had to think.

From her tree, Nimian could see the village. She thought back over everything she knew about Moana. Stilts. The house she was looking for was on stilts. Two of them were. The one she wanted was next to the sea, right on the beach, its front overhanging the water. There.

She watched a group of children running. Then two boys moved below her, one leaning heavily on a fat stick. Still she remained where she was. Six men trooped past, carrying axes and spades. An hour or so later, two men walked by, hand in hand, chatting in low voices, laughing. Nimian peered through the trees. Was one of them him? Was that his voice she heard? She stared at the head of hair. No. And the voice was an island voice, not his. But the boy she was looking for would be a man now. Could it be him? No, not him. Another.

Nimian waited until they were far ahead, jumped down from her tree and set off on the road after them. She looked at their footsteps. Both were in bare feet. She thought about when she had known him. He had always worn shoes.

The men turned off the road onto a track between the trees and Nimian let them leave her behind.

She sat down and ripped a dead, dry, brown leaf into many pieces. She kicked a stone with her toe. Inside her worn red trainers her feet were hot. No wonder everyone was barefoot. She tried to forget the conversation she was about to have – what would she do if he wasn't here? – but she couldn't. She took a notebook out of the satchel on her back and started to doodle.

Hours later she heard footsteps on the road. She looked up and saw a man she recognised.

'Vete.'

'Do I know you?' the man asked.

'We met this morning, remember,' Nimian replied. 'You gave me a lift here.'

'Ahh, you must mean my brother. You are the beautiful girl he told us about.'

'It wasn't you? You look identical.'

'A family trait.'

'I'm Nimian.'

'I'm Vete.'

'Another one?'

'They call me Vete Beni.'

'Hi.'

'What are you doing sitting here alone on your first day in the village?'

'I'm looking for someone.'

'Who?'

'His name is Arun.'

'Then he isn't from Moana.'

'He was born here. I thought he might have come back.'

'Yes, there was an Arun, but that was years ago. There's no Arun now. You're looking in the wrong place.'

'I can't be. He has to be here . . .'

'Maybe he, whoever he is, is sitting outside your house right now, wondering where you are.'

'You don't know Arun.'

'No, which is why I know you won't find him here. This is a small village. Listen, why don't you come with me. Have some tea. You look upset.'

'Thank you, but I'll just stay here for a moment. It is a lot to take in.'

'Well, I'm in the big house if you want me.'

'Goodbye. Beni, sorry. You're really sure he's not here. Arun?'

'I swear on a year's worth of fish.'

'He could have a new name. He's got straight black hair and . . .'

'There are no Moanans with straight hair here. Look at our curls. You're definitely in the wrong place.'

'Hmm. I suppose I must be.'

'What will you do now?' he asked.

'Oh, I don't know. I'll probably see you later.'

Nimian watched as Vete Beni walked around the corner. As soon as he was out of sight she snapped a branch over her knee. 'Damn,' she said.

Nimian, feeling abandoned, feeling alone, felt too visible in Moana. He wasn't here. He wasn't anywhere. She shouldn't have come – but home had not felt like home without Arun. She missed the space he took up. His tree rapped her window at night. Some of his clothes were still in the drawers in the blue room that Nako had painted for him. She remembered the stormy night when Ioane Matete had knocked on their door with his sodden, freezing, long-haired little son dripping behind him. Nako had tucked them both into the same big bed. She remembered how cold Arun's little boy feet had felt against her girl ones.

She missed his feet. She missed being scratched by his toenails. She missed his arms around her and the way he breathed out through his nose onto her skin. For years she'd only had to reach out to touch him. Where was he?

She waved to Sun and his family as she walked past their house and went straight to the beach. Her arms and legs were stiff. She remembered how, when he'd lived with her, Arun had always swum in his clothes:

'It's the island way,' he'd tell her.

'We're not on an island now,' she'd reply.

'Yes we are! Everything is an island. The sea is all around.'

She walked into the sea fully dressed as he must have done, as her mother must have done all those years ago. There was a small piece of land offshore. She'd try to get all the way out there. She cast her mind back over Arun's stories. Had he ever mentioned this island? She didn't think so. Maybe from there, with a different view of the village, she would think of where he could be if not here. She felt her clothes grow heavy with water, lifted her legs off the floor and started swimming.

THE MOST BEAUTIFUL VILLAGE COMPETITION

The light made the dew on the grass sparkle, the spider webs on the huts look like silk curtains and it even turned the wallowing pigs into creatures of nobility. The sleeping villagers woke to smells of cooking wafting on the wind and women shouting orders. Here someone was scrubbing, there putting a final touch to the flowers on the tables, but underneath all the hustle and rush, a murmur of excitement could be heard. It was the day of the Most Beautiful Village Competition.

The judges arrived with a crowd of spectators about three hours later than expected. Some of the men were drunk by then and a pig had already been eaten. Tamatoa and Mano, whose eyes these days rarely left the sea, looked inland and spotted the group walking down the road. They raced around the houses with the news. Nearly the whole village went to greet them: Lisi wearing a beautiful white dress her father had brought back for her mother, red flowers in her hair and black shoes on her imperfect feet; Ama holding her hand, hiding behind her sister, gazing around in dreamy delight, excited by the colours of the flags being waved and the noise of cheering and singing; Mano and Tamatoa together, laughing, jumping, limping; Angel supporting Kara who moved slowly, leaning heavily on his arm, struggling to walk; Laita and Tom Havealeta with Fono and Vahine Vata, chatting together in a close circle of four; a horde of Zeno Tatafus talking with the Unga wives; Lave, Mori, Hosea Unga and their twelve adult sons mixed in with the Vetes; and a big group of children, playing together by the side of the road. Only two people were not there: Ioane Matete, still sitting in his chair and Meleane Vata.

Tom Havealeta acted as village spokesperson. He led the judges – five businessmen from Laumua – around the houses, offering them drink and food as they went. Tom turned the tour into a gentle amble around Moana and both the villagers and judges relaxed into the sound of his voice and the warmth of the sun. He was careful to show them the best of the village, to point out that the trees were bursting with fruit, that the sand was gleaming. He took them to see the animals. One judge picked a guava and gave it to a little Unga boy.

'Who is the white girl?' the first judge asked.

'She has come to live with us. She chose this island over all others.'

'I want to speak with her.'

'She, unfortunately, does not understand us yet.'

'Where is she from?'

'I'm not sure.'

'The sea,' Lisi said.

'Our mother sent her,' said Ama in a moment of courage.

The judge looked down at the two girls who had spoken. He had heard about Moana, so cut off from the rest of the world for so long that it had its own beliefs, its own connection to the wind and the waves and the land and the sand; that there were people here who thought that a human world existed below the sea. He had attributed this to boredom, to the madness that comes from being trapped in a small place, to poor teaching of the Christian message. And he had thought that by now, after three years of road, all this would have gone. But when he heard these girls speak he understood that the rumours in the town about strange village women, women both mad and alluring, were both incorrect and exactly right. He was captivated by Lisi, by her beauty, her belief and her innocence and found he believed her completely. The white girl was from the sea, so be it.

The group passed the Vata house, and Meleane slipped out of the back door and ran to the road. She was not sure why she was avoiding the crowd. Since she had heard about the competition she had looked forward to the dancing, to participating, and the judges looking on. Now it was happening she wanted to hide. They would not be back to the road for a few hours. She found a rock and sat down. Time passed.

A man came round the corner and walked towards her.

She looked up at him, shading her eyes from the sun.

'Is this Moana?' he asked.

'Yes.'

'I don't recognise it.'

'The road is new.'

'Are you new?'

'Yes. I just moved here.'

The man was standing in front of Meleane so that he blocked out the sun. Dark bags hung under his eyes and his skin looked tired. His long black hair was brown with dust and his clothes ripped. He had a scar that wound right around his neck.

'Can I sit next to you? I've been travelling a long time.'

'Yes, sit.' Meleane got up and the man brushed against her as he sat down.

He looked up at her. 'There's room for both of us.' He smiled and his face lit up. He was young. 'This is really Moana? I'm really here?'

'Yes. I could bring you some food?'

'Yes, please.'

Meleane hurried to the nearest house, the Havealetas'. She scurried into the deserted kitchen and loaded a plate with left-over bits and pieces from the feast. She filled a bottle with water from the rain tank.

When she returned, she gave him what she'd collected.

'I won't eat until you sit with me.'

Meleane opened her mouth to answer—

'—Please sit down,' he interrupted, 'because I'm starving.'

Again that smile. Meleane sat down, careful this time not to touch him.

'This is special food,' the man commented as he looked at the number of different dishes on his plate.

'Today is the Most Beautiful Village Competition.'

'Is Moana going to win?'

'I don't know. It is more beautiful than where I am from, but I've not seen most of the island.'

'You look to me like you've seen more than most.'

'Then you are not a very good judge of people. I've seen very little.'

'Perhaps it's better like that. I think I've seen too much.'

There was a pause.

'Do you like the food?' she asked.

'Yes. Did you make it?'

'No. Would you like some water?' Meleane offered him the bottle. He took it and, opening his throat wide, poured it down, not stopping until it was empty.

'Thank you.'

'You have a cut on your ear. Shall I look at it? I think it should be cleaned.' Meleane gently raised her hands up to the side of his head. He moved his arm and stopped her, held her hand in his and looked into her eyes.

'It'll heal. What's your name?'

'Meleane,' she said, taking her hand back.

'Meleane,' he repeated. 'Meleane, you look like the island, do you know that? Everything about you is from here.'

'Where else would it be from?'

'Other women are from different places and some

from nowhere at all. They simply exist. They are their
own bodies and nothing else. But I can see the roots
growing out of your bare brown feet. Look at the soles
– they're the same colour as the earth.'

'Is that a bad thing?'

'No, Meleane, right now it is a beautiful thing. It tells
me I'm back.'

'Back? I don't know where you are from, lots of places
maybe but not here.'

'How do you know?'

'Well, your hair is too straight – no one lives by this
sea and has hair that straight or that black. And your
eyes are not island eyes. I can see green in them. No
islander has green eyes.'

'My eyes are brown. The green is a reflection of all
the things I've seen. I'm a traveller and you are not.'

'You must have stories from all over the world.'

'They all begin here.'

'Did you know someone from the island?'

'Yes. He brought me up with tales of mermaids.'

'Is that why you're here? To find him?'

'Yes.'

'Who is he? Shall I take you to him?' Meleane began
to stand up.

'No,' he gently pulled her down, 'I can wait a little
longer. And I'll find him myself. But first I want to talk
to you more. Tell me a story about the island.'

'There are no mermaids in my stories,' Meleane told
him. 'I'm from inland.'

* * *

Later on that day the judges went to the Unga house-hold and sat down on the floor so that Tom could introduce them to everyone, one person at a time. When Meleane's name was called, she was there.

And the stranger was on the beach, gazing at the house with the stilts, the one that seemed to sniff the sea. He paused at the side door, stepped over the pig board and entered.

Ioane Matete slowly raised his head and groaned, 'Arun.'

'What happened to you?'

The words came slowly. 'You're . . . back.'

'Sorry it took so long.'

Ioane fixed his once powerful stare on his son, breathing deeply. 'I couldn't,' his chest rose and fell, 'come and get you.'

'Have you been like this all these years?'

'In this chair, yes.'

'What happened to you? What happened to your eye?'

'You . . . lose things . . . as you get . . . older.'

Arun could hardly understand his father. He came closer and crouched down.

He said, 'You could have phoned Nako. We thought you were dead.'

'I was, Arun.' Ioane's head fell to the side. He took his time to right it again. 'I am.'

'Get up.'

Ioane breathed heavily. 'I can't, Arun.'

'You can. Get up.'

'I can't. Look at me.'

'Get up.'

Ioane struggled and fell back. He tried again, using all his strength. When he was up, his son turned and took his weight.

'Let's go,' Arun said.

He dragged Ioane Matete down to the beach, pulled his grandfather's boat off the sand and lifted him in.

'Put your hand in the water.'

Ioane flopped his hand overboard and felt the sea for the first time in many years.

'Here.' Arun picked up an oar and brought it down with a smack on the surface. A wave of salt water hit Ioane in the face. He spluttered and coughed like an old man. Then he laughed a new laugh that was strange to Arun's ears.

'It's . . . on my skin, Arun – there's sea . . . on my skin.'

'Of course there is. What have you been doing sitting up in that house?'

'You're talking,' Ioane paused, trying to catch a string of saliva from escaping his mouth, 'like a man now, Arun.'

'Eight years have passed, Ioane. I'm eighteen.'

'No.'

'Yes. Tell me about the house. How is Amalia?'

'Dead.'

'Oh,' Arun paused, 'and Angel?'

'Alive.'

'Good. And you said there were twins. How are they?'

Ioane's voice was raw and his words increasingly unclear. 'Lisi is beautiful . . . The boy . . . useless.'

'Useless? I see you're as affectionate as ever. When did my mother, when did Amalia, die?'

'There was a baby,' Ioane rasped. 'I don't remember.'

'I have another brother?'

'A . . . girl.'

'What's her name?'

'Ama.' A cough. A pause for breath. 'Her hair smells like Amalia's did.'

'Did she ever see you like this?'

'Amalia? Yes.'

'It's a strange sight, Ioane.'

'Where have you been . . . Arun?'

'You keep saying my name.'

'You're here.'

'Your voice sounds awful.' Arun could hear his father's every breath. 'Maybe we should get you back. You must be missing your chair.'

Just as the judges were leaving Moana and the villagers were exchanging satisfied glances amongst themselves, three stray dogs pounced on a group of the village chickens. They ripped the birds to pieces and decorated the paths with feathers, the grass with blood and the beach with entrails. But the dogs did not eat the birds. Smelling meat, the Matete pigs came running. They shunted the dogs out of the way and began to eat them themselves. The villagers of Moana looked on aghast. So did the judges.

a reunion

'Brother,' said Arun as Angel entered the room.

'Arun!'

They ran to one another and hugged. Angel looked into his brother's dark eyes. He saw the five-year-old Arun staring out of the adult's face.

'It really is you!'

'It is. I was worried you wouldn't be here.'

'Where else would I be?' Angel thought for a moment and then asked, 'How was the sea?'

'Blue, brother, as blue as it could be.'

They both laughed.

'These are the twins.' Angel ushered them forward.

'Lisi and Tamatoa?' Arun asked.

They nodded.

'I'm Arun. I'm your brother.'

'Hello,' they said, confused. His name was familiar, but how could this man with his strange accent and straight hair, be their brother?

'You were born with the mangoes,' Tamatoa remembered.

'Was I?' Arun asked Angel.

'Yes.'

'You'll have to take me there, Tamatoa. I'd like to see where I was born.'

'Can you swim? You have to swim to get there.'

'I can sail.'

'This is Ama,' Angel said.

'Hello.'

Ama took hold of Angel's hand and hid behind him. 'You can't be scared of me, little girl,' Arun said. 'We're family. I've come a long way to meet you.' He turned to Angel. 'Amalia died.'

'Yes. How did you find out?'

Arun pointed to their father who was sitting as he always did in his chair. 'Ioane told me.'

'He spoke to you?'

'Yes.'

'Just now?'

'Yes.'

'I haven't heard him speak in years. We thought he couldn't.' Angel faced his father and said, 'So, Ioane, you've been pretending.'

Ioane Matete raised his head and his eye met Angel's eyes. Arun spoke for him. 'I took him out to sea. I wore him out. Brother, you should have taken care of him.'

'He never told us where you were, Arun. We asked every day and he never breathed a word. And now you tell me he can speak!'

There was a movement at the door and Kara appeared. Her skin was almost green. She coughed.

'Who are you?' Arun asked.

'Her name is Kara,' Angel said. 'We found her on the beach a few days ago.'

'She's from the sea,' Ama added.

Arun bent down in front of his youngest sister.

'Is she, Ama?' he asked.

'Yes,' she said quietly.

'How do you know?'

'She was on the beach. And she speaks differently. And she hasn't seen sun so she must have been under-water,' said Ama.

'Well you know what, Ama? I can speak to mermaids. Maybe I'll talk to her. Would you like that?'

'Maybe she has a message from Amalia.'

'Maybe.' Arun turned to Kara and asked her a question.

'You speak English,' she said.

'Yes. Why are you here?'

'I thought I'd drowned, then I found myself on a beach and your brother was taking care of me.'

'Are you alone?'

'I must be. My family is dead. If they weren't they'd have come to find me.' She turned away for a moment.

'I'm sorry. Are you okay?'

'Sometimes I am. Sometimes I'm not. Do you know your ear has blood all over it?'

'Yes.'

'Shall I take a look at it for you? I could clean it.'

'Okay, if you want to.'

'What did she say?' Ama asked as Kara left the room.

'You're right,' Arun replied. 'She's from the sea. She has a message from Amalia but she's not going to give it to you just yet. It's not the right time.'

'Where has she gone?' Angel asked.

'She's going to clean up my ear.'

'What happened to it?' asked Lisi.

'Arun, I can't believe you're back,' said Angel.

'Believe it, brother.'

The family sat in the front room in a circle on the floor, Arun with his back to the side door, facing his father's chair, Angel next to him looking out the big front windows to the sea, Lisi leaning against Ioane's legs. Tamatoa was next to her with Ama beside him, edging closer and closer to her new brother.

Kara decided to leave them to talk.

'Will you still be here tomorrow?' she asked Arun.

'Yes. I'm home now. This is my family.'

'You're their brother?'

'That's right.'

'Can I speak to you tomorrow? There are some things I'd like to know, and some things I'd like you to ask him.' She nodded at Angel. 'Is that okay?'

'It's fine.'

'Goodnight Arun.' She turned to the others. 'Goodnight.' Angel caught her eye and smiled.

'Arun.' Ioane spoke and his children jumped. 'Arun,' the voice repeated. 'Take me to the other room.'

This was not a voice that Angel recognised. Nor the

twins. Nor Ama who was hearing her father speak for the first time. The change shocked them all and they were silent. Arun got up and, putting his father's arm over his shoulder, helped him to move.

When Arun returned, Angel said, 'He has never spoken to us.'

'Did you speak to him?'

'He has never walked.'

'Did you lend him your shoulder?'

Angel said nothing.

'Shall we go up to the plantation, brother?' asked Arun.

'Not tonight. I need to sleep.'

'You want to dream of the white girl, you mean.'

Angel laughed. 'Yes, that's what I mean. You can share my *fale*.'

'No, I need to be outside.'

'Be here in the morning?' It was a question.

'Yes.'

'I'm glad you're back.'

'Me too.'

Arun walked through the village, not yet ready to accept the night. He looked into every house he passed, trying to recognise the faces he saw there. Nothing was familiar. 'I'm home,' he said to himself, suppressing the image of a white cottage on a cold green hill and the face of the girl who lived there. He thought he might go up to the plantation, but did not want to be alone. The sky was clear, the moon was out. He turned his head up to let its light cast shadows on his face. It was the same moon he'd looked at an ocean away.

In the nearest house he noticed Meleane, brushing her brown hair, looking up at the stars. She glanced down and Arun didn't know if he was pleased she'd seen him or not. She opened the window.

'Are you okay?'

'I'm going for a walk,' Arun replied.

'Shall I come with you?'

'I don't know. Do you want to?'

She hesitated. 'Yes.'

'I think I should go alone. It's late.'

She started to close the glass.

'No, come,' he said. 'I'm sorry.'

'No, you're right. It's late.'

'Open the window again.'

She did as he asked. 'What do you want?' she said.

'I'm going to kiss you before I walk away.'

Meleane did not reply but Arun imagined that in the darkness he saw a rush of red reach her cheeks. He climbed up the side of the house, until he was level with the girl. He wanted to reach out and touch her hair, to feel its softness, to know he was home. He wanted to kiss her gently, to just touch her lips, but as soon as she was close to him, he saw the need for romance in her eyes and it made him angry. He thrust his tongue into her mouth. He bit her lip until she bled. She pushed him away from her, then reaching forward she moved a strand of his dark hair away from his face. Arun tried to read her eyes but failed. She reached out her arm

and stroked his cheek. Confused, he dropped back to
the ground.

'You are the first man to kiss me,' she said.

'Goodnight Meleane.'

'Goodnight.'

Arun Matete walked up to the coconut plantation.
He sat down amongst the trees and for the first time in
thirteen years, cried.

The next day the news came through that Moana
had won the Most Beautiful Village Competition. The
villagers did not know what to think.

THE BEGINNING OF IOANE MATETE

Ioane Matete was tired. It was the middle of the night and he was lying on his mat. Arun was back. His son was back. Had it really been eight years? He slowly shook his head from side to side. He had been sitting in his chair for too long. It was time to make himself better. He'd do it at night, get his strength back while everyone slept. He started with his toes, tried to feel them and make them move on his command. How had so much time passed? It seemed to Ioane that it was only yesterday he was lying here next to his wife. Amalia was dead. Amalia, Amalia. When he could walk again, he would visit her grave.

His big toe moved backwards and forwards and Ioane smiled. He moved on to the next one. So his eldest son thought he had been able to speak all this time. He hadn't been able to speak. He hadn't been able to do anything other than think about the past.

* * *

They had decided to take the truck back to Laumua. Ioane Matete drove, with Arun Nepali, his loyal friend Arun, sitting beside him. Ioane had started giving him lessons. Everyone should know how to drive. He showed him the gears, explained about the clutch, demonstrated how the lights worked. When they arrived at a long deserted stretch of road by the beach, it was Arun Nepali's turn.

He was a fast learner and Ioane a patient teacher. Arun was a natural driver, cautious, careful and responsible. He drove up and down, making only minor errors, laughing and joking. They had fun.

It grew dark. Ioane Matete swapped places with his friend. He smiled at Arun. Ioane remembered his friend smiling back. He set off as fast as he could. The old truck strained under the speed, its frame rattled, its engine roared. It had spent years at the bottom of the sea and was not used to racing. The boys whooped as the wind rushed through the air. 'This is why you learn to drive!' Ioane Matete yelled.

A dog. Faulty brakes. A split-second decision. They swerved off the road onto the beach and felt the truck jump as if they had driven over a log.

Ioane Matete kept working on his toes. By the end of the week he could move them all. By the end of the following week he could turn his ankles. And each day, as the sun rose, Ioane Matete fell asleep.

NIMIAN'S BOAT

Arun put his hand into the pocket of his jeans and pulled out a photo, folded and creased from many viewings.

The photo was of Nimian's back. She was sitting, facing away from the camera, the girl he had first known. He remembered when she'd given it to him. It was when she was afraid that Ioane Matete would take him away.

'I hate having my picture taken,' she'd said. 'But I had one taken for you.'

'It doesn't show your face.'

'I know.'

'So, how do I know it's you?' he had asked.

Nimian took the photo from him and examined it. She scrunched up her nose in concentration. Finally satisfied, she turned around and separated her top from her trousers. 'Look. I have this big birthmark here, just above my hip. Check in the photo. Is it my back?'

Arun looked at it. 'It's you. Your birthmark looks like a boat.'

'Now you won't forget me, ever.'

When she realised that Arun was not going away with his father, Nimian tried to take the photo back. Arun hid it and was glad he had, for soon afterwards Nako found the two of them naked in bed together, playing. He was moved to a room of his own and Nimian never gave him another photo; not even when he told her he was going to look for Ioane Matete.

THE MERMAID

Angel walked back to the village that evening, stiff from his day on the plantation. He rolled his shoulders and shook his head. He needed to be with Kara, to ask her about Amalia and about the sea. He wanted to tell her his plans, how he was going to build her a house on the hill, how they'd get married and have children the colour of beach coral. He wondered if she would be awake when he returned to the house. He had carved, on a coconut shell, their two faces, and he imagined how she'd smile when she saw it.

Water was trickling from the Havealetas' gutter as Angel entered the village. He let it fall onto his head, scooped it under his arms and onto his face. Clean. He was ready to see her now.

She wasn't in the house.

'She went to find you, I think,' Lisi told him.

Angel ran outside and looked for her. She was not on the beach. He hadn't seen her in the village. Was she back in the sea? He stopped. The door to his *fale* was open. Was she waiting for him there?

Angel looked down at the girl lying on his mat. Her eyes were closed. There had never been a woman in his *fale* before.

'Kara, are you awake?' he asked her.

There was no reply.

He sat next to her and looked down at her white face. She was paler now than she had ever been. He put his hand to her forehead. It was cold. He touched her neck and her wrist and all he felt was her soft skin, icy like the sea in the dead of night.

'Kara,' he whispered.

He lay beside her and took her body in his arms. He knew then that the people from the sea could not visit the land, that it dried them out, that the water left them. And when it was gone, they died. They died of thirst. Or perhaps of longing, he thought.

At dawn, just as the sun was rising, Angel carried Kara to the shore. The sun was sitting low on the water and Angel turned the dead girl to face the light.

'Did you come to the surface to see the sun?' he asked.

He left her on the sand and pulled his grandfather's boat down the beach. Once it was floating in the shallows he took the girl in his arms and placed her gently in the bottom. She was heavy.

As he pulled at the oars, he told her about the sea stories his mother had told him and he had told his sisters. 'She sent you, didn't she?'

Angel shook his head. The sea couldn't have meant him to love this girl. It wanted her back. But Angel also knew that the ocean never made mistakes. 'You only drown if the sea wants you to,' he thought, and Kara had survived long enough to kiss him. He did not understand.

'You'll be home soon,' he said.

Angel moved quickly through the water. On the other side of the mango island he saw a boat and an old man, dressed in a black coat.

'Angel Hoko,' the man called out.

Angel stopped rowing and let the boat catch up with him.

'Do you remember me?'

Angel shook his head.

The old man said, 'I will take Kara into the sea.'

Angel looked into the man's wrinkled face and felt a weight lift from his chest. He wouldn't have to watch her sink. 'Thank you.' He lifted Kara up. 'Why could she not have stayed longer?'

The old man took Kara in his arms but did not reply.

'She was here for a moment and now she is dead. Why? Surely she could have stayed with me, just a few days more.'

Again the man said nothing.

'Now everything has changed.'

The man spoke softly. 'You should not grieve, Angel. Yes, everything changes. Look at the water, look at how it is never still. In each moment it changes, is that not so?'

'Yes, but that is water and I am a man.'

'The water changes, but every day when you go down to the sea, you recognise it, you still know it is your friend. It changes but it does not change. And so do you. You are like the sea, Angel Hoko.'

A wave splashed against Angel's boat, rocking it.

'Go home. Let her go,' said the old man, drifting away.

'How's Amalia?' Angel called out, but there was no reply. He was alone on the ocean.

Angel rowed slowly back. The tide was against him. After an hour he was only level with the mango island. He decided to stop and eat some fruit. Then, perhaps, he might be ready to return to Moana.

He picked a mango and held it in the crook of his arm as he had once held Ama as a baby. He looked up at the sky and wished it wasn't so clear. He felt his throat tightening. He wanted to cry but could not.

'The island is beautiful, isn't it?'

At the sound, Angel's heart leapt. There was something familiar about that voice. He knew it couldn't be Kara's and yet . . . Had she come back to him? Was such a thing possible?

'Kara?' he said. 'Where are you?'

'I never expected this,' the voice said, 'that I'd like it here. That I might want to stay.'

'You mean here, on land, with us?' As he spoke, in his excitement, Angel addressed the trees and the sand and the water as if giving thanks to all the things that had ever looked after his family, as if giving thanks to his mother who lived in the sea.

'I mean here in Moana.'

'With me?'

'With the village and, if you're from the village, then with you as well, I suppose.'

He heard the girl laugh. It was a laugh like seawater breaking over stones half-buried in the shallows. 'Kara? Have you come back? Have you really?' Angel put his arm up to his forehead and looked into the sun. He could see a girl leaning against a tree. Was it Kara? Could it be her? He took a step forward. No, not Kara, he thought, not Kara. It isn't her. He slumped down onto the sand. This girl is not as white as Kara, and besides she speaks our language. But who then? Who had Amalia sent in her place? 'What is your name?'

'I'm Nimian,' the girl said in that voice that sounded at once so familiar to him and yet so distant. It was a voice of the island and not of the island, a voice of somewhere and of nowhere.

'Nimian.' He played with the name on his tongue. 'Nim-i-an', he repeated. 'Did Amalia send you?'

Nimian looked at Angel, and frowned. 'No.' She reached out a hand and touched his arm. 'Come out of the sun. It's nice in the trees. But watch out for snakes.'

Angel shook his head, 'I want to go back. Will you come with me?'

'I'm not sure,' Nimian replied. She wiped her eyes with her forearm.

'Why are you crying?' Angel asked.

'I'm lonely.'

Angel leaned forward and kissed her gently on the lips, 'Please come with me, Kara.'

Nimian put her hand on his bare chest. 'Nimian not Kara. But yes, I'll come with you.'

Nimian let the man settle her into his boat. Her head was as confused as a whirlpool. She had just let herself be kissed by someone whose name she didn't even know. She smiled. Perhaps being kissed by strange men was what happened on her mother's island. She wished someone had told her more about this place. If not her mother, then Ioane, not that he talked much. All she had were Arun's vague memories from childhood and stories of mermaids. She had come here to find Arun, but instead had been picked up by a man with a swarm of identical brothers, had been told that no one resembling Arun had been in the village for years and years, and had spent time on this tiny islet eating mangoes. Now, when she was wondering what to do, she found herself in a boat being paddled back to the village by a man who called her Kara. Well, Arun was not here but she'd promised herself, and the promise was unbreakable, that she would not return home without him. Without him, she had no home worth going back to. And if he wasn't on the island, well she didn't want to be, wasn't going to be, alone any longer. Perhaps this man was as close to Arun as she'd ever get. Perhaps she should make do with him and be happy.

Angel smiled at her and she smiled back, not sure whether to encourage him or to turn him away. But when they arrived on the shore and he took her hand

and led her to his *fale* she did not fight him. Nor did she resist when he kissed her again.

She pushed the man gently and he made a show of falling in a heap on the ground. Laughing, she lowered herself onto him.

AT THE *FALE*

One side of Arun's head was throbbing as he walked into his house that evening. It was too much to take in – being back in Moana, his father, Angel, the twins, Ama and the girl Meleane. He thought he had left his headaches in a cottage far away, he thought the sea had cured him of what Ioane Matete said was the disease of staying still. But now, his head hurt. He massaged it with two fingers, enjoying the pain that came from pressing down hard. He had spent the afternoon walking up and down the beach, the road, the clifftop. He was dripping with sweat but didn't feel tired. Had Moana always been this small?

At the kitchen door his sisters looked at him. Lisi opened her mouth then closed it again.

'You can say it,' said Arun.

'You stink!' said Lisi. Ama giggled. 'What have you been doing?'

'Walking.'

'Running?' Lisi asked.

'Walking fast.'

'I'm just cooking. Are you hungry?'

Arun looked into the pot. 'No. Where's Angel?'

'I think he's in his *fale*.'

'I'm going to take him to Laumua, dancing.'

'We can dance here,' Ama said. 'Laita knows all the island moves. You don't have to leave again, Arun.'

Arun smiled at his sister. 'I'll come back. That's not the kind of dancing I'm talking about. I want to go to a club, throw myself around in the dark, drink whisky. There has to be one in Laumua.'

'Can I come?' Lisi asked.

'And me?' Ama added.

'You're too young,' her sister told her. 'Just me.'

'Neither of you,' Arun said. It's not the sort of place a man goes with his sisters.'

'You've been away so long it's hard sometimes to remember you're my brother,' said Lisi. 'I'm sure I could forget just for one more night.'

Arun laughed without mirth. 'No, Lisi. You girls stay here, do girl things.'

Lisi picked up an egg and smashed it into a bowl.

Arun walked to Angel's *fale*. Yes, dancing was the answer. He loved the dark of a dance floor.

'Angel,' he called as he pushed at the door. He saw the naked back of a girl, and his brother's legs. 'Oh, I'm sorry,' he said.

Back outside he stumbled down to the water's edge. Oh, how his head hurt. He thought of Kara and his brother and laughed. So, such things go on even in Moana. He was pleased for Angel, though he didn't know anything about the girl, apart from their one conversation. But she was pretty in a way. And she'd seemed to like Angel.

He walked along, his feet splashing in the water, thinking of this and that, but what kept coming back to him was the picture in his mind of what he'd seen. He took the photograph out of his pocket. That back? Nimian? Not possible, surely. He massaged his head again and dipped it into the water. Perhaps his headache was making him crazy. How could Nimian be here? He must be wrong. That must have been Kara. So he told himself, but still the thought persisted. Nimian! Even in shadow, even in the darkest room, he would recognise it, that birthmark, that boat floating above her hip, he would know that shape anywhere. Why was that back with Angel? Why? He ran to the *fale* and slammed the door on its hinges.

'Nimian!'

The couple jumped, gathered themselves, stared at the doorway.

Nimian seeing him, stood up, naked and distraught. 'Arun! Is it you?' she ran to him, but he put out a hand.

'What are you doing?' he asked her, his head hurting more than ever. He was oblivious to her nakedness, he only wanted to hear something that would allow him to forget all that he had seen.

'Arun,' Angel said gently, his face blushing. 'What is it? What is the matter?' He draped his *sulu* around Nimian.

'What are you doing?' Arun asked again.

'Arun! You remember Kara? This is Nimian who has been sent by our mother to take her place.'

'I couldn't find you,' Nimian said quietly.

'That's my brother,' Arun replied.

'I came here for you.'

'Arun,' Angel said, 'what is happening?'

'This isn't Kara, brother.'

'I know—'

'No, you don't. Where's Kara?'

'I put her in the sea and she came back to me.'

'This is not the same girl, brother. This girl isn't for you.'

'Why not? I love her.'

Arun looked at his brother, at his eyes filled with confusion and realised then, for the first time, that there was only one person he loved more than Nimian. 'Then she's yours.' He turned to leave the *fale*.

'No, Arun,' Nimian said. 'Where are you going? I've been looking for you. I came here to find you.' She grabbed at his arm, trying to stop him.

'Stay with him, Nimian. You've been in his *fale*. That's it.'

'What do you mean, Arun? That's what? Arun wait.'

But Arun left the *fale* and put his head in his hands. He walked up through the village and saw an old truck sitting near the road. He climbed into the front seat and looked down. The keys were in the ignition. 'Only on an island like this,' he thought. He turned on the engine and drove down the long road to Laumua.

* * *

Nimian pulled her clothes on.

'How is it that you know Arun?'

'I have to go.'

'Will you come back?'

She did not reply but ran to the door. Arun was nowhere to be seen.

Angel put his head outside. 'Are you okay?'

'Yes. I . . . I can't come back.' Nimian sat down on the ground outside the *fale* with her back resting against the wall. She knew that Angel was watching her and tried to hide the waves of regret crashing inside her. She had finally found Arun and . . . what must he think of her. She'd been searching for him for so long, thinking only of finding him and bringing him home. Why had she given up so easily? Why had she followed this other man home? Suddenly she realised who the man was and groaned. 'Oh! Arun called you brother. You're Angel Matete.'

'I'm Angel, yes.'

'Arun used to talk about you all the time.'

'How do you know Arun?'

'Your father brought him to us when he was a boy. We grew up together.'

'Ah, so he was like your brother.'

'Yes, no, I don't know,' she replied – but the other words she might have used, the words of love and longing, did not come out. Seeing the need in Angel's face, his hope and his desire, she choked them back. 'He's gone and won't return.'

'He will. My brother is home now. You can wait for him.'

'Where?'

'Anywhere. Here.'

'With you?'

'If you like. I am the brother of your brother. My mother looks over us both.'

'Does she?'

'Yes.'

'Nothing else will happen between us, Angel Matete. You do understand that?'

'I understand that my mother has sent you.'

'I came to find your brother. I didn't know who you were. I'm sorry.'

'I understand that you belong here.'

'Do I? I don't know where I belong anymore.'

'Here.'

Then, not quite knowing why or whether she should, she came to him and discovered that it was there, in the small space of his *fale*, in the nest that he made for her with his arms, that she felt safe. 'The brother of my brother, I like that,' she whispered and fell asleep.

early morning on the beach

At dawn Angel went to the sea. It was a still day. He walked to the far side of the beach and sat on the wet shore. The water lapped at his ankles. The old boatman had told him to let her go, but now Angel wished he had not. If he had taken her out to sea himself as he had planned, he would have known where she was. He could have rowed out there now and spoken to her. He had so many questions.

He wrote the name 'Kara' in the sand. How easy he had thought it would be. The sea had given her to him, placed her in his arms. They would have married and had children. But now she was gone, and Nimian was with him in her place. It was strange. It was hard to understand.

Angel Matete looked out to sea. He remembered how easy it used to be to turn off the voices in his head. But today was different.

He stood up, brushed the sand off his legs and walked

a little way along the beach. On his return he saw a shape in the water. He knew who she was. He ran as fast as he could into the sea.

'Kara,' he said as he grasped her in his arms and dragged her to the shore. 'You're back!'

He looked down at the dead girl. Her long light hair was straggly and matted. Her skin was paler than ever. Her eyes were glazed and unfocused. There was a crab attached to her body, nibbling at her. Angel threw it angrily away and held her to him. He kissed her forehead.

'Kara,' he said again, scarcely able to believe she was there. 'You're back. Thank you.' He kissed her again. He brushed some hair from her face. A little came off in his hands. 'I'm sorry I gave you to the boatman. I'll take you this time. I'll put you in the sea myself.'

He picked her up in his arms and carried her to his grandfather's boat. Angel Matete, with great ceremony, put Kara back in the ocean, just beyond the mango island.

Furniture

Arun Matete was gone for two weeks and his family began to think he had left them for good.

'He wouldn't do that,' Lisi said. 'He'll come back. He promised.'

And he did, with a truck and a trailer full of furniture.

'Where have you been?'

'Shopping,' he told them and started unloading.

The first thing out was a big double bed. 'For Ioane's room,' he instructed Angel, not looking in his brother's eye. 'He's too old for the floor. And there is a small one for you girls. And some sofas for the main room of the house.' Arun had also brought a table for the kitchen and linoleum for all the floors. 'I've been getting splinters in my feet,' he told his family. 'I'm not used to wood anymore.'

The family carried everything into the house and placed it where Arun said it should go. They put a radio in the main room and a motor in Amalia's father's boat. They hung up curtains and assembled shelves.

Angel stopped himself from asking why they needed all these new things. His brother was back, that was all that mattered. He watched Arun lower their father onto his bed.

'I thought you'd left,' Ioane Matete said to his son when they were alone.

'When I leave you're coming with me.'

'Good. Soon I'll be ready.'

'Don't take too long. Things have changed everywhere except in Moana. When I arrived, the house was as it was when I was five. We all need to move on. Nothing should stay the same.'

'This is a good bed,' Ioane said.

'Far too good to be slept in by one lonely old man.'

'When you marry it's yours. Until then you're on the floor, my son.'

'Goodnight Ioane.'

'Goodnight Arun.'

That night Lisi and Ama slept on a bed for the first time in their lives and Tamatoa on a sofa. All three were kept awake by the softness and wished they still had their reed matting. Ioane Matete lay back, shut his eyes and went straight to sleep.

SPIDERS

Most mornings Nimian woke up alone in Angel's *fale*. She was glad of this. It allowed her to brush aside what might have happened in the night, allowed her not to remember him stroking her hair and kissing her face as she fell asleep. When she woke up alone she could forget that she had spent the whole night lying on his arm or had felt through the haze of sleep his hand caressing her skin, slipping under her clothes. Waking alone it was possible not to remember that sometimes she would move a little as he touched her so that his fingers ended up on the base of her spine or the side of her breast.

Nimian rolled onto her back and stared up at the thatched ceiling of the *fale*. Each day there were at least two spiders up there and today one was carrying an egg sack. When Nimian had first seen a spider like this she had thought it was carrying a shell, thought how strange it was that a spider should collect the very same thing that she put in her pocket each day on the beach. But now she knew. It was just one of the many things she now knew about Arun's island. She knew that soon she would wake up to a room full of baby spiders. She knew that she should ask Angel to remove it – but she did not want to. She was attached to the spider and although she knew that no good would come of its little babies, she could not get rid of it.

She lay watching the spiders. She didn't want to get out of bed. She didn't want to leave the *fale*. She wondered what the villagers thought of her. Perhaps now they imagined that all foreigners acted like this – they look for one boy and live with another. How had it happened?

She had to speak to Arun.

When she found him, Nimian told Arun, 'I can't do this anymore.'

'Then why do you?'

'Tell me how to change it. Tell me how to go back.'

'I can't. You're with Angel.'

'You could tell him that I was never your sister. If you felt something for me you would tell him.'

'He's my brother.'

'Your older brother. The brother you have told me stories about for years. The brother who used to look after you. Don't you think he deserves the truth?'

'I can't hurt him, Nimian, I just can't.'

'And nor can I.

'You should have thought of that before you slept with him.'

'I didn't know who he was then. Arun, please, I don't want to hurt him and I don't want to hurt you.'

'So what are you doing in his *fale* every night?'

'Nothing! We sleep, Arun, that's all. I know the rest of the village don't think so but you should. I'm not from here, Arun. I can be friends with a man. Angel is my friend. I'll stay with him while I wait for you.'

'Go home, Nimian, go home.'

'Not without you.'

'I'm home already.'

'No you're not.'

a new beginning

It was a windy morning, very early. Angel walked across the sand to the place he had found her, airing the heat of the night out of his bones. There had not been a day this overcast for months. Angel watched goose bumps cover his arms and was glad the weather had finally broken. He was ready for change.

He felt happiness rising inside him. He looked around. There was no one on the beach. He jumped in the air and threw his legs over his head. He landed and stumbled. He frowned. That was not very good. He did it once more and landed well. He smiled.

Angel felt full of energy. He wanted to call out in a loud voice, whoop loudly, but knew that to do so would end his morning alone. He sat down on top of his boat and pulled his legs to his chest.

Suddenly Angel tore down the sand as though he were racing a crowd of boys. He tried to think of when he had last run. Ages ago, not since he was a child, anyway.

Angel realised he had been too old and too sensible for too long. It was time to play.

Something caught his eye. Her body. Kara's. Angel stood a few metres from her. Her corpse smelled and he saw that she had lost two fingers from one hand.

'What have they been doing to you?' Angel asked, panic rising inside him. Why was she back? He looked down at the woman he had loved and didn't know what to do.

'Thank you for sending me Nimian,' he said to her, and then a thought crossed his mind. 'I haven't forgotten you, Kara. I never will. Is that why you are back?'

He sat down next to her and put his head in his hands. Should he bury her? Can women from the sea be happy in the soil? He touched the water that was lapping up next to him.

'Amalia,' he asked the waves, 'what should I do?' As though in answer, the next wave that broke on the shore came higher up the beach and seemed to drag Kara back into the sea. 'Okay.'

Angel carried the body to his boat. He put her in the bottom and pushed out to sea.

'Please make there be enough wind, please wind, blow,' he said to himself as he raised the sail.

Angel looked down and saw she was lying awkwardly with her arm trapped under her.

'Sorry, Kara,' he said, gently picking her up. He cradled her head against his chest and kissed her hair.

'I'll take you home, Kara,' he told her.

Once he had passed the mango island, he continued rowing for another two hours, then he lowered her into the sea.

THE PLANTATION

Angel waited for Arun on the road, his mind full of Kara. He sniffed his hands. He had washed the smell of her skin off his fingers, her hair off his lips. He was clean. Arun would not know that he had been with a dead woman that morning. He saw his brother run up, past the Havealeta house.

'Sorry,' Arun called. 'I couldn't wake up.'

They moved away from the village in silence, Arun yawning and stretching at the sun, Angel concentrating on each step, anxious to have his spade in his hand and begin work. Today they would dig yams. Angel thought about what Lisi would do with them. He remembered Amalia's cooking. Perhaps if Lisi had spent more time with her mother she would make spicy yam curry or soft *lovo*-cooked yam, or even yam fried up into chips, hot and crunchy. But Lisi would probably boil it until it was dull and tasteless. Angel remembered Kara eating Lisi's food. Pushing it around her plate. They had pretended it was because she was still ill. Perhaps she was. She had died the next day.

They arrived at the plantation.

'What today, boss?' Arun asked.

'Yam,' Angel replied.

'Oh good.' Arun smiled at his brother. 'Lisi will make us yam goo.'

The boys set to work.

Arun's head was full of Nimian. He could not think straight, knowing she was on the island. He put his hand into his pocket and with his thumb stroked her photo. He should have told Angel what she meant to him. He shouldn't have secrets from his brother. In his head he never had. Sailing with his father, he'd climbed to the top of the ship's mast and searched for a little island, somewhere in the middle of an endless ocean, that had his brother on it; so he could tell him what it was like to see the world, so that he could be back in Moana again. Even when Nako's cottage was his home and he thought he would never again return to the island, he'd shut his eyes and be on the earthy floor of the plantation, his brother beside him, their hands joined, looking up at the island's sky, listening to bird-song, one bird at a time. He looked at the man working next to him. If he could not tell Angel about Nimian, his brother was a stranger. He had to speak.

Angel could not stop thinking about Kara, beautiful decaying Kara. He knew that the spirits take many forms. Would she be there again tomorrow, waiting for him? He should ask Arun to wake early – they could walk the beach together. If she was there, Arun could answer the question that was lapping at his mind. Why was she coming back to him? Why had his mother sent him Nimian? His brother would know: he had seen the world. He had to speak.

'I see Kara,' Angel said, but Arun did not hear him for in the same moment he also spoke. 'Nimian is—'

The boys stared at one another. Arun spoke first. 'I did not hear you, brother.'

And Angel replied, 'Nor I you. What was it you said?'

Arun's eyes wandered along the creases of his brother's forehead. Lisi and Ama had told him that Angel had never been seen with a girl before. Could Nimian be his first? And what did Angel have in his life, working day by day, year by year, on the plantation? If Arun told him that he loved Nimian, his brother would feel awkward, perhaps ashamed. He didn't know what Angel would feel. But maybe if he said nothing, something good could happen.

'I asked why the Ungas are not here today.'

'Funaki had a baby,' Angel replied. 'But she is too small. They think she won't survive. There may be a funeral tomorrow.'

'Oh. I've never been to a funeral before.'

'Never?'

'No. I'm lucky I suppose,' said Arun, absentmindedly. 'Death is the one thing I haven't seen.' He looked up at Angel. 'What was it you said before, brother?'

'Nothing,' Angel replied. How could he tell Arun, who had not seen a stranger die, let alone their mother, that he had held a dead girl that morning and was in love with her corpse?

His brother raised an eyebrow.

'Well, just that we should get some more yams.'

Ioane's arms

In the years that had passed, Ioane Matete had given the victims of the crash a life, a story of their own. Sitting in his chair he'd gone over and over it. Ili and Salote he called them, and he believed they were in love and about to become lovers. In his remembrance, in his dread, he saw Ili ask Salote to walk with him. He saw the girl blush and agree. He imagined the boy taking her hand as the sun set. As they searched for certain stars, Ioane pictured Ili gently brushing Salote's neck with his lips. He saw them lying in the sand and as they kissed for the first time, Ioane Matete watched his teenage-self hit them with his truck.

Once his feet were working again, Ioane Matete moved on to his arms. One day, when the rest of the family were out of the house, he spoke to Arun.

'Take me in the boat today but tell no one. You sail out beyond the mango island. I'll row from there. My body is getting stronger. My arms are ready for some exercise. Come on.'

'Why is it a secret?'

'A man's recovery is something private, Arun. Can I trust you?'

'You know you can.'

Arun held his father around the waist. Having checked that the shore was empty, the two stumbled down the beach to the water's edge.

'I wish your legs were ready too. I'm looking forward to that.'

Ioane laughed with his son as he sat panting in the boat. Arun pushed out into deeper water. Once he had regained his breath, Ioane said, 'When I first took you away with me, you were scared each time you couldn't see the sea. I spent years lifting you up and showing you the horizon, pretending that the blue in the distance was water. It's your turn now to lift me.'

'I remember that,' Arun said. 'It took me a long time to realise that you were making it up. That was a good lie, Ioane. The world was so large!'

'My world feels small now. I only see half of it.'

'You don't need two eyes to look around your bedroom. Shall I take you back there?'

'I'm not complaining, Arun. Tskk. Let's get going.'

Arun raised the sail and they sped away from Moana. On the far side of the mango island, Arun moved his father to the middle of the boat and handed him the oars.

'Keep up with the current,' he told Ioane. 'If we move

too far from this spot I'll raise the sail and bring us back.'

'Don't touch it unless I tell you to.'

'It's time I attached this motor,' Arun said, kicking the one that sat underneath him.

The first time Ioane Matete rowed, the boat was washed far out and Ioane, exhausted, slept for the rest of the day and all that night. The next morning he asked his son not to go to the plantation.

'Take me to the ocean, Arun. Help me row.'

Again they were washed away. And again. But Ioane Matete did not give up. His arms were getting stronger.

THE WATERFALL

Angel took Nimian by the hand and led her out of the village. He had a bag over his shoulder, filled with clothes for them both, enough water to last a couple of days and food. She looked at him with a question in her eyes and he looked back at her, telling her not to ask it.

They walked along the road without talking. He was barefoot and silent, but her trainers scuffed the ground and kicked the coral along the path. Angel stopped and turned back to check on Nimian, who was a few steps behind. Her face was red from the sun. She was slightly out of breath.

'It's too hot!' she told him.

He pulled her off the road and into the thick trees. She let out a shriek, but laughed when she saw that they had passed through into a clearing. On one side the plants had been trodden down. Angel led the girl towards them and along a path.

'I've never brought anyone here before,' he told her.

'Why are you bringing me?'

'You're not anyone, you're my one,' he said.

Nimian paused. 'Angel, you don't have to share everything with me.'

'I want to share this.'

They walked through the trees, climbing over fallen branches and fighting through the thick grass. Angel was glad to see that Nimian was smiling and her face less rosy. She was a girl for sand and sea breezes not for the heat of inland. He thought about the day he had first found Kara on the beach. She too was from the sea.

The path moved slowly uphill and turned from a walk into a climb. Angel kept trying to help Nimian, but she shrugged him off, preferring to pull herself from branch to branch.

'I've never seen a girl climb like you do,' he told her.

'Have you ever seen a girl climb?'

'No.'

'You've never left the island,' Nimian said quietly to herself. 'There's a lot you haven't seen.'

As they reached the top, Angel put his hands over Nimian's eyes. Then he removed them. She smiled. 'Pretty nice.' They looked out over the island; the land coated in green, the sea a bright turquoise blue with dark rocks and coral visible even from here.

'This is the best view,' Angel told her. 'Look there,' he pointed below them, 'that is Moana. You can just see our house; the tide is so high that it looks like it's going to come in through the window. And there, all that land is our plantation. You can't see the different trees from here, but we have everything: coconuts, bananas, yam, breadfruit. We get mangoes from that island there, can you see it?'

'That's where we met.'

Angel paused. 'Yes, of course,' he said. Casting his eyes out to sea he was surprised to see someone on the water. 'Look, a boat. It must be the old boatman.' He thought of Kara's body, smelling of seaweed and rotting flesh. He wondered if she was finished with him yet.

Nimian turned around and kissed him gently on the cheek. He took her hands in his and used them to point.

'Can you see the cliff? Look, that one there is the end of the island. Do you see now where Moana is? But around that one is Laumua. Look at the sea and, there, the coral. Only a few people can row that pass. The boatman, some of the Tatafus, Ioane and perhaps Arun. And see the villages all clumped together on the other side of the island. It shows you how isolated we were before the road came.'

They stayed for a while, looking out over the island and the ocean. Angel stood behind Nimian, his arm over her shoulders, breathing in her light hair and scalp. He smelt the skin on her shoulder; her strange skin with its strange smell. He wondered what he smelt like to her.

'I like it here,' she said.

'I'm glad,' he told her. 'There's more. Follow me.'

Angel took Nimian's hand again and led her around a rock that jutted out over the edge of the hill.

'Don't fall,' he said, 'but try not to look either. I want to surprise you. Here.'

In front of them was a spring that rose from the earth and then tumbled over the edge of the hill in a waterfall. There was a pool a short climb below.

'Away from the beach, this is my favourite place on the island. No one comes here, except me. We can be alone.'

'Alone, eh?' Nimian smiled and moved slowly towards him.

'You're beautiful,' he told her.

'Be quiet.'

Her hands moved under his T-shirt. He pulled it up over his head and flung it to the ground. Holding his hand, Nimian started to make her way down to the pool, throwing off her shoes, her shirt, her skirt, her pants. Angel watched her naked body. He had never been alone with a girl like this before: in the middle of the day. Not when the girl was alive. Nimian slid into the pool, shrieking at the cold and then turned to splash him. He followed her down, but she shook a finger at him and pointed at his clothes. He took off his shorts.

Angel regretted that they had left so late. The sun was setting and she was hidden from him by the water and the night. And the dark made him imagine strange things, things that he did not want to imagine, things that he wanted to put behind him. He imagined that her hair was Kara's, that her flat stomach wobbled as

Kara's did, that her lips were Kara's lips, that her arm was the same one that had clung to him that day on the beach.

Later, huddled together in a blanket, they cooked Spam and noodles on a fire of driftwood. They ate in silence, watching the fire burn and light up the moonless night. Angel was happy. Happy to be with her, naked and alone, away from his *fale* and family. Away from Arun and Ioane and the eyes of the village upon them. He knew that he would ask Nimian to marry him so that when the sun rose she would be there and he would kiss her on that day and the next and forever, and never again have to look at Kara's bloated face.

'This is forever,' he said and as he spoke the words he did not think of Kara. He had Nimian for the rest of his life. There was no need to hurry. He imagined their baby, a little pale thing that would be able to swim before it could walk, that would love the island, the sky and the sea, as they did. A baby with her bright eyes. A baby that would grow up as he had – with sand between its toes and the sea on its skin. A boy that he would take up to the plantation with him, or a girl who would always be in the house when he got home. He moved the blanket and kissed Nimian's stomach gently.

She laughed. 'That tickles.'

'Just in case,' he replied.

'In case what?' she asked.

He kissed her again. They lay down next to one another and fell asleep under the stars.

* * *

233

Nimian woke up the next morning with a sore back from lying on a stone. She felt a knot in her stomach and didn't know why. Angel was already awake. Sometimes she couldn't believe how beautiful he was. His body was much more beautiful than Arun's, taller and broader. She imagined what Arun would look like now without his clothes. No, Angel was better, the better brother. She was angry with Arun for leaving her to look for Ioane Matete and then not fighting for her when she finally found him again. She couldn't imagine being angry with Angel. But when he kissed her, she didn't kiss him back. Something he had said last night came back to her, a single word: forever.

'Angel, do you love me?' she asked him.

'Of course I do.'

'How do you know?'

'You're naked in my arms. I know.'

'Where I'm from that doesn't really mean anything. We've just started this. Don't rush.'

'You love me too, Nimian,' he told her. 'I know you do.'

She took a deep breath. 'Do I, Angel? Or do I like you?'

He held her to him and kissed her head. 'You love me. Love is just a word, Nimian, that means you want to kiss me and hold me and be with me. Is that not true?'

'Yes. But . . .' Nimian gave up. 'Shall we swim again?' She did not bother to get dressed but began to walk, as she was, to the bottom of the waterfall. Angel stopped her. He handed her clothes to her.

'Where are we going now?' she asked. 'I don't want to go back to the village just yet.'

'Come with me,' he said.

He led Nimian away from their camp, away from the waterfall, away from Moana and the view of the sea, down the other side of the hill. Below them the land was thick with trees and all that could be seen was green with the grey of the road snaking through it. Before they rejoined the forest, Angel stopped. There was a hole in the ground into which he crawled. She heard a splash. By the time Nimian got onto her hands and knees and peered in, he was nowhere to be seen.

'Angel,' she called out. Her voice echoed.

She wriggled through the entrance and saw in the dim light that they were in a cave full of water and that Angel was below her, swimming. He pointed around him. She made out the shadows of fish. Angel held his arms out to her.

'Will you catch me?' she called.

'Always.'

She rolled her eyes, took a deep breath and threw herself in.

THE FEAST

The villagers didn't like Nimian sleeping in the same *fale* as Angel. They were not married. It was not right.

'She is not from here,' Tom said. 'There are different rules for people from overseas.'

'To her, we are married already,' Angel explained.

So they shrugged their shoulders – it was just another change that came with the road – and decided to have a feast to welcome her to Moana.

They dug a hole in the ground and lit a fire with stones in it. Later, once the fire went out, some of the heated rocks were placed with grass inside the stomach of a pig. They wrapped the pig in coconut palms, surrounded it with vegetables in tinfoil and used the remaining stones to create a wall around everything. The villagers covered the whole pit in banana leaves and heaped soil upon it. As it got dark they roasted a few more pigs on the beach. Laita led the village girls in a dance and Hosea Unga, the men.

'Can I talk to you?' a man asked Nimian.

'Of course! You speak my language! Hello. Who are you?'

'I'm Laita's husband. I'm Tom.'

'I'm Nimian,' she told him.

'I know that. Everyone here knows that.'

'So tell me who you are.'

'You mean how it is I can talk to you? My father was a missionary. He moved to Laumua, married my mother and had me. I learnt my English from him. We came to Moana when we married.'

'Are you a missionary?'

'No. I'm an islander.'

'Can't you be both?'

'No. My father soon forgot why it was he came to Laumua. His God mixed with the spirit of the island. He started telling stories, stopped preaching. He died many years ago. I have been meaning to come and speak to you since I heard you had arrived.'

'I'm glad you came over.'

'I wanted to ask how you learnt to speak our language.'

'I . . . It was in a past life.'

'You knew someone from here?'

'I'm your opposite. My mother was from Laumua, though I didn't grow up there. We had our own private language at home. My mother liked that.'

'Ahh, so you're an islander at heart.'

'Not yet, but perhaps I'll become one, like your father.'

'I'm sure you will! Now, I've got a pig to kill.'

'Really, don't we have enough meat?' she asked.

'There is never enough meat.'

'Can I watch?'

'You can help. I need someone to skin it.'

They walked up into the village towards the pigsty. Tom jumped in and caught a squealing piglet. Nimian sat down and watched as he slit its throat and drained the blood. He cut down the belly of the beast and took out what was inside. Nimian averted her eyes, willing herself to be fascinated by the feast unfolding around her; the food piled high on coconut palm tables, the people singing and dancing, the sea splashing against the sand and the clear night sky.

'This is Arun's island,' she thought.

Tom put the dead animal and a knife on her knee.

'It's only a little one,' he told her, 'it shouldn't take you too long.'

Nimian pictured supermarket pre-packed meat. She held the pig at arm's length and ran the knife over its skin like she was brushing its fur. She didn't want to look. Slowly the hair came off and it grew balder and balder.

'Don't forget the face,' Tom called as he walked back to the beach, and Nimian moved the knife up to the pig snout and stroked it over the skin. She looked into the animal's eyes and gagged.

'No, this is too disgusting,' she said to no one. She stood up and was sick into the sty. The other pigs raced over and tasted their new food.

She felt a hand stroke her hair.

'I'll do it,' said Meleane.

'Thanks,' Nimian replied. 'I'm not very good at this.'
Meleane handed her a cloth to wipe her mouth.

'I'll just head back down the beach,' she said. 'Is that
okay, Meleane?'

There was a circle of people sitting on the sand.
Someone was playing a ukulele and everyone else was
singing. At the end of each song, a story was told or a
conversation began. Nimian sank down into the sounds
of the voices. She drowned out the words and relaxed
into reading faces. She tried to imagine how it would be
if she couldn't understand. Who would she like just by
looking at them? Angel sat down next to her and immediately was asked to tell a story. She saw a smile start in
his eyes as he began to speak and saw the audience respond
with smiles of their own. She watched how they listened
to him and she found herself listening too, entranced by
his words, absorbed by the story. It was a tale about the
island, like everything in Angel's life. She felt as if she'd
heard it before. Beautiful landscapes, sea people – were
all the stories here the same or was this one that Arun
had told her long ago? She looked up and saw that he
was also watching his brother. What would she think of
Arun if she were seeing him now for the first time? That
he was dark and unfriendly and hiding something. His
eyes turned to her. She smiled and he held her gaze, then
stood and walked away into the village.

'Nimian, sing for us,' Tom shouted from across the
circle. 'Sing!' And the rest of the villagers took up
the chant.

Nimian's face dropped. 'I wish I could, Tom. And I'm not being shy or anything. It is just I really can't sing. Really. Not at all.'

'Sing!'

'No, no. I can't.'

'Sing.'

'Honestly, it would hurt your ears.' Nimian stood up and backed away from the circle. She moved around to where Lisi was sitting and put her hands on her shoulders. 'Lisi will sing. She has a beautiful voice.'

Nimian silently begged for them not to ask her any more but Vete Tatafu called out, 'sing' again, and would have carried on had Lisi not begun to hypnotise her listeners.

Nimian paused for a moment, then shook herself free and fled from the circle. She ran back towards the house and crept underneath it.

'Who are you hiding from?' a voice asked.

Nimian screamed. 'Arun, what are you doing here?'

'I thought they would ask me for a story soon. Why are you here?'

'They asked for a song.' Nimian laughed. 'And I am a truly awful singer.'

'I know, I remember.'

There was an awkward silence.

'Arun—'

'How did you escape?'

'Lisi rescued me. She started singing. She's my new favourite person in the world. Arun, can I ask you something?'

'No,' he replied.

'No? Really?'

'Really. When people say that, it's because they want to ask me something they know I don't want to tell them. When you ask me . . . So, no.'

'Okay. But just so you know, you can ask me anything and I'll tell you.'

Arun sighed. 'I already know everything I want to know about you.'

'Everything?'

'Everything that matters.'

'I love you, Arun,' she said.

'Don't say that.'

'I came here to find you.'

'My brother loves you.'

Nimian thought about this. 'Yes, perhaps. But that was an accident. An accident that shouldn't have happened.'

'But it did and it's too late to wish it hadn't. We're on the island now. Angel thinks you're going to marry him.'

'No he doesn't,' she said, laughing, her face blushing red. *Forever.*

'And so does the village.'

'Does it matter what they think?'

'Things are done in a certain way here.'

'I wouldn't have thought you were one for traditions. Is this really what this is about?' She looked at his face in the darkness. 'I thought you didn't want me anymore.'

Arun felt the flush of anger surging up his neck. 'A

tradition is something old, something from the past that is kept alive. This is not a tradition, Nimian. This is a way of life. It is fine for me to do what I like – I'm going to leave. And for you too. You're not from here, there are different rules. But this is Angel's life, Nimian. Respect it!'

'You're angry.'

'Why him? Of all people, why my brother? I told you about him, is that why? I told you about my brother and my island, so you've come here, to . . . You knew it was him didn't you? That first day.'

Nimian stared at Arun as though he were a stranger. She moved away from him and Arun grabbed her arm. She shook him off. He pulled her to him and held her tight against his chest. She struggled to get away but he did not let go.

'Arun,' she said, but her voice was muffled by his clothes.

'Good night, Nimian,' he said, releasing her.

Nimian was alone. She wiped her eyes on her arm and made her way to Angel's *fale*. She lay down on the floor but could not sleep with the memory of Arun's arms around her. A few hours later Angel stumbled in. She wanted him to hold her, to kiss her, to change how she was feeling, but he had been drinking *kava*.

Nimian watched him for a while. She tried to control the pounding in her heart by matching it to the rhythmic rise and fall of Angel's chest, but she couldn't calm down. She was angry. She would go and look for Arun. There were things that had to be said.

Nimian felt comforted by the sand on her soles and the sheen of the moon on the water. Her heart calmed down. She walked ankle deep in the sea, looking down for the shape of a jelly or stone fish. She stubbed her toe on a rock and swore loudly. The darkness was intense, the light in the sky did not quite reach the earth and the only brightness was the glowing of the fire from the feast at the other end of the beach. Nimian looked and saw that two figures were still sitting beside it. She hoped Arun was not one of them. She wanted him to be alone.

Nimian stopped walking. She did not want to be noticed. She turned her back to the village and looked out to sea. At that moment she thought she could watch the water for an eternity.

'I suppose if I stay here,' she thought, 'that's what I'll do.'

She found a dry piece of sand and sat down. She thought about Angel. She reflected on how, in some ways, he was perfect: beautiful, kind, in love with her. Perfect in most ways. In all ways. And she loved him. She loved his voice, his smile, the way he looked at her, the way he cared for his family. His family: Ama, the twins and Arun. Arun. Why had Angel kissed her that day on the mango island? Why had he taken her home? She shouldn't have let him.

'I thought you'd gone to sleep.'

Nimian jumped. 'Arun!'

'There is something I want to ask you.'

'Is there?'

'I want to know if you love Angel.'

'Love?' Nimian asked. She said it once in the island tongue and once in her own. 'Which kind do you mean, Arun? The easy kind they use here or our kind?'

'He loves you. Do you love him?'

'It's a big word. You know that.'

'You said you love me.'

'I have known you forever, Arun. What is between us is in our bones.'

'Then leave him, now.'

'I can't hurt him like that.'

'Yes, but you will. All dealings with you end up hurting.'

Nimian looked at him sadly. 'Don't, please.'

'Long ago, Angel and I were alone against the world. I thought I could return to that again. In my head, the island was always the same; cut off with Angel waiting for me. Now I'm back, and instead of my brother and my mother, there are the twins, Ama, the road and you.'

'You must have expected that the island would change. Time passes, Arun.'

'Expected you to be here with Angel?'

'No, but the rest.'

'I should have, but I didn't. I expected I'd return and Angel would be alone on the beach, sitting, watching the waves as he used to. I'd walk with him up to the plantation and we'd talk about the sea and the world.'

'You can still do all that.'

'No, we can't. How can Angel talk about the world?

He's never even been to Laumua. How can I tell him where I've been when he's in love with you?'

'You could talk about the island.'

'How can I do that, when I've seen the world? I'd imagined returning home with Ioane and watching him and my mother reunited. Instead I came home alone. She's dead. He's half dead.'

'You were never angry with Ioane for taking you away and leaving you with us. I would have been.'

'Why?' Arun asked. 'Everything about who I am comes from my travelling. Besides I loved being with you and I hated her for letting me go.'

'But now you don't?'

'Sometimes.'

'Why did she?'

'What?'

'Let you go?' asked Nimian.

'You know why, Nimian. Because she had her Angel.'

'I'm sure she didn't want to.'

'Would you give up your baby?'

'She didn't give you up. You went with your father.'

'Would you ever leave your baby with its father?' Arun asked.

'I don't know. I can't imagine it. But I don't have a child.'

'Don't. Unless you want it to hate you.'

Nimian said nothing, her head bowed, feeling his hurt.

'I'm going back to the fire,' said Arun. 'It's time you went. My brother will be waiting for you.'

Nimian watched him walk away. She noticed for the first time that he was the only person in Moana who wore jeans, the only man who had long hair. He would leave soon. She wondered if, when, he departed, he would ask her to go with him. Would he let her know his plans? She imagined waking one morning to find him gone. She put her hand to her chest and gulped back the panic that was rising within her.

She thought of Angel as the boy that Arun had described, sitting still on the beach and staring at the sea. She envied his quiet, the peacefulness of his mind. She was full of questions. He just watched. She tried to emulate him. She looked at the sea, at the waves, at the beach.

'Perhaps this is easier in the day,' she thought, 'when the water isn't hidden by darkness. Or perhaps I am just not good at turning off the voices in my head.'

Nimian decided to stay until she stopped noticing herself. She would sit still until she forgot that her legs were wet from the sand and that the mosquito bite on her wrist was itching. She would sit still until she was able to see each wave that broke on the shore, until she could follow its progress from the beginning, through every ripple, to its end. She dug her toes into the sand. She counted waves, one, two, three – up to ten and then shook out her legs. She would try again tomorrow. It was time to go to sleep.

Back in the *fale*, she lay down next to Angel and felt him stir. She moved closer to the heat of his body and put her head on his chest.

Ioane's Legs

Ioane remembered the smell. It was as if he were still standing there in front of them. Death has a smell that no breeze can carry away. The boys looked on what they had hit: a couple, locked in an embrace, boy trying to shield girl, girl frozen in surprise, both joined together to die, their bodies crumpled by the weight of the destroyed vehicle.

Ioane Matete knew now that he could have lived with killing them. It had been an accident. It was not the sight of them dying that had followed him around for all these years, it was not the few words that he heard them cough to one another that haunted him.

'We have to leave,' he had cried, and grabbed Arun Nepali, trying to drag him away.

'No!' Arun stared at him as though he had never seen him before. 'We need to get help.'

'We need to leave. If we don't, what will happen to us?'

'Get help, Ioane, for God's sake, get help. I will stay with them.'

'I can't, Arun. I can't.' He remembered Arun's last words, carried to him in the wind as he ran.

'You did this, Ioane. You.'

But Arun was the only one who knew that Ioane Matete had been driving the truck and Ioane did not tell the rest of the village. The families of the couple thought it was Arun, the foreigner. The owner of the truck thought it was Arun, the foreigner. All of Laumua thought that Arun, the foreigner, who couldn't drive, had killed two of their own. Ioane Matete said nothing.

Ioane had never seen his friend again and hadn't made a single friend since.

Ioane Matete's arms were now strong. He could row against the current by the mango island. He could raise the sail in a fierce wind without help. Ioane Matete could lift rocks and heavy chairs above his head. It was finally time to fix his legs.

He started at night again, slowly lifting them away from the mattress, first the right and then the left. And then he relearnt to walk as a baby learns, hauling himself up by the furniture, using his arms to support his weight. Eventually he called for Arun and, when the rest of the family were out, the two of them walked around and around the house.

THE ISLAND'S WOMEN

On the night of the feast, when Angel Matete slept with a day's worth of *kava* in his blood, he had a dream. In his dream he pictured what was to come. He saw his own death, his body sinking down into the water, like a bottle full of sand, from his grandfather's boat. There he saw Kara as he had seen her on the beach, rotten and dismembered. But when he reached out to her, the light from the surface made her beautiful again. She had been waiting for him. He saw the house she had prepared, the children they would have, everything there except him. 'Don't rush,' he heard her whisper, 'just keep me in the sea.'

He woke up the next morning and understood that Kara would be on the beach again, waiting for him. He found her in the same place on the sand. He lay next to her, half in, half out of the water, and imagined he had woken beside her that morning and every other one. Her eyes had been eaten, her body was full of water and all her clothes had been ripped away. Algae made her slippery to touch and shells had attached themselves to her feet. But the biggest change was her smell, which was more powerful than the stink that came from bursting the intestines of a slaughtered pig. Angel vomited. As the sun rose off the water he picked her up, took her to his grandfather's boat and once again put her back in the sea as far beyond the mango island as he could row.

'See you tomorrow, Kara,' he said, wishing her gone.

The day after the feast, Meleane slept late. She had stayed by the fire until its embers burnt away and the sun had started to rise over the island. Now, lying in her bed, she did not want to wake up. She clutched at the night before, scared that if she properly opened her eyes, it would become the past, no longer happening. She wanted to be back on the beach in the dark, watching the stars, listening to the island's songs and the villagers' stories. She wanted to feel once again that moment when Arun had sat down next to her. His face had been tight and angry when he'd first arrived, his fist tense as if he was waiting to jerk a fish out of the water. Slowly it had loosened up, relaxed, and he had smiled at her.

'Okay, Meleane,' he had said. 'Okay.'

Later on the men had moved to the Ungas' house to drink kava and the women had slowly drifted off to sleep but Arun had stayed with her by the fire. And even once he'd left, he'd come back. He'd come back to her.

Meleane kicked off the blanket. It was too hot in her little bedroom. She stood up and opened the window. He had once kissed her from this window, she thought. She touched her lip where he had bitten her.

'Meleane, get up!' her mother, Vahine, called out to her.

She got dressed and went outside.

'Zeno Tatafu has had a baby,' Vahine said.

'What's she called it?'

'Vete of course, it's a little boy.'

'She'll be pleased,' Meleane said. 'What will we take them?'

'No one in this village makes reed mats any more. I thought we would start, Meleane. Not everyone likes having beds. Mattresses are too soft for some of our older neighbours. Let's try and start one today. If it's awful, well, we'll find something else.'

'It will take weeks!'

'The baby isn't going anywhere.'

'Okay. I'll go and collect leaves.'

'Perhaps the Matete girls can help you. Zeno told me that their mother used to weave.'

'I'll ask them.'

Meleane smiled to herself. She wondered if Arun would be there. Perhaps he would be back and the girls still at school. She'd sit with him before they came home. And maybe Teacher Zeno would want to talk to Lisi. Ama would wait for her. They'd be very late. Angel would be held up on the plantation as well and Nimian would be out somewhere. And she would talk to Arun for hours as she had last night and he would look her straight in the eyes when he spoke and not allow anyone else to join their conversation. They had been sitting so close together that their legs were touching.

She walked down through the village to the Matetes' house. The tide was high, the front wall was wet with spray from the sea. She went through the side door into the main room.

'Hello,' Meleane called out. There was no answer. 'I'll wait,' she said aloud, and sat on the sofa where she imagined Arun sat, his legs firmly on the ground, leaning back, looking around him.

'Who are you?' a croaky voice asked.

Meleane jumped and looked around her. The room was empty as it always was, nobody there except for Ioane Matete sitting in his chair in the corner.

'Ioane, did you just speak?'

'I asked who you were,' he replied slowly.

'I'm Meleane. I've never heard you say anything before.'

'You've never come and sat in my house alone before.'

'I'm sorry. I'll go.'

'No, stay. Get me some water, I'm thirsty.'

Meleane hurried out to the kitchen and grabbed a glass, then ran around to the rain tank.

'You suit this house, Meleane. You remind me of Amalia.'

'Your wife?'

'Yes. And of another woman I once knew. You look just like the first girl I fell in love with.'

'Amalia used to make mats didn't she? I've come to ask your daughters if they know her secrets.'

'They won't. Neither of them knew her.'

'Not even Lisi? We're not sure about how long the leaves need drying for.'

'No!' Ioane shouted. 'She's my daughter—' He started to cough and wheeze.

'I'm sorry,' Meleane said, 'I didn't mean to upset you. I really should go.'

'Sit down. My son brought these chairs. They used to sit on the floor.'

'Arun?'

'Yes. My son. He's a traveller, Meleane, and a traveller needs someone to come home to.'

'Arun isn't planning to leave.'

'But he'll leave nonetheless. There isn't much time.'

'I'm, I don't know—'

'Don't pretend with me Meleane, not with me.'

'Do you really think I suit this house? I do love it here. There are no ghosts. In our home, we can feel the people who used to live there. Did you know them, the doctor and his wife?'

There was the sound of feet approaching the house and Arun came inside.

'Hello, Meleane,' he said and saw how she kept glancing at his father. 'Ioane, I thought you said you were only speaking to me?'

'I've made an exception. Now, son, take me out in the boat. Is the motor working?'

'Perfectly.'

'Let's go. Come and visit me again, Meleane.'

'It's a windy day,' she said. 'Do you really think you should go out now?'

Ioane raised an eyebrow at Arun and they both laughed at her.

'Go inside, little girl,' Arun said.

Meleane watched them from the window. She saw Arun help his father into the boat, the two of them talking. Both their faces were animated and Meleane wondered how it was that she had ever thought Ioane was as good as dead, how she had not known that he could speak and hear and understand. She thought about everything he had said. Perhaps Arun had talked about her. She closed her eyes and let herself dream. When she opened them again the boat was far out to sea, the hum of the motor hard to hear. Another boat was on the water, a row boat.

Ioane had said that the girls did not know how to weave. There was no reason to wait. Meleane let herself out of the house and decided to go and pick the leaves she needed. She walked up through the village, waving at the little kids leaving school, watching her brother Mano and his friend Tamatoa climb out of a low window.

She smiled. 'Even Mano has secrets.'

She walked past the rock where she had first met Arun, in amongst the trees, and found the *pandanus*. She had nothing to cut them with, so started breaking leaves off with her hands. She watched the blood rise to the surface of her fingers. She ran back to the village and borrowed a machete from the Havealetas' house. She cut into the tree, working with the natural spirals in the wood. It was slow work but she collected a small bundle. It was a start. She tied them together and set off back to the village.

She imagined the mat they would hand to Zeno. It would be one for the baby to crawl around on, one where he could sleep. It was Zeno's first child. As she walked by the Tatafu house she looked in the window to see if she could see the new mother. As it was nearly midday the house was full of the family, all the women and their children getting ready to sleep. Meleane waved and kept on walking.

How strange to hold a baby in your arms for the first time. A new life. Not just for the baby, for you as well. Arun had not been a first child. First Angel, then him. First one then another. What does it change to have the second? And if that second baby was Arun?

Meleane left the *pandanus* leaves in a pile by her door and went inside. Her mother was nowhere to be seen. Meleane was glad. She wanted to dream. She went into her bedroom, lay down and stared at the ceiling. On it she saw pictures of her future. She watched them eagerly.

Angel found Kara the next morning and the morning after that and all of that week and the next and the next. First she returned with no arms, then no legs and one morning just her torso appeared on the sand. Angel imagined her head sitting in the stomach of a shark. Flesh had fallen in great chunks from her skeleton and she smelt of something so much worse than death. But each morning Angel picked her up, held her to him and returned her to the sea.

'This time you'll stay with your family under the water,' he told her, although each morning a part of him hoped to find her again. The smell no longer bothered him, nor the decay. She was his mornings; he her visitor, she his. But he could not understand why she returned.

'Amalia,' he would say to the ocean, 'why are you sending her back? She needs to join you now. Look after her for me. Kara, wait for me there. You have to be patient. It's not my time yet.'

'What do you do each morning?' Nimian asked Angel one day. 'You hardly sleep anymore.'

'I go to the beach.'

'But why? Why not lie here with me?'

'You're asleep.'

'Yes. Haven't you ever just lain next to someone and watched them?'

Angel did not reply.

'Who is on the beach that early?'

Angel thought of telling Nimian about Kara, thought about asking her what to do, asking how he could make her stay in the sea where she belonged. Instead he said, 'No one but me. And sometimes the boatman.'

'The boatman?'

'He sails around here from time to time. He lives on the sea.'

'He lives on the sea?' Nimian asked incredulously.

'But I haven't seen him recently,' Angel muttered, more to himself than to her. He remembered the last time he had spoken to the boatman. *Let her go.*

He looked up at Nimian and smiled. 'Okay, tomorrow I'll stay with you.'

Ioane Matete Wakes Up

The day that Ioane Matete stood up with no support at all from Arun, it started to rain. Unusual rain, constant rain. It rained and it rained and it rained.

Ioane felt an itch on his knee. He shook out his leg to relieve it, and then the itch moved to the back of his thigh. At first it was enough just to put his hand under his leg and pinch the skin, but soon he had to scratch.

Ioane straightened himself up. He kicked out his legs. He felt strong. He heard the sounds of his children in the kitchen. He walked through to them.

'Why aren't you up on the plantation, Ioane?' he asked Angel. Angel, Nimian, the twins and Ama jumped. They looked in astonishment at Ioane Matete standing there.

'My name is Angel,' his oldest son, finally finding his voice, corrected him.

'That was the name your mother gave you. To me, you are Ioane.'

'To myself, I am Angel and I will be Angel to you.'

'Will you now?' Ioane stared balefully through his one eye and took a step forward.

'Ioane,' interrupted Arun. 'It's too early for all this. But, Angel, it is long past dawn.'

'Yes, I'm going,' said Angel.

'Tamatoa, you go with him,' Ioane ordered.

'I go to school in the morning,' Tamatoa replied.

'Not any more you don't. You're old enough to work.'

'I don't need Tamatoa's help,' said Angel, 'I work the plantation with the Ungas. And Arun.'

'Stand up, boy.'

Tamatoa picked up his stick and stood up.

'You're right, Ioane –' Ioane Matete said to his eldest son.

'I am Angel.'

'– He's weak. He'll be no good. Tamatoa, you can take the boat out. Bring home some fish. Use the motor, those arms of yours can't row.'

'Go to school, Tamatoa,' Angel said quietly to his brother.

Tamatoa nodded.

'You, girl,' Ioane pointed to Ama. 'How old are you?'

Ama took Angel's hand and he answered for her, 'Ama's eight.'

'Ama,' said Ioane, 'you'd better get your books. School starts soon.'

'What about me?' Lisi asked.

'You, my daughter, will stay here. There is food to make, the house to clean, mats to prepare. Your mother used to make mats every day. Go and see Meleane Vata, she'll help you.'

'Yes, Ioane.'

'And you . . .' Nimian was sitting with her back to him, hoping not to be noticed. Recently she had started eating with the family in the kitchen because Ioane Matete had not been in there for years. She had frozen upon hearing his voice, praying that he would not see her. She was not ready to see the man who had left her mother behind. She did not want to see the man Arun had left her to find. 'Who are you?'

Nimian turned around. 'Hello, Ioane.'

'What are you doing here?' he asked in her language, his certainty disappearing into a frown.

'I came to see your son.'

'How long have you been here?'

'A few months.'

Ioane turned to Arun. 'You didn't tell me she was here.'

'I know. She's with Angel.'

Ioane looked at his eldest son. 'Why—'

Arun spoke in a cheerful voice. 'So, Ioane, you've given everyone else jobs, what are you and I going to do today?'

Ioane looked at him in confusion, then said slowly, 'It's raining, we're in port, what do you think?'

'*Kava*. I'll tell the neighbours.'

'Lisi, you'll serve. Arun, it's time she was married. Bear that in mind when you invite the village. Make sure there are a few possibilities. She's the most beautiful girl on the island; we should be able to choose anybody we like. Lisi, do your hair,' Ioane said distractedly. Nimian had stood up and was leaning against Angel.

'And remember not to give your father a full cup. He's not had a high tide for years now,' said Arun.

Ioane laughed. 'Your father can manage perfectly well. It's your brother who's never been able to drink much. Ioane, Tamatoa, Amalia, why are you still here? You, Nimian, go! I'll talk to you later.'

Ioane Matete watched his children leave the house and stood outside the door looking at the rain. The ground was slowly turning to mud.

'Ioane?' Lisi said.

'Do you smell this?' Ioane asked.

'What?'

'The ground, the earth. This is how it smelt the day I married your mother.'

'Angel told me to go to school. Should I?'

'What did I tell you to do?'

'To stay here.'

'So, Lisi, there you have it; two orders. Which do you obey?'

'My father's?'

'It's not a test, Lisi. It's up to you. I married your mother when she was sixteen. You're nearly that age. What do you think will help you more: going to school, a day of reading books that you could read here, or getting to know some of the men in the village, meeting your husband? Perhaps you think you are too beautiful to need to serve at a *kava* party. Perhaps you think men will fall in love with you without wanting to speak to you even once.'

'No, I don't think that. I'll get ready.' Self-consciously she pushed her long hair from her face. 'And Ioane?'

'Yes?'

'Are the Tatafus coming?'

'Some will. Which Vete are you hoping to see?'

'Well, it's just that I've heard that Sun . . .' Lisi was embarrassed.

'Go and get changed. I'm sure Arun will bring him.'

Ioane wondered if he wanted Lisi to marry a Tatafu. He was sure that no Vete was good enough for his daughter but it occurred to him there could be advantages. He would obey his father-in-law. The Tatafu household was full so he would make the couple move in here.

He imagined how it could be in a few years: Lisi and Ama here, having children. That would be good. Ioane Matete scratched his head. Nimian. She was not with Arun. Strange. Arun had loved that girl from the moment he'd first seen her at Nako's house. What could have happened? Still, he thought, it was for the best. Nimian was not the type of wife he wanted for Arun. He needed a girl like Amalia: a girl to cook, clean, have children – not ask questions and not demand to come with him when he left. Imagine if he had married Nako! No, Nako, Nimian, they were good for a year or two, but not as wives.

Arun would marry Meleane and she would live here in this house, while his son travelled. Meleane would make a good island wife. Arun would live the life he had been born to, the life Ioane had lived: in ships, in foreign countries, but always with a family on the island, in the village of Moana, to come back to.

Nimian. What to do about her? He didn't want her getting in the way. Angel, so it seemed, was in love with her. He could use that. He would talk to Nimian.

Yes, Ioane thought, it is all going to work out. He wondered if he would again be a part of his son's travels. Perhaps. He felt stronger than he had in years. One day, he would sail again. This rain: it made him want to be on the ocean.

Ioane Matete watched as the rain grew heavier. The mud pile at the top of the village began to spread. Pigs wallowed happily. He smiled. The island knew he was back.

Arun invited the village and the villagers came: the Tatafus, the Ungas, Tom Havealeta, Fono and Mano Vata. Lave Unga and his sons brought a bunch of *kava* roots.

But before they could join them, Ioane needed to take his second son aside. 'I think it is time we spoke. Don't you, Arun? You've been keeping secrets.'

Arun nodded slowly. 'But let's walk. It's complicated, now that Nimian is here.'

'That's something else you should have explained to me. Start from the beginning, tell me everything. Where have you been, my son?'

'Well, you left me with Nimian and her mother.'

'Nako was a beautiful woman. But tell me, did she treat you well?'

'Very. Like a son. I liked living there. I was the man of the house.'

'But you were so young.'

'I didn't feel young. I felt like it was time I was a man. And Nimian and I, we did things that . . .'

'Made you one?'

'Yes. Later. I stayed there for years, Ioane. You didn't visit at all in the last three.'

'Has it been so long?'

'It's been even longer than that.'

'Which room was yours?'

'I moved into the attic.'

'With the view of the sea?'

'Yes. I could see ships coming and going on the horizon. I imagined you on one of them.'

'It made you restless watching water.'

'And you calm. I liked it there. It was my home, but I still waited for you to come back.'

'Do you hate me for leaving?'

'I don't hate you, Ioane. We are travellers. We see the world the same way, you and I, and that's our burden.'

'It is. Our burden and our blessing.'

'Two years ago I came to look for you.'

'Two years?'

'I had no money and no idea where you were. I went to everywhere you ever told me about, Ioane, and more places besides. I've seen the whole world.'

'And then you came home.'

'I came home and you were waiting.'

'I was.'

'And Nimian was here.'

'Tell me why.'

'She came to find me. But I . . . Angel's looking after her.'

Ioane Matete stopped and pulled at Arun's hand. He opened his arms and held his son. 'You gave me my life back, you know that don't you?'

'Did I? Well I'm glad then. Ioane?'

'Yes.'

'Angel doesn't know that Nimian and I were . . .'

'One?'

'One.'

Ioane Matete put his arm around his son. 'She'll be gone soon.'

'She can stay. I don't care anymore.'

'She'll go.'

'Ioane, you and I, we're not the type to sit around talking. Let's go home. They'll have drunk all the *kava* before we get there.'

Later that day, once the men had stumbled back to their houses, Ioane Matete lay down in the middle of the main room of his house and watched the ceiling sway back and forth. In his mind was Nimian. When she walked in he asked her, 'What took you so long? Where have you been?'

'Dancing with Laita and some of the village girls. It seems that's what the women do when the men are drunk.'

'The women should have been working.'

Nimian raised an eyebrow.

'What are you doing in Moana?' Ioane asked as he slowly stood up.

'Living, being an islander.'

'You'll never be an islander.'

'Why's that?' asked Nimian.

'Because to be an islander you need to be planted here and take root here. You're not from here, you never will be.'

'Is that so? And you would know, I suppose.'

'I would. I do. Tell me, Nimian, what are you doing here?'

'What am I doing here? What are you doing here, Ioane? You should be with Nako.'

'My sons and daughters are here,' Ioane replied. 'What are your plans for Angel?'

'It's . . .'

Ioane Matete grabbed her arm and pulled her towards him. 'You and Arun?' He put his hand around her throat and pushed down with his fingers. He pulled her hair back with his other hand forcing her to look in his eye.

She gasped, 'We were children.'

'And now you are with his brother?'

Ioane moved his hand to her mouth. Tears started to stream down Nimian's cheek and she pounded with her fists against Ioane Matete's chest, trying to escape.

'That makes you a whore. What's wrong, Nimian? You don't like this?' He fixed her with his eye. 'I am going to move my hand from your mouth. You'll stay quiet, won't you?'

She nodded.

'I want you to get off this island. Do you understand? Take Angel with you if you want to but leave Arun alone. Never come back.'

'Let me go now,' she said quietly and this time it was Ioane who agreed. He removed his hands and watched as Nimian ran to the door. There she turned around. 'I'm no worse than you, Ioane Matete.'

Ioane looked at her. 'That's not good enough for my son.'

In the kitchen, Ioane said, 'Lisi, my lovely, what is that wonderful smell? I'm hungry, please tell me it's food.' He rubbed his forehead then looked up and smiled at his daughter.

Lisi beamed. 'It is; fried fish and boiled yam.'

'My favourite.'

Lisi gave her father a plate of food. 'I'm glad you're better,' she said. 'I know you've been here but I've missed you.'

Arun came in as she was speaking. He punched his father lightly on the arm, 'Yes. It's good to have you back.'

Ioane smiled at his children. It was good to be back. It was good to be out of that chair. He was tired of sitting, tired of watching, tired of going nowhere. From now on he would act.

THE RaIN

The rain lashed the island for fifteen days and fifteen nights. At first the villagers stood outside and bathed in it – as good as a waterfall shower. But, as it continued, Moana began to flood and one by one the residents retreated indoors. The phone line grew damp and stopped working, the power and water supply were cut off and the older inhabitants were reminded of the years before the road when they had lived without contact with the wider world.

The rain came down as though it would never stop. It blocked out the sun and the village grew cold. The pigs sneezed and the cocks crowed in the middle of the day. The village men, forced outside to search for something dry to burn, came back shivering and empty-handed. The women knitted until supplies of wool for their babies ran out. No one slept in the middle of the day anymore.

There was only one person in Moana who was glad

of the rain: Ioane Matete. He did not want it to stop. The rain was making him strong. Whenever he saw Nimian, he whispered in her ear, stroked her neck and watched her green eyes glaze over and go dead. She would leave soon.

One day Tamatoa was walking along the shore when he saw Nimian crying. He watched her holding her knees as she sat on the wet sand, head lowered, shoulders hunched.

She reminded him of his mother, sitting on another beach, when he had been much younger, crying in this same way, on the day his father had returned all those years ago. Like Nimian his mother had dug her toes deep into the sand, like Nimian she had hidden her head. He wondered what it was that had made Amalia stop crying, and remembered: a mango. Angel had given her a mango and his mother had smiled. He would bring Nimian a mango. A mango would stop the tears.

Tamatoa walked to the Vatas' house.

'Mano,' he called out, and his friend yelled at him to come in.

It was cold and damp inside the house and a smell of rotting permeated the air. Tamatoa wanted to go back outside as quickly as possible. He preferred being cold in open spaces.

'What do you want, Toes?' Mano asked.

'I'm going to swim out to the mango island. Will you come?'

'Not now. My father's driving the truck to Laumua.'

'I need to go out there now.'

'Why?' Mano asked. 'We haven't been there since, you know. Since the Most Beautiful Village Competition.'

'I know. But I want to go back.'

'That trip didn't end well.'

'You were fine.'

'Why do you want to go back there, Toes? I don't, ever.'

'I need a mango.'

'Okay, well, go then. But take someone with you and watch the tide.'

'I always do.'

'I know. It's just me that's an idiot. See you tomorrow?'

Tamatoa hobbled back into the rain. He circled the house and went to the furthest part of the beach from his family. The tide was turning; it was just beginning to go out. The sky was full and heavy and the rain was falling.

'I'm wet anyway,' he told himself.

He sat down on the sand and took his mutilated foot in his hand. He rubbed it hard as he studied the sky. There would not be a storm. It would just rain and rain and rain.

He walked into the water and let it help him towards the mango island. He fixed his eyes on its shape in the distance, lifted up his legs, and swam. He would soon be there.

The waves were rolling high on the ocean and Tamatoa bobbed with them up and down. His leg was hurting. Since the rain began no one had slept properly. Tamatoa realised he had never been so tired. He had to shut his eyes. He would soon be there.

His legs found the bottom and he pushed against it. Once on the sand he collapsed and fell instantly asleep. He awoke breathing water through his nose. Hazy with sleep he opened his eyes, crawled further up and shut them again.

The same thing happened.

Again.

And again.

Tamatoa forced himself to wake up properly and saw that he was right up the beach, almost in the trees. He looked down at where he had first slept. It was not there anymore, only sea. He looked up. The sky was still dark. It would not stop raining.

'The water is going to keep on rising,' he said out loud.

He knew he couldn't sleep on the sand. He would climb a mango tree, sleep a little more, pick some fruit for Nimian, then wake up and swim back to the island. Behind the rain, he knew that the sun must be setting. He climbed the highest tree he could find, settled onto a wide branch and slept.

Tamatoa dreamt that night of being born, of toes, of the sea and the shore, of Mano and his brothers and sisters. His whole life returned to him in pictures. He saw his parents; his mother holding him, his father picking him up and changing his clothes. He saw his school and the island families. He saw his kitchen and the main room he slept in. And then Tamatoa dreamt of pushing his feet into Lisi's and waking covered in blood. He saw his mother's face leaning over him, holding a machete. The place where his toes should be hurt. He cried out in pain. He woke up.

'It's only a dream,' he told himself and reached for his foot. He held it tightly in his hand and squeezed. The pain intensified. Tamatoa opened his eyes wide and looked around him. He was up a mango tree. Next to him was a small black snake. He looked down. There was water everywhere.

'Are you escaping the flood too?' he asked the snake.

The snake looked at him.

'Did you bite me?' he asked.

The snake looked away.

'Am I going to die?'

The snake slithered along the branch.

Tamatoa felt the poison move through his body to the rhythm of his beating heart.

HUSBANDS AND WIVES

The rain afforded a certain amount of freedom to the young people of Moana. On a sunny day the village was always full of family and friends and everything they did was visible. But with the rain keeping most people inside, it was now possible to move around unseen. Vete Sun Tatafu was determined to use the dark days to talk to Lisi Matete, the most beautiful woman in the village, whom he wanted more than anything to become his wife.

He slipped out of his house and down to the shore, where he sat on the beach and waited. Sun had been watching Lisi for years. He knew her routine. After lunch she walked the beach and if the rain didn't keep her away, today he would walk with her. It would be the first time they had been alone together. He rehearsed what he would say.

There was a sound from the Matete house and a figure stepped over the pig board.

'Walk with me,' Ioane Matete ordered and Sun fell in step beside him. 'Why are you waiting outside my house?'

'I'm not, Ioane. I was just sitting on the beach.'

'Then why have your eyes been fixed on our door?'

Vete Tatafu looked at Ioane Matete and decided to tell him the truth. 'I was hoping to talk to Lisi.'

'Is that the right way to talk to a single girl? Alone on the beach?'

'No. Sorry. It's not,' Sun said. 'But . . .' He gulped. 'I want her to marry me.'

'Why would she accept you?'

'I love her.'

'Why would I want a Tatafu to be my son-in-law?'

Vete did not know what to say. He hadn't expected this. He was in love. 'Well, erm, Lisi would have plenty of family,' he blurted out. 'And I can give her things. We trade. We're doing well.'

'Lisi already has a family. There are just a few of us. We stick together. There is no possibility of Lisi moving out.' Ioane paused and looked Vete Sun Tatafu straight in the eye. 'But you can live with us after the wedding.'

After Ioane Matete had dismissed his future son-in-law, he made his way up through the village to the graves. The villagers stared. 'Ioane can walk,' they said to each other in wonder. He had never before visited the grave of his wife. On it he found a single fresh white flower, put there by whom, he did not know. Ioane picked it up and smelt it. It smelt of her.

'Amalia, Amalia,' he said. 'Are you asleep?'

Ioane Matete lowered himself onto the ground beside her and lay on his back, letting the rain tap on his eyelids, his hands cushioning his head.

'Arun has come home,' he said. 'He has travelled the world as I did. You'd be proud of him, Amalia. He is just as we always wanted our son to be.'

A mosquito landed on Ioane's arm and he watched it bite him. When he was sure it had drunk his blood, he slapped it. He held his arm out in the rain and watched the red stain wash away.

'Lisi is getting married, Amalia. I have accepted Vete Sun. You always said a Tatafu boy would make a good husband. And she seems to like him. They'll live in our house. There will be space once Arun and I leave again. Lisi will miss you at her wedding, Amalia. She is beautiful, you know.'

Ioane Matete moved a few paces from Amalia, to a tree that protected him from the worst of the weather. In spite of the hard ground and drops trickling onto his face, he was soon asleep. He dreamt he was in bed with his wife.

NIGHT

Meleane sat on the beach that night and watched the waves. The sun had just set. It was not like her to be out of the house after dark, but she hadn't been able to sleep.

'Perhaps I'm finally becoming a villager,' she said to herself. 'The sea is getting to me.'

But it was the rain that had kept her awake; her house was damp, and the ocean was louder than normal. Meleane worried they would all be flooded. She wanted to be awake in case the water crept up in the dark on the Matete house. She knew that Angel trusted the sea, that he was convinced it would never hurt his family, but Meleane knew he was wrong. The Matetes would be the first to drown.

The sand was wet and Meleane regretted that she had not brought anything to sit on. But then her bed was wet too and all the furniture in the house and the grass in the village and – everything. Meleane could not remember being dry. She looked down at her hands. Would her bones soften, like a chicken-leg left in water? Would they disintegrate and leave her with flapping skin? Easier for someone to eat, she thought. She squeezed a finger with her other hand. The bone was still firm. She looked over at the house on the shore. There was someone under it. Arun.

The night was his time, his alone, but on this night everyone was awake. Inside the house, Ioane was talking to himself in a loud whisper as though he feared the dark. There were noises from the girls' room too, quiet frantic voices, Tamatoa's name said over and over again. But the main room was empty; Tamatoa was nowhere to be seen. Arun had walked past Angel's *fale* and heard the moans of Nimian. He dreamt of making her make that sound, of stroking her pale skin, kissing her lips. He imagined her naked inside the hut, beside his brother's naked body.

And now Meleane was also awake. He remembered when he'd first seen her at night, on the day of his return to the village. Before Nimian came back. She would moan for him if he wanted her to. He spat on the ground. His spit added to the rain. He noticed something wash up on the beach in front of him. It looked like a stick.

Meleane's world paused as Arun moved towards her, his dark eyes boring into hers as though attempting to see right into her mind. She tried to smile but could not. She glanced down at her bare feet, at her brown toes. When she raised her head he was on the sand beside her.

'I've found three snakes,' he said.

Meleane froze. 'Where?'

'Dead ones. Over there.' He pointed down the beach.

'That's strange.'

'What are you doing? Why are you awake?' he asked.

'The rain,' she said. 'Everything is wet.'

'It's not dryer out here, Meleane.'

'I know.'

'Look there!' Sitting down beside her, he pointed at a shadow in the sea. 'I bet that's another one.'

'Where do you think they came from?'

'Where everything comes from.'

'The Matetes and their sea.'

Arun smiled at her. 'Do you remember when I kissed you, Meleane?'

'Yes.'

'I won't bite this time.'

Meleane felt Arun's hand around the back of her neck, stroking it, gripping her hair. She let herself be pulled forward towards him and kissed. She breathed in deeply through her nose and moved her mouth with Arun's. He sat up onto his knees. She clung to his neck with one arm and reached for his face with the other.

Arun pulled away from her, just far enough to say, 'The last time you touched my face, I expected to be slapped.'

Meleane saw something out of the corner of her eye. 'Look, another snake.'

She felt herself pushed down. She watched Arun as he lowered himself onto her, his arms on the sand above her shoulders, his legs forcing hers apart, his mouth descending.

She struggled to free herself. 'Wait, Arun,' she whispered. 'I can't— We're not—'

'Yes, you can. You will.' He kissed her again.

Arun had found a way to get Nimian out of his head. When he was kissing Meleane he was not thinking about her. When he was ripping open her *lavalava*, he could see she was not Nimian. Meleane was an adult with fully formed breasts and hair where Nimian had once had none. Meleane was being touched for the first time, by him, just as Nimian had been, but Meleane responded as a woman. With Nimian it had been a child's game, played under the tent of their covers by candlelight – not silent and secretive on an empty beach in the rain, lapped by a sea of snakes. Nimian had not been hungry and anxious like this. She had not pressed herself against him as Meleane did. Nimian had not demanded love. She had never stared up at Arun with wide trusting eyes. She had never brushed his skin with her lips. Nimian had bitten his nose and tickled him. She had laughed at his body and been surprised by her own. Nimian and he had wrestled and joked and screamed and laughed. With Meleane it was not a game, it was serious, it was life – and because it was so different, Arun did not think about Nimian at all.

Finally Meleane understood that he loved her. The way he looked at her, the way he kissed her, told her everything she needed to know. Meleane lay back on the sand and was warmed by Arun's body. He took off his clothes. She had never seen a naked man before. She imagined what it would be like to see him in the light, to see that silhouette in all its detail. She knew she would one day; they'd wake up in their own room with the sun shining down on them.

Arun started kissing her body and his kisses grew hard and his teeth bit down on her skin.

'You said you wouldn't bite me, Arun,' Meleane whispered when he drew blood.

His fingers tore at her flesh, his nails ran down her back. He squashed her down into the sand, trapping his hands under her. She became aware of each grain of sand that was pressing into her back and each of his nails as they carved patterns into her skin. Meleane wondered if he was writing something. Would she wake up tomorrow with his name in blood on her back? She moved away from him.

He held his hands up. 'Come back.'

Arun turned Meleane onto her front. He was tired now and didn't know what he was doing. He looked at her back and was glad of the dark. If this back was Nimian's back, what would he do then? He would not hurt her. He would kiss her tenderly on the shoulder and smell her beautiful skin. He would hold her hips and stroke her stomach. He would whisper that he loved her. He would whisper that he hated her for what she had done to him with Angel. He would move gently with her, make sure she felt as he felt, make sure she knew he had forgiven her, make sure they came together. He imagined all this, then withdrew from Meleane and collapsed on the sand.

Meleane lay next to Arun. She wrapped her fingers around his and thought how gentle he had been at the end. He did love her.

'Arun,' she said.

'Yes,' he answered.

'I'm cold. Will you hold me?'

She moved her head onto his chest and he wrapped his arms around her.

'Arun?'

'Yes.'

'There are more snakes now.'

'Yes.'

'Arun?'

'Meleane, I have to sleep. Just lie quietly for a while. Okay?'

'Okay.' She kissed his chest and they both fell asleep.

When Arun woke, it was still raining and still dark. He moved Meleane off him, and left her on the sand. He stood up and put on his jeans. The beach was now black with the bodies of snakes. He laid his T-shirt and Meleane's dress over her and walked away, above the tideline. He wondered if snakes were still poisonous once they'd drowned.

The beach held no secrets for him. He had come to know Moana in the dark. But the snakes had changed the landscape and he felt afraid. He had slept with Meleane. They'd make him marry her. The sea looked cold.

Meleane woke up alone. She pulled her dress over her head. She was about to run home when a thought made her pause. Where was home? Where did she belong? She was a woman now.

She walked to the Matete house, staring at the ground, watching where she trod. She did not know where Arun slept, so she crawled underneath the house, where she had seen him sitting. She wrapped his T-shirt over her shoulders, curled up and dreamt of snakes, alive and dead and dying. And while she was dreaming, a body washed up on the beach.

a Death

As the sun rose, Arun dug a grave for Kara while Angel, with his head between his knees, told him everything that had happened.

'But why didn't you bury her, brother? If not when she died, at least the first time she was washed up.'

Angel stared up at the sky and wondered if the clouds were finally beginning to clear. There was a spot of blue on the horizon. He rubbed the rain into his face. 'She was from the sea, Arun. I thought she had to go back there. Amalia—'

'Those were just stories, brother. Just Amalia's stories.'

'I believed them. I do believe them. You don't drown unless the sea wants you to, Arun.'

'But this girl did die. A long time ago. You know that.'

Angel lay back on the grass next to his mother's grave. 'Don't tell Nimian.'

Arun lowered the box with Kara's remains in it deep into the ground and covered her over with earth. 'Shall we say something?'

Angel shook his head. 'I've been talking to Kara for too long.'

'It doesn't matter, brother. She's gone now.' Arun stood up and walked towards Angel. He put his arms around his neck and held him to him. 'You should have told me. I could have helped you.'

'I'm going back to the *fale*,' Angel said. 'Nimian wants me to be there when she wakes up.'

Arun watched his brother walk away and said goodbye to Kara in her own language, wondering how he could contact her family – if she had someone looking for her. She'd said her boat had capsized. He would go to Laumua. When he had last been there, one family had been trying to bring the internet to the island. He hoped they had. Then he might be able to trace her. He marked her grave and sat next to her in silence. She was alone, far from home, on the other side of the world. He knew what that felt like.

Angel decided not to go straight back to his *fale*. It was only five in the morning; Nimian would not wake for some time. He would go to the beach and walk to where he normally found Kara. He imagined what that might be like, not finding her body. He breathed in deeply. The air was fresh, alive.

The beach was not as Angel had imagined, but it was black with snakes. Where had they come from, what had happened? He looked up. The rain had stopped.

He put the palms of his hands out. Nothing. Whatever it was, it was over, he thought. The rain, Kara; finished, done with.

Angel arrived at the far end of the beach. A dead body was waiting for him. He shook his head.

'She is in the ground. Arun put her there. I saw him, I . . .'

Angel covered his eyes with his hands to shield himself from his madness. 'Too late,' he thought. 'I am already mad.'

The corpse was lying on its front. Angel saw dark hair. Not Kara. He flipped the body over.

Tamatoa.

toes

On the morning of Tamatoa's funeral, the sun was out. It warmed the bodies of the people of Moana but their hearts remained cold, pierced by icicles of grief. They buried him in the little graveyard behind the school, next to his mother, his grandmother and the grandfather he was named after.

Lisi stood at the back of a crowd of people and stared at their heads. Her face was pale, her cheeks dry. He's dead, he's dead, he's dead.

The previous day her father had accepted on her behalf a proposal of marriage from Vete Sun Tatafu, and he was next to her. She ignored him. Her toe hurt, she needed Tamatoa's feet to push against.

'Tamatoa Matete is on his way to heaven,' Tom said at the front. 'And there he'll be as he was here, young, bright, loved. Tamatoa lived a whole life on earth so he'll be whole up above. We should rejoice. Let's sing a song to send him on his way.'

And Tom lifted up his voice and sang and the villagers joined in. The pieces of glass that decorated the grave glinted in the sunlight and a flower grew out of the ground. Lisi saw her brothers smile. Her brothers – now she only had two. 'Whole in heaven,' she thought. Tamatoa had never been whole. She had his toes.

Mano Vata sat on the beach where Angel had found his friend's body. The sand had been cleared but still snakes were being brought in on the waves. He waited for them and, when he saw one wash up, he rushed at it and hacked it into pieces.

'I didn't go with him, I didn't go with him,' he said with each blow. He banged his fists on the ground. 'I should have gone with him. Why did I go in the truck? I'm sorry, Toes.'

A breeze blew and Mano turned his head away from it and saw the villagers moving from the graveyard to the Matete house. He saw Ioane, standing tall and proud, smiling. He saw Angel and Arun talking sadly and Nimian following them. Next came Ama, small, alone. And after the rest of the villagers was Lisi, limping heavily, looking like a wounded ghost.

'Okay, Toes. I'll look after her for you. Don't worry.'

As the villagers ate the food that Laita Havealeta had brought down to the Matete house, Lisi went into her bedroom and drew the curtain. She lay on her bed and shut her eyes.

'Lisi?'

'What do you want, Sun?' she asked without moving. 'You shouldn't be here.'

'We're getting married. I had to come and see if you're okay.'

'No you didn't.'

'Lisi—'

'What?'

'What can I do?'

'Nothing, leave me alone. My toe hurts.'

'I could rub it for you. That might help.'

'No. I don't show people my foot. It's ugly.'

'Don't say that, Lisi.'

'Why not?' she asked.

'Because your foot was what connected you to Tamatoa, so how can that be ugly? Lisi, you don't have to be perfect.'

'You only love me because I'm beautiful. I've seen you watching me.'

'Lisi you are the most beautiful woman on the island and I'm going to be so proud when you're my wife and I come home to you every day. But I don't only love you because of that.'

'What else then?'

'You're right, I do watch you. You swim every afternoon when the beach is empty and I watch you. You cook all the time. You look after your family. You love your brothers, when most women only talk to other girls.' He looked at her. 'Show me your foot.'

'No.'

'Show it to me.'

Sun Tatafu reached out to Lisi's foot and took hold of it. She didn't protest. He slipped off her delicate white shoe. Four perfect toes and a space were pointing towards him.

'It's beautiful, Lisi,' he told her as he raised her foot to his lips and kissed the gap where Tamatoa's toe had been. 'You're beautiful.'

'I'm not whole,' Lisi said and started crying. 'Only Tamatoa can make me whole . . . He's dead, Sun. Tam's dead.'

'I know.' Sun held her to his chest and let her cry. 'And it's horrible and sad, and you should cry for him. But Lisi, my Lisi, don't cry for your foot. You don't need to as long as you're with me. I love you exactly how you are. Let me make you whole. In a different way.'

'Tam has my toe and I have his. And now we are lost to each other forever.'

'He knows you would have done anything for him.'

'I still would.'

'Pray Lisi, and he'll hear you in heaven.'

'Won't he need his toes up there?'

Mano Vata watched Lisi when she came out of her bedroom. 'Her eyebrows are like Tamatoa's,' he thought. 'She raises them in the same way, the left one higher than the right. He always did that, when I said something stupid, or surprised him. Her eyes are almost the same as well, unblinking like his. She limps too. It was never just him. Perhaps they are not so different. Okay,

Toes, I'll talk to her, as soon as I can get her on her own.'

Lisi Matete saw Mano's eyes following her across the room. 'They're still watching me,' she thought, 'even as I cry for my brother they watch me. And Mano, anyone but Mano. Tam's friend, he called himself, after he stole my brother from me. Tam would have been with me, if it hadn't been for Mano, not swimming, not drowning. Not being washed up in front of Angel. He wouldn't be dead if he'd stayed with me. And my toe wouldn't hurt. We'd be here, together now, without all these people, curled up, comfortable, looking out at the water.'

Lisi walked around the front of the house and took water from the rain tank. She looked out at the ocean and screamed at it.

'I hate you,' she told the waves. 'I hate you,' she told the spray. 'I hate you,' she shouted at the current and the tides. She glared at the mango island and cupped her hands around her mouth. 'I hate you, mangoes. I hate you, island.'

'Lisi?' Mano had walked around the side of the house. 'Are you okay?'

'I'm fine, thank you Mano. I'm great!'

'Lisi. He was my friend. And I think he wants me to make sure you're alright.'

Lisi looked at Mano Vata and saw the compassion in his face.

'Thank you, Mano. You were a good friend to Tam.'

'You didn't like it.'

'He left me.'

'I'm sorry.'

'It wasn't your fault. But, Mano . . .'

'Yes.'

'There is one thing you can do for me. If you will,' Lisi said.

'Anything.'

'Bring me a really sharp knife.'

Mano looked at Lisi. 'Why?'

'I have a mango here. I want to eat it. Tam died on the mango island. I'll say goodbye with it. In the kitchen, there is one next to the pans. A machete. Will you bring it out? I don't want to go inside.'

'Okay, Lisi. Wait here. I'll be out soon.'

Mano Vata ran around the house and went straight to the kitchen. It was empty except for Ama sitting hunched up in the corner, drooping like a wilting leaf. He heard her sniff.

'Are you okay, Ama?' Mano asked.

'Yes,' she replied. 'But I'm sad.'

'Where are the pans?'

'There. What are you looking for?'

'Lisi asked me to bring her something. I have to go. Do you need anything?'

'No. I'm fine.' Ama wiped a tear from her eye and smiled.

Lisi saw that Mano had brought the right machete, the sharpest they had.

'Thank you.'

'So where is this mango?'

'Can I eat it alone? Please. I'm sorry it's just too private, even for you.'

Mano sighed. 'Okay, Lisi, as long as you promise me something.'

'What?'

'You'll come and find me afterwards. And if you ever need anything, you'll let me help you.'

'I have everything I need, Mano,' she said, 'but thank you.'

'Okay. Bye. See you in a little bit.'

'No, Mano, not in a little bit. I don't want your help or your friendship. He was my twin. You don't know anything about it. Go away!'

Lisi went and sat under the house, where no one could see her. She took off her shoe and looked at her foot. She held the machete in one hand and it in the other.

'It's just like opening a coconut,' she said to herself. 'One sharp hit and off it comes. You'll soon be whole, Tam.'

She took a deep breath.

'One, two, three.'

She brought the knife down sharply. She screamed. Blood was everywhere. She wiped a spurt of it from her eyes and looked down. Her toes were on the sand. She smiled through the pain. She'd cried out but she didn't think anyone would have heard her. She wrapped up her foot and poured the water she'd taken from the rain tank onto the toes.

'You won't want them bloody, will you Tam?' she said, ignoring the tears that poured down her face. 'Ow!

Tam, that hurts. I hope the snake didn't cause you so much pain.'

She pushed herself up to standing. She had to walk to his grave. She placed her injured foot on the ground and tried to put weight on it. She passed out.

When she came to, she heard Sun Tatafu calling her name. He could help her.

'I'm here,' she called out, 'Help!'

Sun crawled under the house and saw Lisi covered in blood. He immediately took her in his arms.

'What's happened? Where are you hurt? Who did this to you?' He kissed her head and stroked her hair. 'It's okay, I'm here, I'm here.'

'I'm okay,' Lisi said, even though the pain in her foot was unbearable and she could hardly focus on anything else. 'I cut off my toes. I have to give them to Tam. Will you carry me to him please? He can be whole now. I can help him.'

Sun looked at Lisi in horror. He dropped her back onto the sand.

'You did this? Lisi, you did this to yourself? You've turned yourself into a cripple. How do you expect to walk now?'

'You love me. It doesn't matter.'

'I can't marry a girl who won't be able to lift her own children. I can't marry a girl who would cut off her own toes. I won't have a mad wife, Lisi. I'm sorry.'

Vete Sun Tatafu crawled back out onto the beach. Lisi fainted again, and didn't come to until dark.

* * *

Mano Vata went into the house.

'I'm sorry, Toes. I tried. She doesn't want my help.'

He was about to go into the main room when he remembered Ama crying in the kitchen. She was still there, a lump in the corner just as he had left her.

'Hasn't anyone been to see you?' he asked.

Ama said nothing.

'Can I stay?' Mano asked. Ama nodded. He sat down and put his arm around her.

Ama said, 'Before you came to Moana, sometimes, when Lisi went off to play, Tamatoa stayed inside with me. We had lots of games. I wish I could play with him a little bit more.'

'Were they good games?'

'They were the best.'

'Maybe you could teach me some one day.'

'You don't need to say that. I'm ten now. I'm not a baby. You don't have to look after me.'

'Ama, I used to play with Toes too. We spent a lot of time together, didn't you notice?'

'Of course I did. You were always together.'

'Well, who am I going to play with now? Toes used to look after me, stop me doing too many silly things. I think I'll get in a lot of trouble now he's gone.'

'Okay, Mano,' Ama said, 'I'll look after you.'

'Do you promise?'

'Yes.'

'Forever and ever?'

'Yes.'

Mano reached for her hand and squeezed it. She laid her head on his shoulder.

Lisi Matete woke up to a damp cloth on her forehead. She opened her eyes and saw Meleane looking down on her.

'Sun left me.'

'Lisi, is that why you did this?'

'No! Tam needs to be whole. I had his toes. I wanted to give them back.'

Meleane looked down at the girl who just a few moments ago she thought was dead. 'Okay, Lisi,' she said, 'in that case we better put them in his grave, don't you think.'

'You'll help me?'

'Of course.'

'What time is it? Where is everyone? We don't want to be seen. I think they'll all be like Sun. No one will understand.'

'It's late,' Meleane told her, 'everyone is in bed. Here, crawl out. Then you can put your weight on my shoulder and we'll walk together. But then you're going with me to see Mori Unga.'

It took a long time for the two girls to reach the graveyard. The shovel was still there from earlier. Meleane began to dig. Lisi drifted in and out of painful sleep. Eventually they hit wood, and Meleane slipped down into the grave and cleared the earth from the whole of the coffin.

'Don't look when I open it, okay? Just pass me your toes. Promise me.'

Lisi stood back, glad that she did not have to go down there. She heard the sound of wood scraping against wood and Meleane breathing hard as she worked.

'Now give me a hand and let's get out of here.'

Lisi lay on her stomach and reached into her twin's grave to pull out Meleane.

'No more of this, Lisi,' Meleane said. 'Nothing like this again. Ever, okay?'

'I had to take care of him,' said Lisi. 'There was no one else.'

'Well, now I have to take care of you. And I need you to promise you'll not do this, or anything like this, ever again.'

'You're going to look after me?'

'Of course I am. You're not alone Lisi. I won't let you be.'

'Why, Meleane?' Lisi asked, 'I've never been nice to you, you don't owe me anything and you didn't really know Tam.'

'Because, Lisi, I need you to look after me too.'

'Why? What's the matter, Meleane?'

'I'm having a baby. I'm a Matete now and I'm going to need the help of my sister.'

'Arun?'

Meleane nodded. 'But he doesn't . . .'

'I'm so sorry.' Lisi took hold of her hand and smiled up at her. 'I'll look after you, and the baby, forever.'

'And I'll look after you, Lisi, while your foot heals, while you cry for Tamatoa—'

'While I tell my father that Sun won't marry me anymore?'

'Forever!'

'Forever.'

And both girls stood up and made their way, supporting each other, away from Tamatoa's grave, and across the village, to the Unga household to wake up Mori and Funaki.

MELEANE AT THE MATETES'

The food in the Matete house improved once Meleane started living there. She added herbs to the pots when Lisi wasn't looking or took them off the fire before they burnt. The family stopped avoiding meal times and all the Matetes, as well as her brother Mano, trooped into the kitchen at midday and in the evenings.

Meleane felt at home in the house by the sea and she knew it was where the baby swimming inside her needed to grow up. But since that night on the beach she had hardly seen Arun.

'My son has spent too long indoors in his life,' Ioane Matete told her. 'He needs to be outside. He is not ignoring you, Meleane.'

'I need to speak to him, Ioane. But—'

'Speak to me instead.'

Meleane shook her head. 'There are some things I cannot tell you,' she said, looking at the man sitting in front of her. The thought of that eye turning angry was frightening.

'Talk to me, Meleane.'

Again she shook her head.

'Okay then,' said Ioane Matete. 'I shall talk to you.' But he stopped when Ama and Mano came in the room. 'Let's go out on the boat.'

Ioane stood up and offered his arm to Meleane Vata. She took it and felt him pat her hand. Meleane looked at Ioane. She wondered how old he was. Sometimes he felt like her father or grandfather, but other times, like now, as she watched him drag the boat from the sand onto the water and saw the muscles in his arms flex, she didn't know what she thought. Arun had eyes that aged him. Ioane's one-eyed gaze was strong.

Meleane jumped into the boat and sat facing the island. She watched Ioane punt the boat out of the shallows, then turn on the engine. The noise of the motor comforted her.

'Meleane,' Ioane said and she looked up at him. 'You do not want to talk to me about my grandson that is growing inside you. You do not want to talk to me about being unmarried. You do not want to talk to me about not knowing what to do. But as I told you, you can speak to me about everything.'

Meleane looked into the sea and saw the fish swimming below the surface. In that moment she longed to tip overboard. She imagined the weight of her baby dragging her to the bottom of the ocean. She would not have to have this conversation then.

'The answer is simple, Meleane,' Ioane continued. 'You will marry Arun. I know you love him. The wedding will be in one month. On the day I married Amalia.' He paused. 'Don't cry, Meleane. I hate to see my daughter cry.'

'Ioane . . .' Meleane began, but then failed to find an end to her sentence.

'It's okay. But this evening I want you to move back home. And do not tell anyone about the baby. When you are married you'll live with us again and your baby will be a Matete. Now let's catch some fish.' Ioane threw a line out the back of the boat and sped out to sea.

That evening, Angel went with Meleane back to her house, carrying the few clothes she had moved to the Matetes'. They walked slowly, taking the longest route.

'I don't think we've ever spoken before,' Meleane told him.

'It's my fault,' Angel replied. 'The first day you moved here I meant to go and see you. But I had to work on the plantation, and the next day . . . Well, things happened and now here you are, about to become my sister.' Angel looked at her gentle face. 'My brother is lucky,' he told her. 'Soon he'll have everything a Moanan man could ever want. A beautiful island wife, who'll live with him in this village of ours, and give him children and grow old with him.'

'Thank you,' Meleane said.

'It's true,' Angel replied. He thought about Nimian. Perhaps he was lucky too. Perhaps Arun's happiness was not out of reach.

THE WEDDING OF ARUN MATETE AND MELEANE VATA

On the morning of her wedding, Meleane Vata woke up in her parents' house for the last time, ran to the window and looked outside. It was a beautiful calm day, the sun was shining over the village – Moana at its best.

'That's lucky, isn't it?' she asked her mother. 'Or is it? Will I be happy?'

'It's lucky,' Vahine Vata assured her. 'Your father and I married on a day exactly like today and we've been happy for years. Now get dressed.'

Meleane went into her bedroom and pulled her mother's old wedding dress over her head. It was a little tight over her stomach and breasts.

'My mother wasn't pregnant when she married,' Meleane thought, and smiled because the village did not know that she was already carrying Arun's baby. 'My husband, Arun Matete.'

Meleane had still not spoken to Arun since the night

they spent together. She did not know whether Ioane had told him about the child.

'But that's not why he's marrying me,' she told herself. 'He loves me. It's only been three months since Tamatoa's death. The family are still mourning. That's why he hasn't spoken to me. How could he? Besides, Nimian has been comforting him, just as Mano has been looking after Ama and I've been looking after Lisi. But soon, when we're married, I'll be able to give him all the comfort he needs.'

She imagined him laying his head on her lap, running her hands through his thick dark hair, their baby climbing all over them, Arun catching him in his arms and throwing him up in the air. She imagined the child squealing with pleasure and her husband smiling and turning to her for a kiss.

'We're going to be a family,' she said aloud and hurriedly brushed her hair.

'Remind me, Ioane, why I'm doing this?' Arun Matete asked his father.

'Because, you were foolish enough to get her pregnant.'

'She's pregnant?'

'Didn't I mention that before?' Ioane smiled.

'She's pregnant?'

'Yes, Arun.'

'How do you know?'

'I know. Do you want to go and ask her?'

'So,' Arun counted in his head, 'in six months I'm going to have a baby.'

'Yes.'

Arun turned white.

'Arun. Why are you worried? This is how I always said it would be. You have an island girl. She gives you children. And you travel. I'm feeling pretty well; I think we can go again in under a year.'

'Children?'

'Of course, Arun. One son to take care of the plantation, one to travel with you.'

'Two sons?'

'And a daughter, to look after you when you are old.'

'And a daughter? Ioane, I can't have a daughter.'

'Perhaps that's wise,' Ioane said, more to himself than to his son. 'I always thought daughters were the greatest joy. So beautiful, so loving, the best of my children. But then they embarrass me; hack themselves to pieces, ruin their chances of a decent husband. My daughter will be living under my roof until I'm long gone.' He looked at Arun and spoke loudly once more, 'No, stick with sons. Look at you. I tell you to marry and you agree without even knowing why. You, Arun, are what a man hopes for in a son. I'm proud of you.'

'She's pregnant?' Arun repeated.

'Get dressed. We need to be down on the beach soon. Did you know I married your mother there? In a great storm.' Ioane Matete looked out the window at the beach. 'Years later I found some glass buried in the sand. I think it was from the lightning.'

'Glass?'

'When lightning hits sand, that's what happens.' Ioane Matete went into his bedroom and came back with something in his hand. He gave his son a knobble of glass. 'Take it, it's yours.'

Arun looked at the glass his father had given him and ran his fingers over its soft sides. It was as beautiful as lightning. 'I wish there was a storm today. It's too calm, Ioane. Do you remember days like this at sea? The sails slack, being stuck in the middle of the ocean, just waiting for a little wind.'

'You never did like those days.'

'Nothing can come of them, can it?' Arun put the glass down by the window. 'Angel says I was born in a thunderstorm. Were you there?'

'No. Babies, Arun, are not something that men need worry about. I came back when you were five. We'll do the same with this child.'

'To take it with us?'

'To see what kind of boy it is. You were always meant to travel. I saw that the first time I saw you. But your brother – he was his mother's child. Useless.'

'What if it's a girl?'

'Then you beat your wife and have another. She needs to give you boys.'

'Ioane, I don't love her.' Arun thought of Nimian but then shook her out of his head.

'One day you might.'

'And if I never do?'

'It doesn't matter.'

'I can't just be with Meleane if I don't love her.'

'Who said anything about just being with her? Only on the island, Arun. We'll travel. You can fall in love with a new girl in every country. But only one on the island. Do you remember some of your aunties? Beautiful women, from here, there and everywhere. Easy come—'

'—easy go,' finished Arun. 'Did you love Amalia?'

'Yes, in a way. She was my wife. She was mine.'

'Meleane is mine already.'

'Make the most of that, Arun. A wife is the only woman in a man's life who says yes to his every request.'

'An island wife, maybe,' said Arun thinking that Nimian would never be like that.

'A Moanan wife, yes. Now are you dressed? Let's get you married.'

Meleane Vata walked down the beach on her father's arm, passing all her friends from the village: the Tatafus, the Ungas, Laita Havealeta, Nimian and Angel Matete, Ama, Mano and her mother Vahine, and finally Ioane Matete and Lisi. Tom Havealeta was at the front waiting to perform the ceremony.

And then he was next to her, pledging his life to her, looking her straight in the eye. In no time their fingers were tied together and they were man and wife. Arun kissed her then, on the seashore, in the sun, as the waves purred against their toes and for years afterwards Meleane remembered this as the happiest moment in her life.

'I love you, Arun,' she whispered to him as the villagers went into the Matete house.

Arun reached down and ran his hand over Meleane's stomach.

'I hope I won't disappoint you,' he told her. 'I'll do

the best I can, but . . . Meleane, I'm worried I won't be enough for you. I'm not a good man. I'll leave, you do know that don't you? I'm a traveller.'

'But you'll come back?'

'Yes.'

'Arun, you're all I've ever wanted.'

'You're having a baby.'

'I tried to tell you.'

'Sorry. I was coming back, you know. That night on the beach. I hadn't left you. I was coming back, but then, Tamatoa . . .'

'It's okay, Arun. It doesn't matter. Come on. Let's go in.'

'The last time the whole village was here was for the funeral feast.'

'This house has seen a lot of tears, now it's time to laugh. So stop looking so miserable. Come and eat.'

'Okay,' Arun said, smiling. 'You go ahead. I'll be there soon.'

Meleane skipped into the kitchen where Lisi and Ama were serving food.

Arun Matete walked up to the plantation, sat down on a log and put his head in his hands. He cried for his dead brother, for Meleane and for himself. He cried because he felt trapped on the island, more now than he ever had before. He cried because he knew that leaving would hurt his wife. He cried because he would not come back. He cried because he was like Ioane.

And crying, he remembered his mother crying when he was a baby and himself crying because she was crying. And who stopped him? Angel. 'Come cry to me,' Angel had said – but he never had. Yet Angel had unburdened himself to him, had told him about Nimian and Kara. He would do the same. If Angel came up here now, perhaps he could teach him to love the island, and then perhaps he could stay after all and become a villager and care for Meleane. If Angel came now they would lie on their backs and look up at the trees and see the beauty of life, and time would stop. Angel would show him and Arun would do what he said and be happy.

There was a rustle in the bushes, the sound of someone approaching. Arun smiled as he waited for his brother.

Nimian entered the clearing.

'Arun, what's wrong?' Nimian said and ran to him. 'Why are you crying?' She knelt down next to him and put her arms around his neck. 'It's okay, Arun. Whatever it is. What's wrong? Can I help you? Don't cry, don't cry,' she repeated and between each sentence she kissed his cheek and touched his tears with her lips.

Hopelessly, Arun put his arm on her back, under her T-shirt. He stroked her skin, feeling for her birthmark, pulled her closer to him and kissed her.

Meleane Matete encouraged all her guests to eat. She moved around saying hello to everyone so that no one noticed that she herself was not eating. Her baby was making her sick and it was all she could do not to throw up all over the pork.

'Meleane,' Lisi whispered, 'you keep holding your stomach. People will notice.'

'I'm going to be sick. There's no hiding that.'

'Let's go for a walk.'

'I can't, I'm the bride.'

'You can. Ama,' Lisi called to her sister who was chatting to Mano. 'We're just going to walk across the beach. You're in charge.'

'Okay,' said Mano.

'Let's go.'

Meleane took Lisi's arm and supported her friend as she hobbled down, using Tamatoa's stick, to the wet sand.

'I'm supposed to be holding you up, you're the sick one,' Lisi said as, breathing heavily, they reached the sea.

'We're both useless. Let's just sit a while.'

They sat in silence for a few moments, watching the sun dance on top of the water.

'Can you believe I'm married?' Meleane asked.

'It's great . . . Sister.' Lisi squeezed her arm.

'Do you think Arun is happy?'

'If I were you, I'd enjoy Arun when you can, but don't rely on him. You're a Matete now and you should know that. It's the same with Ioane. I love my father, Meleane, I always have, but he has not spoken a single word to me since Tamatoa's funeral. He and Arun are travellers. They only really love their boat.' After a pause she added, 'And each other.'

'That's what Arun said to me today, but I don't think he's going anywhere. We're about to have a baby.'

Meleane suddenly grew pale, sat up on her knees, turned away from Lisi and threw up.

'Are you okay?'

'Yes. Now I am. Shall we go back to the feast?'

The girls stood up and, leaning on each other, made slow progress returning.

Arun Matete felt a hard slap around his face.

'Finally, a girl who will hit me,' he said quietly.

'Why did you do that, Arun?' Nimian asked. 'Why now?' She kissed him again.

'Do you really want an answer to that?'

'Yes. You got married ten minutes ago. Of course I want an answer.'

'As soon as I go back to that house, I have to start acting like Meleane's husband.'

'You should have started already.'

'I've always been slow off the mark.'

Nimian smiled. 'Arun, we can't do that again. We've left it too late. Meleane . . .'

'Angel?' asked Arun.

'No. Not him. He's not you.'

'I should have kissed you that first day. I should have torn you from Angel's arms.'

'You've forgiven me?'

Arun reached into his pocket and brought out the wrinkled photo of Nimian's back.

'You kept it. I hate that photo.'

He flattened it out on a rock, trying to rid it of its creases. 'It's my favourite thing in the world.' He put it back in his pocket, then said sadly, 'Meleane's having a baby.'

Nimian took his hand in hers and played with his thumb. 'Let's go back to the house. Your family are waiting for you.'

Nimian stood up, held her hands out to Arun and pulled him to his feet. He put his arm around her shoulder, drew her to him and breathed out through his nose onto her temple. They walked down into Moana.

The wedding feast went perfectly. The sun continued to shine all day, and the villagers danced, ate, talked and sang. Arun and Meleane Matete were given gifts: from the Tatafus some baby clothes for when they started a family; from the Ungas a carving of a woman dancing; the Havealetas gave them a book Tom had found in Laumua about ships from all around the world; Meleane's father, Fono Vata, built his daughter a chest to keep all her clothes in at her new home and the Matetes killed five of their best pigs.

Arun and Meleane spent the rest of the day in one another's arms. They danced together and sang a duet. They kissed, knowing it was the only time in their married lives when they would be able to show any affection outside their home. Asked about when they wanted to start a family, Arun assured everyone that he planned to have one right away and when Meleane blushed, the villagers assumed it was natural shyness at the thought of the night to come.

Halfway through the feast, Ioane Matete found his youngest daughter Ama and told her to move out of the little bedroom. From now on it would be his, to let Arun and his wife have the room he had once shared with Amalia. Ama and Lisi would sleep in the main room, on the sofas, or the floor like Tamatoa had. The girls moved their clothes, their father's clothes and made up the big double bed.

That night, once everything had died away, Arun and Meleane walked, hands held, into their room. They slept together for the second time. Arun did not bite or scratch and when Meleane woke up the next morning, she was in his arms, and the sun was falling on their faces.

At his brother's wedding, Angel Matete realised he had never been in love before. He looked back on his time with Kara and saw that it was madness, not love. She was just a girl who died. He should have listened to the boatman and let her go right at the beginning. It had not been love. Love was what Meleane and Arun had. Love was a future. Love was life.

And at the wedding feast it seemed to him that Nimian was the most alive of all the guests. He had not seen her for most of the day, but when she appeared, her eyes were shining. He watched her dance. He watched her laugh and sometimes, when she thought no one was looking, he watched her cry with happiness. He had seen her paddle in the shallows of the sea and raise her head to watch the moon rise. There was life in her and Angel wanted to share it.

LIA MATETE

Meleane named her baby Lia, after her grandmother, Belia Vata, and Arun's mother, Amalia Matete. Lia was a healthy girl, the villagers said, considering she had been born three months early. But Meleane, knowing that wasn't true, worried about her daughter's tiny body and frail frame. She stayed in bed with her for a whole month, trying to feed her up, waited on by Lisi, visited by Ama and Mano.

Her room became her sacred space, her little baby kingdom, but she liked it the best when Arun came in after a morning on the plantation and flopped down beside her for his rest. Then she would put the baby on his stomach and watch her as she rose and fell to her father's breath. Meleane craved time with Arun and would not let herself fall asleep when he lay beside her. She was awake after lunch each day, and all through the night, and only shut her eyes in the afternoon, when she knew he was out on the boat fishing and would not be back for hours.

Almost despite himself, Arun Matete had grown to like his pregnant wife. Her stomach, so round and full; her breasts, larger and firmer every day; her smell, of something alien and sweet – Meleane was not like other women he had lain next to. She was his wife and he could not help but reach out and touch her whenever she was near. He was intrigued by her, this woman who loved him. And she never tired of him, never turned away from him. His father was right; his wife always said yes.

But now Lia was born, and suddenly Meleane's stomach was shrinking not growing, her breasts always had a baby on one of them and when he approached her there was a tiny little sleeping figure in the way. His daughter had taken his wife from him and try as he might not to let it happen, his mind kept wandering away from Meleane and back to Nimian and the day of his wedding.

Angel Matete liked the sound of crying babies. He remembered Arun crying as a child and then the twins howling for months on end. But Lia cried like Ama had, small whimpers, the cries of a child who does not want to disturb anybody – it was this sound that made Angel long to give his niece everything in the world.

He needed to talk to Nimian, to ask her to be his, to have children with him. But somehow the time never seemed right. Did fish talk about laying eggs? Did plants decide to release their seeds onto the wind? No, these things happened as naturally as the tide turning – so

Angel did not worry that he did not ask her. All would happen as it should. And once she was pregnant, Angel would marry the mother of his child, and his own family would begin.

Nimian looked at Meleane, Arun, Angel, Lisi, Ama and Mano and saw an island family. She hovered at the door while they all sat on the big bed together and played with little Lia. She only ever entered if she heard Ioane Matete moving around behind her. She saw Lia's whole life as it would unfold. Lia was a girl, she would grow up to become a woman, a wife. She would have children of her own. There was nothing else. Nimian had been fooling herself imagining that she could stay here with Angel and Arun. Ioane had been right to ask her to leave. How was it possible for Meleane to hold that baby in her arms and not to cry when she thought about its future?

Nimian knew now she was not meant to stay on the island. What was she doing here? She did not love Angel, she never should have gone to his *fale* on that first day. And she could no longer bear to watch Arun being a husband and a father. It was time to say goodbye.

saying goodbye

Nimian woke up next to Angel, as she did every morning, but she did it this morning for the last time. She turned to face him and kissed his eyes until they opened; brown, quizzical, kind. He yawned, stretched his arms and pulled her to him and she held on to him as though she would never let go.

'I love you,' she whispered into his chest and was glad when he did not hear her lying to him. Eventually he drew away.

'I have to go to the plantation,' Angel said. 'What are you doing this morning?'

'I have to tell you something.'

Angel's face broke into a huge smile and he jumped across the bed and kissed her. 'You're going to have a baby?'

'What? No!'

'Yes,' he said.

She touched him on the chest by his heart. 'Go, go,'

she told him. 'We'll talk about it when you get back.'

'Okay,' he said, kissing her one last time. 'I'll see you at lunch. Lisi is making mango juice for little Lia. I imagine that's what we'll get.' He laughed. 'Are you okay?'

She nodded.

'It's just you look sad today.'

She kissed him again. He got out of bed, dressed and with one final kiss left her.

'Goodbye, my angel,' she wrote after he had gone.

Arun woke up next to his daughter and wife. Both were already awake, the baby feeding, the mother looking down at her child.

'Morning,' Arun said groggily. He had been drinking *kava* the night before. He put a hand to his mouth, kissed it, then touched Meleane gently on the cheek.

'Good morning, Arun.'

The baby stopped feeding and gurgled in her father's direction.

'This little thing loves you, you know,' Meleane told him. 'Look, she has eyes for no one else.'

'Then she has very good taste,' Arun replied. 'Now then, I want a kiss from both my girls. I'm off to the plantation.'

He leant over, rubbed his nose against Lia's tiny snub, jumped out of bed, walked around to the other side and kissed his wife.

'Actually, I've got something for you,' he said and put a piece of glass in Meleane's hand.

'What is it?'

'It's from my parents' wedding. It's lightning. Ioane thinks it's lucky. I hope it looks after you.'

'I love it,' Meleane said.

'I'm sorry,' Arun told her.

'What for?'

'Nothing, everything.'

'You keep on thinking you're going to disappoint me, Arun. You never have.'

'I've got to go. Goodbye.'

He kissed her once more and left.

Nimian walked into the kitchen and ate breakfast with the girls.

'What are you going to do today?' she asked.

'School,' said Ama. 'Mano's coming to get me in a moment.'

'You spend a lot of time with Mano.'

'I know. We're going to marry once I'm old enough.'

'I'd give it a few years,' Nimian said.

'Exactly, in a few years I will be Ama Vata.'

'It's all arranged?'

'No. But he loves me.'

'Well, Ama Vata, good luck with that. Mano's nice.'

At that moment Mano entered the room.

'You're speaking about me,' he said.

'Ama was just telling us you're taking her to school,' Nimian said.

'Yes. Let's go.'

Ama stood up and the two of them hurried out.

'What about you, Lisi?'

'Meleane and I are going to weave mats, if Lia lets us. It's a perfect day to sit with the windows open and enjoy the sea breeze. It hasn't been this calm since the wedding.'

'That was a beautiful day, wasn't it?' Meleane said, more to herself than anyone else. 'Lisi, I want to take Lia into the sea. Will you help me, you're much better at swimming than I am?'

'I'm not sure that's true anymore,' Lisi said, 'but I'd love to come.'

'Sounds like the perfect day,' Nimian said. 'But where's Ioane? Won't he be around the house?'

'He seems to spend all his time out in the boat at the moment,' Meleane answered.

'I think he's about to take off again,' Lisi added.

'That'd be good wouldn't it?' Nimian asked.

'No!' Meleane shouted, then checked herself. 'I mean, no. It's just, he'd make Arun go with him. I know he would.'

'Arun can make his own decisions,' Nimian said.

'Everyone has somebody they can't say no to,' Meleane said quietly.

'I'd better go,' Nimian said. 'Goodbye Lisi. Goodbye Meleane, goodbye baby Lia.' She bent down and looked once more at the little girl. Then she walked to the top of the village, past Tamatoa's grave and out onto the road.

Arun Matete, beneath a coconut tree up on the planta-tion, said to Angel, 'The sea is blue all around the world. But only in certain lights. When you sit on the beach at Moana and look into the distance, sometimes it is so clear it looks green, doesn't it? And then there is a colour clearer even than that, when the sea must be colourless because it is possible to make out each fish, each rock, each piece of coral. Well, there are other countries where they have seas of all different colours, blue seas and green seas and grey seas on which the sun hardly ever shines and seas with so little air to breathe that they gasp like dying fish.'

'What are you talking about, Arun?'

'Wouldn't you like to see all those seas?'

'Why? You're here to tell me about them.'

'I'm leaving.'

'Are there more seas to see?'

'Come with me.'

'No, Arun, I can't cross the ocean.'

'Brother, I'm telling you, you can.'

'It is enough for me to hear it from you.'

'But why take my word for it?' Arun asked.

'Look at the horizon. What is there?'

'Sea, more sea and a rising sun.'

'The sea is infinite,' Angel said, 'and everlasting.'

'I remember being at school here, years ago. Teacher Zeno told us it was not. That was the first time I believed Ioane would take me away.'

'And you wanted to go with him. Whereas I knew Zeno was wrong. For me the sea is the end of the world.'

'I'm leaving Ioane behind, brother. Look after him.'

'Why?'

'Because he'll be angry.'

'No, Arun, I mean, why are you leaving him behind. He thinks he's going with you.'

'He can't. It's his turn to stay behind. Just promise me you'll take care of him.'

'He won't let me,' said Angel. 'And even if he did, I couldn't. We can't even be in the same room together.'

'But do it anyway. Go beyond all that. Speak to him. Take him out with you, don't leave him in the house to rot. He's not good at staying still.'

'Will you come back for him?'

'No.'

'And Meleane and Lia?'

'They have Lisi.'

'Is there no one who you mind leaving behind? Me, Nimian—'

'Only you. But you and Ioane will take care of each other.'

Angel raised his eyebrow.

Arun said, 'Promise me.'

'Okay, if I must.'

'Now I'm happy, brother, for I know you're a man of your word.'

'And I know you lie, Arun. So I'm not going to believe that you won't return.'

Arun laughed and hugged him. 'Goodbye, brother.'

'Goodbye, Arun.'

Nimian was waiting.

'Okay?' he asked her.

'Okay.'

'We'd better leave then. Last chance to change your mind.'

Nimian looked around her at the village, at the home of the Havealetas, with its mud pool and pile of logs outside. At the pigs and chickens running wild. At the paths of sand and coral.

'I wish we could see the house from here.'

'We'll never see it again,' Arun replied.

Nimian thought about Lia, who would never know her father. But she took his hand and led him down the road. 'She'll have an uncle,' she thought, 'the best uncle there is and aunts and a mother and that's enough. It has to be enough.'

They walked on and did not once look back.

JOINING THE SEA

For the first time, Ioane Matete and Angel had the same thoughts. They were fish, suffocating on land, about to be killed by a blow to the head. They were mangoes that had fallen into the sea and were sinking. They were lost souls, abandoned by the ones they loved.

'Come on, Ioane,' Angel said.

'Where are we going?'

'To die.'

'Good.'

'Help me with the boat.'

Ioane Matete and his son worked together, for the first time, pushing the boat into the Pacific Ocean. They sat down side by side, turned on the engine and moved away from the island.

'Here,' Angel said, after a few hours had passed.

'Here what?' Ioane asked, looking around him at the vast empty sea.

'Here we die.'

Ioane nodded.

'The tide will take our bodies back to Moana. They'll bury us next to Tamatoa and Amalia. Dying at sea is a Hoko tradition. It's how my grandfather ended his life and his father before him.'

'I am Ioane Matete.'

'Then find your own way to die.'

'No, it's a good idea, Angel. My time has come.'

Saying that, Ioane stood up, looked as if there was something he wished to add, and then, without a word, stepped over into the water. Angel also got to his feet. He took one last look at all that was around him and consigned his body to the deep.

Angel opened his eyes and mouth and felt the water take him. He saw the sea, coral and fish, the shadow of a shark, light falling through the water and below him the hair of Ioane Matete waving as if bidding him goodbye. And he realised he was a fool. She was just a girl he'd hardly known. There was so much to live for.

He felt someone take hold of each hand. Kara, Amalia . . . So his mother had been right after all.

THE ISLAND

Meleane Matete woke up to a tug on her smallest finger. It was midday and she had just fallen asleep. She looked around and Lisi, Ama and Mano were pointing at her daughter. Lia was standing up.

'Look at her,' Lisi mouthed.

Meleane looked while Ama called Lia. The little girl walked unsteadily towards her aunt.

'She's walking!' said Meleane as everyone clapped.

Almost at Ama, Lia stopped and looked around, smiling proudly at her family. She turned towards the door, wobbled and fell over into the arms of her uncle.

'Careful,' Angel said as he picked her up and pretended to dry his wet hair on her stomach. 'When did you start walking?'

'Today,' Meleane told him, holding his gaze with her lively brown eyes.

'This is cause for a celebration,' Lisi announced. 'I'll fry some fish. Oh, but we're out of oil.'

'The Tatafus told me yesterday they have a spare canister,' Meleane said.

The girls all looked at Mano.

'Okay. I'll get it. Fish it is and then a swim in the sea.'

'Yes!'

'And Lisi,' Mano said, 'the Ungas and I picked yam yesterday. Make some of that as well.'

'Okay. I will.'

And the family prepared lunch.

Photo courtesy of Hannah Stumpp

Originally from Scotland, Madeleine Tobert spent several years in the Pacific islands. She tried to leave but found she just couldn't. She now lives in Auckland with her Fijian husband. *The Sea on Our Skin* is her first book.

acknowledgements

A big thank you to Richard Francis and all my workshop groups at Bath Spa University. To Frankie, Toni, Natasha, Lianna and Hannah for taking the time to give me their comments. To Phoebe, Wouts and Richie, my research buddies. To Tale, Jone and all of Vorovo-ro's Team Fiji for their many stories. To Pandy, for help with the title. To Savenaca, a wonderful distraction and occasional inspiration. To my agent, Judith Murray, for faith and expertise. To Helen Coyle for wonderful edits. To Lisa Highton and the crew at Two Roads for giving a home to the Matetes. And most of all, for more than could ever be written on one piece of paper, to Mikey.

TWO ROADS

stories . . . voices . . . places . . . lives

Two Roads is the home of great storytelling. We publish stories from the heart, told in strong voices about lives lived. Two Roads books come from everywhere and take you into other worlds.

We hope you enjoyed *The Sea on Our Skin*. If you'd like to know more about this book or any other title on our list, please go to www.tworoadsbooks.com or scan this code with your smartphone to go straight to our site:

For news on forthcoming Two Roads titles, please sign up for our newsletter.

We'd love to hear from you

enquiries@tworoadsbooks.com   Twitter (@tworoadsbooks)

facebook.com/TwoRoadsBooks